MW01129087

DISCLAIMER

ISBN (Large Print): 978-1-957207-00-1

ISBN (Paperback): 979-8748084239

This is a work of fiction. Names, characters, businesses, places, events, and incidents are either the products of the author's imagination or used in a fictitious manner. Any resemblance to actual persons, living or dead, or actual events is purely coincidental.

MY SON'S
SECRET

Jews, the Third Reich, and a Web of Secrets
Book One

USA TODAY BESTSELLING AUTHOR
ROBERTA KAGAN

PROLOGUE

November 8, 1938

KARA SET the modest cake on the table in front of her blond-haired, blue-eyed son. She studied him and marveled at how much he looked like her. "Our precious son is two years old today," she said, smiling at Abram Ehrlich, the child's father. Abram, with his black, wavy hair and dark eyes stood at her side, his face shining with love for her and their little boy.

"Are you ready to blow out the candles?" Kara asked as Abram began lighting the three candles. "Look, you have three candles. One for each year of your life and one extra. That one is for good luck." Kara ran her fingers through her son's blond curls.

"Bubbie, you blow candles."

Hoda Ehrlich laughed. "Karl, of course I will help you," she said. "What a big boy you are now. Every day you grow more and more handsome. Soon you'll be a fully grown man."

Karl giggled.

Kara stood back and watched. Her heart swelled with love for the people who were with her in this small kitchen. It was hard to believe that a few years ago she'd lived a completely different life.

1

She'd grown up in a Gentile home. Her parents had instilled a great fear of Jews in her and her sister. But now, these people, who were Jewish, were her family. And even though her mother-in-law had been against her and Abram's relationship in the beginning, Hoda had become Kara's best friend and strongest supporter.

When the people in the Mitte, the primarily Jewish sector of town, where they lived, had begun to spread cruel gossip about Kara, it had been Hoda who had stood up for her. No one but Abram, Kara, and Hoda knew that Karl was born out of wedlock. But they guessed, and they talked. And it took Hoda to openly put them in their place to stop the gossip.

"All right. Are you ready?" Hoda said, turning to look at Karl as she gently put her arm around his shoulder.

"Yes, Bubbie, let's go," Karl said with the kind of enthusiasm only a two-year-old child could exude.

"One, two, three . . ." Hoda said.

Just as they blew the candles out, there was a thunderous crash in the street. It was louder than anything Kara had ever heard. She looked at Hoda and then at Abram. Karl was stunned. He turned white, then he let out a shriek and began to wail.

"Shaaa . . ." It's all right, Hoda cooed, picking the boy up into her arms.

Abram turned to the women. "You two stay here. I'm going to go out and see what's happening."

"Don't. Stay here. You must not go outside," Hoda warned.

"It's all right, Mother. I'm just going to go into the store and look out the window so I can see what's going on in the street."

As Abram left, they began to hear shouting in German, not in Yiddish, which was uncommon in this part of town. It sounded like a mob of drunken men. They were singing something about Jews and a knife. Then there was a crash of glass shattering.

Karl screamed again.

"Hold him," Hoda said as she handed Karl to Kara. "I have to go and see if Abram is all right."

Kara cuddled Karl in her arms. He was terrified. His eyes were opened wide, and he was screaming and crying.

Hoda left the kitchen and ran down the hall and then out into the bookstore. But she was only gone for a few minutes before she and Abram returned. "There is some sort of violent demonstration going on outside in the street," Abram said, trying to stay calm. "The best thing for us to do is to go back into the bedroom and hide in the closet."

"Who is responsible for all of this?" Kara asked.

"I don't know who they are. They look like a bunch of hoodlum boys and young men. They aren't wearing any sort of uniforms," Abram said, "but we have no time to talk about this right now. Please take the baby, and go into the bedroom with Mother. I'll keep watch out here."

"Oh no, you must come with us," Kara insisted. "Please, Abram."

"I have a gun, Kara. I know how to shoot. I'll be out here in case they try to come in. But I would feel much better if I knew that the three of you were hidden. Now, listen to me. The three of you should be able to fit inside the closet in our room. Move the clothes if you have to. Do whatever you must but go quickly. While you are in there, try to keep Karl as quiet as you can. Try telling him a story to calm him down. I know it will be hard with all that is going on. But do your best." He smiled at her, but his lips were trembling. "Go," he said.

She didn't move. Instead, she stood staring at him, tears filling her eyes.

There was another crash, which sounded like a large plate-glass window had been broken outside, then a bout of loud laughter followed. A woman let out a scream. *Was it terror or pain, or both?* Kara couldn't tell. She looked at Abram and saw the fear in his eyes.

"Abram . . ." she pleaded, "please, come with us."

"I can't. Now go. Please hurry," he said firmly.

Hoda put her arm on Kara's shoulder. Then she nodded at Kara and led her and Karl into the bedroom.

Kara was shaking so hard that her teeth were chattering.

"Let me hold Karl," Hoda suggested gently.

Karl curled up in his bubbie's arms as she began to tell him a story. Her voice was soft and filled with warmth and love as she began: "A long time ago . . . the Jews were enslaved in Egypt by a cruel and terrible ruler." Hoda smoothed Karl's hair. Then she kissed the top of his head. "They could see no hope of ever being free."

Karl nuzzled his head on his grandmother's chest. "What happened to the Jews next, Bubbie?"

Before Hoda had a chance to answer, they heard loud footsteps on the hardwood floor. Kara felt her heart pound so hard that she thought it might jump out of her chest. Hoda glanced at Kara, and Kara saw the terror in her eyes. But then Abram flung the closet door open. "Hurry, follow me. We must get out of here quickly."

"Why? Where are we going?" Hoda asked as she stood up, still holding Karl. Then she and Kara followed Abram.

Karl had begun to cry again.

"The mob has set the bookstore on fire. The apartment will be in flames in a few minutes. We have to get out before the smoke blinds us all and we can't find our way out." Abram took Kara's hand and pulled her along. Hoda followed quickly.

Kara coughed as the smoke filled her lungs. The three of them ran out the back door. Then they followed Abram into the alley behind the store, where they ducked into a concrete stairwell a few doors away from their apartment, then ran to the bottom where it was cold, damp, and dark.

"I'm scared, Bubbie," Karl said, his small body trembling.

"I know, my little bubbala. But don't be afraid; Hashem will protect us. Let's pray and ask him to watch over us."

Kara grabbed Abram's arm and held him tightly. She listened as Hoda led Karl in a prayer. It seemed to comfort the little boy, and he laid his head on his bubbie's breast.

The smell of smoke from the many fires in the street permeated the air, and they all began to cough. Karl's eyes were red, and his nose was running. He coughed and choked until he vomited. Then he started crying again.

"No, shaaa, my sweet child. Don't cry," Hoda soothed. "It's all right. Everything will be all right."

"Can't breathe," Karl said.

"I know," Hoda said.

"Eyes hurt too." He rubbed his eyes hard with his small fists. Kara thought her heart would break as she watched him.

"It's all going to be just fine," Hoda said, rocking him. "Shall I sing to you?"

Karl nodded. And Hoda began to sing in Yiddish.

But he kept crying, and each time there was a loud noise he shrieked. Hoda stopped singing and wiped the tears from Karl's eyes with her blouse. Then she lifted his face so they were eye to eye, and she called him "Akiva," which was his Hebrew name. Then she said, "Such a shayna punim you have. But I can't see how beautiful your face is when you cry. Will you smile for your old bubbie?"

Karl's face was red and tearstained, but he smiled.

"You are my heart, little man. When you smile, it lights up my whole world," Hoda said.

They stayed huddled in that stairwell through the night, through the following day, and into the next night without food or water as the world they had known was blowing up around them.

"I'm hungry. I want my birthday cake," Karl asked. He did not understand that their home and everything in it was gone.

"He is hungry. We must do something," Hoda said.

"It's dark now, and I can still hear the sounds of the mob outside, but in the morning, I will go out and see what I can get for us to eat," Abram said.

"How long can this last?" Kara asked.

"Who knows. Until they destroy all of us? I can't say for sure. But we must eat. So, tomorrow morning I will try to find food."

All night Kara listened to the angry mob. She wondered where they found the energy to perpetuate such cruelty. Two days already they'd been at work destroying the Mitte. How could they be so tireless? *Perhaps they are demons.* And tomorrow Abram must venture out of their little safety nook.

Kara could hardly breathe thinking about Abram going outside to find food. *What if they hurt him? I would rather die of starvation than let him face those savages. But the baby must eat, and we must take care of our child. I know Abram, and he will do whatever he can to take care of Karl. He would even put himself at risk. Dear God, please help us.*

The dawn brought a stillness that was as frightening as the violence of the previous night. It was so quiet that Kara felt the hairs on the back of her neck stand up. *Are these horrible predators still out there? Have they fallen into drunken stupors in the street? Will they awaken and hurt my Abram when he tries to go out and find food?* Kara felt Abram touch her shoulder. She turned to look at him. Hoda and Karl had both fallen asleep, with Karl resting in his grandmother's arms.

"I am going to see what I can find for food," Abram whispered.

"I'll go with you."

"Absolutely not," he said firmly. "It's too dangerous."

"It's better if I go alone," Kara suggested. "I look German, and I have papers."

"Absolutely not! If they even so much as suspect that you are living with me—and they might already know it—they could hurt you. I would never forgive myself for allowing you to go. I will go. And that's the end of it."

"But what about you? If it's dangerous, isn't it dangerous for you?" she pleaded in a whisper so she wouldn't wake Hoda and the child.

"Kara, I have a gun. I'll do what I have to do."

"Abram, if you shoot a German, you'll be arrested. And then God knows what will happen to you."

"My love, my Kara," he said, touching her face. "I hate to argue with you. And quite frankly I don't have the time to reason with you right now. We need food. I am the man of this house. I will go and find food." Abram stood up. Quietly, without turning around to look at her, he began to climb the stairs. Kara let out a soft whimper. Then she stood up. Her back and limbs ached from sitting on the cold concrete. But she ran up three stairs to Abram and threw her arms around him, holding him tightly.

"I love you. Please, please, be careful."

"I love you too. And I, of course, will be very careful," he said. Then he kissed her and gently pried her arms from him. "I have to go, but I'll be back as soon as I can."

"Do you promise to come back?"

"I promise."

"You've never broken a promise to me, Abram." She grabbed the sleeves of his shirt and tugged at them.

"And I won't break this one either. As long as I am alive, I will never leave you," he said.

She began to cry. Then as he walked softly up the stairs, she whispered, "Just please stay alive."

CHAPTER ONE

K ARA LAID her head against the cold concrete wall. Tears flowed down her cheeks, but she made no sound. *It's best if they sleep through this,* she thought, looking at Hoda and Karl. She tried to force herself to be optimistic. *Abram will be back soon. I know he will. Dear, sweet Jesus, please, watch over him and bring him back to us safely.*

An hour passed, an hour that seemed like a lifetime, but Abram did not return. *Karl will wake up soon. And then what I am going to do? What am I going to tell him? Where will I tell him Abram has gone? He's going to be hungry and crying. And I can't bear to think of it, but . . . what if something has happened to Abram? How am I ever going to go on living in this terrible world without him? How did I ever fall in love so deeply? What was it about this man that changed me? How, Kara? How did it all start?*

Her mind began to transport her back to the beginning. Kara closed her eyes, and then she remembered.

CHAPTER TWO

Autumn 1928
Berlin, Germany

THE SKY WAS dark with only a thin sliver of moon to light it when eight-year-old Anka Scholz crawled into her ten-year-old sister Kara's bed. "Just listen to them. Mutti and Vater are fighting again," Anka whispered in a frightened voice.

"I know." Kara rubbed her sister's shoulder.

"I'm afraid. I hate it when they fight. It scares me."

"It's all right. You can sleep with me."

"Did you hear that noise? It sounded like he hit Mutti again." Anka shivered.

"Shhh . . . don't listen to them. Pay them no attention. Just lie your head right here on my pillow, and let the sound of my voice be the only sound you hear. Can you do that?"

"I'll try," Anka moaned.

"How would you like it if I told you a wonderful story today, by one of my very favorite authors. I don't have the book so I can't read it to you. But, would you like me to tell you the story?"

"Oh yes, please."

"Well then, you have to pay close attention. Which means you can't listen to anything going on between Mutti and Vater."

Kara felt her sister nod.

The autumn wind howled, then rustled the leaves on the tree outside the window.

"I know we need more money, but where am I supposed to get it? What do you want me to do?" Her father's voice reverberated through the walls as he hollered at her mother, and Anka trembled.

"Remember what I said? Now, don't pay attention to them, Anka. Just listen to me. Only to me," Kara whispered into her sister's ear. "Once upon a time"—Kara felt her sister settle down and curl into her as she continued—"there was a momma duck. She had laid several eggs."

"Eggs for eating?" Anka asked.

"No, sweetie, eggs that would hatch and become little baby ducks."

"I saw little baby ducks once; they were all fluffy and yellow."

"And very cute, right?"

"Yes, they were."

"Well," Kara said, glad that Anka was becoming interested in the story, "one bright summer day the sky was so blue, and the clouds were so white that it looked like a painting. The mother duck was sitting on her eggs, and she realized that they were all ready to be hatched."

"So that means baby ducks are coming?" Anka asked.

"Yes, are you going to keep interrupting me?" Kara said, trying to sound stern but smiling in the darkness. She was glad her sister was engrossed in the story instead of trembling with fear.

Anka shook her head. "No, I promise to stop interrupting; please go on. I will be very quiet. So, what happened to the ducks?"

"Money is worth less and less every day. The children are growing and they're always hungry. How am I supposed to buy a loaf of bread when one loaf costs me an entire day of pay? It was easier a few years ago; I could buy a loaf of bread for thirty-four-hundred marks. But now it costs well over two hundred billion. There just isn't enough money," their mother said pleadingly.

"Don't forget that it's my pay. Not yours. I am the man in this house. You should kiss the ground I walk on because I go to work and I provide for us. Instead, you nag and complain. I happen to know that there are plenty of men out there who have abandoned their families," he said angrily.

"If you gave me your pay it would be one thing, but the truth is, Artur, you have been drinking away most of what you earn. I buy bread when I can. Most of the time I buy flour and make my own. It's less expensive. But do you have any idea how many times I've looked into the jar before I went shopping for food only to find that it's empty, because you drank all of the money away? You don't pay much attention to me, so you probably don't even realize it, but I have been bartering for what we need. How do you think we are surviving—on air? After I finish all of the housework, I am cleaning other people's homes in trade for eggs. I am washing other people's dirty clothes for flour. This is what is keeping food on the table. Not you. Not your job. You spend everything you have as fast as you earn it."

There was a loud bang and Anka jumped. She looked at Kara, who smoothed her hair trying to comfort her.

Then her father growled, "You know what your problem is? You don't appreciate me. You don't appreciate what I go through for this family. You don't deserve me, Heidi. You come from trash and you are trash. My parents told me not to marry you."

"Stop it, please, Artur. Stop it, and try to understand that we need more. I know how hard you work."

"Do you? A fella who works hard deserves to have a beer after work. I give you what I can."

They heard a slap, and then their mother let out a cry.

"It's not your fault," their mother begged. "One day's pay doesn't go very far these days. It's the way things are. It only buys a loaf of bread so small it barely feeds us. I don't mean to hurt your pride, Artur. You're a good husband and father. I know that. Believe me I do, but if we are going to survive, I must find work, real work. A job in a factory maybe. The money I bring in will help our family."

"And what makes you think anyone would hire you? There are men out there on the streets, men who served our country in the Great War who have been beaten down by this economy. They are looking for work. And you can be sure that they're smarter than you, and they have employable skills. But they can't find jobs. So, what makes you think you can? Are you gonna whore yourself out? Is that what you're gonna do? Go to the foreman at a factory and trade him sex for . . ."

"Stop it, please! The children will hear you."

"I know you've done it before. Don't think people don't talk about you. I am so ashamed that you're my wife."

There was another slap and another cry. Anka winced and curled herself into her sister.

"Listen, Artur, I don't know if I can get a job, but please understand that I must try for the sake of the children . . ."

"Do you know what everyone will say about me? Not that they don't say enough already. They'll say that not only is Artur Scholz's wife a whore, but she is working because Artur is a failure who can't support his family. What kind of man does that make me? A failure, yes? Is that what you're saying, Heidi? I'm a failure?"

The girls heard the crisp sound of another slap, and then another. Then they heard a commotion as if furniture had been turned over. Their mother let out a loud cry. Anka grasped her sister tightly, hugging her close. "I'm scared he's beating Mutti again. Last time he got mad like this he broke her arm."

"Shh . . . shhh . . ." Kara tried to distract Anka by continuing the story. "And then the ducks began to hatch."

Another slap, another scream. A loud noise as if something, perhaps a piece of furniture, was turned over. Anka was shaking.

"And you know what?" Kara asked. But her sister didn't answer. "All the ducks looked the same. All except one. This one was different."

"You are nothing but a bitch. All you want to do is break me and shame me. If that's what you are trying to accomplish, Heidi, you've done it. You've done a good job of it. I came back from that damn war with a limp, but I served the fatherland. And, in spite of my limp, I got a job. I am doing the best I can to support you and the children. But you know what? You're ungrateful. Are you sure you're not a Jew, Heidi? You act like one of them. You are nothing but a filthy rat."

"What's a Jew?" Anka asked.

"Listen to the story," Kara pleaded.

"I want to know."

"I've seen drawings of them. They are scary people. They have long noses. Vater says we should be careful of them. He says they trick children into going with them. Then they take them to some dark temple where they drain their blood."

Anka shivered. "Why? Why would they do that? Are they monsters?"

"Vater says they are. He says they need the blood of Christian children for their dark satanic rituals. But I don't believe anything Vater says. Anyway, you are supposed to be listening to the story of the ducks, not thinking about monsters who drink the blood of children. For goodness' sake, Anka."

"I'm sorry, go on . . ."

"And so"—Kara took a deep breath and sighed, then she continued—"all the ducks were the same, but one was different. The others called him the ugly duckling."

CHAPTER THREE

ABRAM WALKED out into the street. It no longer looked like the familiar neighborhood where he had grown up. It looked like a war zone. He glanced around him and the breath caught in his throat. All that remained of the synagogue was a burned-out building. Glass covered the streets. A pool of blood had dried only a few feet away from him, and he wondered whose it was. Then he saw an old broken bicycle that had been perched up against a building. The tires were flat. The seat was cut to shreds. He saw the old bike fall to the ground, and his memory was transported back to his father. Abram remembered that his father had given him a bike two days before the terrible book burning in the Mitte.

It was May 1935. A spring day when the flowers had just begun to bloom, and tiny blades of grass peeked out of the ground. Abram was in the bookstore getting ready to leave. He wanted to take his new bike for a ride when his father came in from outside.

Kaniel Ehrlich grabbed his son's arm. "Abram, lock the door. Then take as many books as you can carry and hide them under the floorboards under my bed. Hurry."

"Which ones, Papa?"

"Anything by an American author. Anything by a Jewish author.

And any book you truly love. They are burning books in the streets. Hurry."

"How much room do I have?"

"Not enough for every book. But take what you can. Now please, Abram, hurry. Those bastards, Hitler's henchmen, are outside. Listen, I know you can hear them."

"How could I not? They're screaming and ranting."

"Well, they've started a bonfire with the books that son of bitch Goebbels has deemed indecent. And we own a bookstore. They'll be here to take our beloved books any minute."

Abram gathered the books he loved first, then he added some Jewish texts for the customers and some books by as many American authors. He could hardly carry them all. But he did and he ran toward his father's room.

In the streets, German people gathered, along with men in brown uniforms, their faces crimson. They were throwing books that they had stolen from the homes of Kaniel's neighbors, onto a large raging fire. It burned angry and red with flames that leapt toward the sky. Hoda, Kaniel's wife and Abram's mother, came running into the living room. "They're coming here. Give them the books, Kaniel. It's not worth getting arrested over. Or maybe worse. Maybe they'll beat you up, or . . ."

"Shaaa, Hoda. It's all right. I will give them whatever they want from the store," he said.

"You sent Abram upstairs to hide books, didn't you?" she asked.

He shrugged. Then he nodded. "We can't let them kill all of these beautiful stories. It would be a sin."

"Dying would be a sin too," Hoda said. She was trembling, "They are not blind. They see that this is a bookstore. They will be here in a minute. They'll be looking for their Traifemeh bicher, the books they have forbidden. It's not worth dying over . . ."

"Nobody is dying. They don't want to kill anyone. They just want the books. I'll give them the books that are on the shelves," Kaniel said in a calm voice trying to comfort her.

The door was flung open. The tiny bell that had been hung on the top of the door to alert the family when customers came, kept ringing as the door hit the wall behind it. Hoda jumped. Abram came into the room and winked at his father who offered him a weak smile. "Good afternoon, Officers," he said, trying to sound calm. "What can I do for you today?"

The Nazis pushed past Kaniel and his family and began to carry out handfuls of books. Abram moved forward. "Why are you doing this?" he said, ready to punch one of the Nazi invaders.

But Kaniel rushed over to his son and held him tightly. "Don't do anything," he gave warning. "Let them take the books."

Abram looked at his father with despair in his eyes, but Kaniel just shook his head. "Let them take the books," he repeated.

A bomb exploded, shaking Abram back into the present moment. Realizing the danger, he looked for cover.

CHAPTER FOUR

Is Abram all right? All Kara wanted to do was cry. But instead, she closed her eyes, and she could see his eyes. Those same eyes that had looked up at her from the book he was reading on that first day she had met him.

CHAPTER FIVE

Summer 1935
Berlin, Germany

FOR AS LONG AS Kara could remember, she and her neighbor Elke Cline had been best friends. They were drawn to each other because they both loved to read, and more importantly, they both loved to dream. The characters from the novels that they read came alive when they discussed them. And they couldn't get enough of romantic heroes and beautiful women. Rare or forbidden books that no one they knew had read, intrigued them. They searched these books out together, sharing them, so they could discuss what they'd read. And so, on one bright sunny autumn day after school had let out, Elke walked over to Kara with a sparkle in her eye. "I have an idea," she said.

"Oh? And what's that?"

"Three weeks ago, I went to the Mitte with my mutter. She was going to see the Jewish doctor: secretly, of course. So you can't tell a soul."

"Of course, you know that I would never say a word to anyone about anything you tell me," Kara said.

"I know that. I know I can trust you. And that's why I thought you might want to try something different."

"I don't understand."

"Listen. While my mutti and I were on the bus, I saw a bookstore, a Jewish bookstore in the Mitte."

"And?"

"And I thought, wouldn't it be fun to explore it. They might have some of the forbidden books that we would love to get our hands on."

"I don't know. We could get into a lot of trouble. And besides, you and I both know that Jews can be dangerous. What if they capture us and . . ."

"You don't believe all of that nonsense now, do you? My mutter's doctor is just like us. He's a nice man. He's very understanding too. I will tell you another secret, but you must absolutely promise never to breathe a word of it."

"I just told you that everything you tell me is between us only," Kara said.

"My mother was pregnant. My parents could not afford another child. Even with all the government help. So, my mother went to see this doctor, and he fixed it for her."

"Fixed it?"

"Yes, he got rid of the baby."

"How? I mean, is she all right? Did anyone find out?"

"She's fine. I was with her. You know how close my mother and I are. Well, she was afraid, but he was very gentle and extremely careful."

"If he were caught . . ."

"Yes, if he were caught, he would have suffered greatly. But it's our secret, right."

"I said it was and it is. I promise you, Elke. No one will ever know."

"So, about the books. Would you go with me to that Jewish bookstore?"

"I'm a little scared," Kara said.

"I know. That's what makes it fun," Elke said, winking at Kara.

"All right. Why not. We could use a little adventure. So, let's go," Kara said, "but first let me find my sister, Anka, so I can tell her that you and I are going to the library to study. That way if my parents ask, she will tell them that."

"Do you want to bring her with us?" Elke asked. "I don't mind if you do."

"No. I think it's better to tell her we're going to the library. Let her go home and do her homework."

"Perfect," Elke said.

After they found Anka and told her they planned to study and that Kara would be home later, Elke and Kara caught a bus to the Mitte.

Kara shivered with excitement as she glanced over at Elke. "It's very different here," Elke whispered.

"Yes, it certainly is. They look so different," Kara said as she glanced at the people around her, "and look at the Jewish stars in the store windows."

"Yes, I know. I told you it would be an adventure to come here."

"Do you think that they will do anything to us? I mean kidnap us or . . ."

"No, I think those are just silly children's stories. When I came here with my mother last week, no one said a word to us."

Kara was intrigued. She would have liked to know more about these odd people. She would have liked to study them, to hear their stories, to know how they lived and what mattered to them. But she knew that her parents would never approve of her being here, let alone trying to talk to anyone. And besides, what if Elke was wrong; what if those stories she'd heard about the Jews were true, and she and Elke were in danger? As they walked in silence, they listened to the people they passed, speaking in a strange form of German. "What language is that?" Kara asked.

"Yiddish. It's a Jew language. But it's close enough to German that you can understand it, can't you?"

"Yes, most of it."

Kara thought about her parents and how they would have responded if they could see her walking with Elke on her way to a Jewish bookstore. Her mother would have scolded her, but her father, a war veteran from the Great War, would have been angry enough to beat her. He was a staunch follower of the new führer, who had made it known that he hated Jews. He said they were the reason that Germany lost the war. He said they were the reason that the German people had suffered under hyperinflation and had been humiliated and reduced to a defeated land. Kara didn't pay much attention to politics. But she was glad that the hyperinflation was over. She had been too young at the time to understand much. However, she had witnessed the effect it had on her parents, and that was enough to let her know that Germany was suffering.

Personally, she could remember a few instances when her mother had begged for a bag of potatoes or flour at the local store. Kara and her sister were always hungry. But when dinnertime came around, her mother said that her father was the head of household and that it was only right that he be served first. "He needs his strength, girls. He has to go out and look for work," her mother, Heidi, said in a sweet voice. But the few times Artur Scholz was able to find a job, he only lasted a couple of weeks before he came home drunk and angry. His excuse was always the same: the boss had let him go for no reason other than that the boss was a louse and he hated Artur.

Artur Scholz never accepted the fault for anything. If Kara's mother even dared to ask him to explain the situation in more detail concerning why he'd been let go, the fights began. Several times Kara and her sister cowered in the corner while her father beat her mother with his belt. A few times he lost control, and Heidi Scholz had ended up with a broken bone. After he beat his wife, Artur would sit in his favorite chair with a glass of schnapps and fall asleep. Hours later he would wake up with his rage gone. Then he would find his wife and get on his knees and apologize to her.

Once, Kara remembered, Heidi had packed the girls up and she'd been ready to leave. Kara and Anka were so glad to be going away from their volatile father. But before they got out the door, Artur had pleaded with Heidi not to go, promising he would never hit her again. And she'd stayed. It was only two weeks later that he broke her arm. But no matter what the circumstances, Kara learned, her father was never to be questioned. For as long as she could remember, Kara knew that everyone in their house was afraid of her father. He was a tyrant who ate most of what little there was. Her mother divided most of what was left between her two daughters, leaving only a very small portion for herself.

Kara hated to see her mother get dressed, because Heidi was so thin that when she saw her wearing just her slip, Kara was able to see her mother's ribs through the thin material.

One of Kara's most painful memories, which still haunted her, happened on a spring day. Anka had been playing with the girl who lived in the apartment next door, so the child's mother had agreed to watch Anka while Heidi went shopping for food. Heidi took Kara's hand and they headed into town. They picked up flour and potatoes. But then they stopped in front of the butcher shop. "You are eleven years old now. You can understand and follow my instructions. I want you to wait for me out here," her mother said in front of the butcher shop. "I am warning you not to move from the front of this store, no matter how long I am gone. Do you understand me?"

"Yes, Mother. But why can't I come in with you?"

"Because I said you can't. That's why. That's all you need to know. Do you understand me?"

Kara nodded.

Her mother walked into the butcher shop. She talked with the butcher for a few minutes. Then she saw the butcher with his bloody apron walk over to the door and hang a sign that read Closed. Then he and Kara's mother disappeared behind the counter. The lights went off inside the store. Kara was nervous.

She tried to peer inside, but it was too dark to see anything. Time passed, and as it did, Kara grew more and more frightened as she waited. Her mind had run away with her, and she wondered if the fat butcher, with his greasy hair and bloody apron, had killed her mother and cut her up to sell as meat. An hour later, when her mother appeared carrying a bag with two freshly killed chickens, Kara had been relieved. But on the way home, when she asked her mother why she had been gone so long and why the entire shop was dark, her mother scolded her for asking and made her promise not to mention the incident to anyone. "Make sure you never tell your father," she said, pointing her finger in Kara's face.

Since Adolf Hitler had come into power, there had been a great improvement in the Scholz household. As the führer had promised, unemployment had decreased, and her father had found work building a hospital. He still drank excessively and spent most of his money at the local tavern, but he was in better spirits. When he came home drunk, instead of beating their mother, he fell asleep. And although under the Third Reich, women were expected to devote their lives to their children and their homes, in order to make ends meet, Heidi was still forced to take in wash and mending for wealthy families.

Kara earned a few marks each month from babysitting the neighbors' children. She gave half of what she earned to her mother and spent the other half on books. She never told her parents what she spent her money on because her father would have been furious if he'd known. She thought that he would have probably beaten her and taken all of her money, telling her to go to the library. And although she frequented the library, she still longed to own her favorites.

Kara was lost in thought as she watched the people walk by with their strange clothes, gesticulating as they conversed in that strange form of German, which Elke had told her was called Yiddish.

Elke spoke, bringing Kara back to the moment at hand. "We'd better hurry and get to the bookstore so we can get home," Elke said, "I must be home in time to help my mother prepare dinner, and then I am going to the Bund Deutscher *Mädel* meeting tonight. Are you coming?"

"I have to. My father insists that I never miss a single meeting," Kara said, adjusting some hair that had come loose from her braids.

"Don't you like it?" Elke asked.

"Not really."

"I think it's fun. We're cooking tonight."

"Yes, I know," Kara said. "The cooking nights are my favorite."

"I love the extra food," Elke said. "I'm always hungry."

Kara smiled. Her friend had always been chubby. Somehow even during the leanest times, Elke found ways to get extra treats.

As they entered, they passed through an even more Jewish sector of town. Kara looked around her. Here the people looked even more unusual. There were men with their long, black coats and beards or curly sideburns who made her shiver. Dr. Goebbels had given the Germans plenty of warnings about the Jews. The others were different but not as different as these, and now as Kara looked around her, she felt a chill run up her spine. She felt so strange here, in her traditional German peasant outfit, here in this part of town where women wore long dresses and head coverings.

"Are you scared?" Kara asked Elke.

"Yes, I am. But I am curious too. Aren't you?"

Kara nodded. But as she glanced at the dark-eyed, dark-haired people, she wondered if they'd made a mistake in coming to this part of town.

"This is it!" Elke said, opening the door to a shop that had strange lettering and a Star of David on the window.

Kara trembled as she looked around. There was no one she recognized, and she didn't really expect that there would be.

"It's all right. Come on in," Elke said.

Kara nodded and then followed her friend inside. A small bell that was attached to the door rang, and a young man about five years older than Kara, with a yarmulke covering his head, looked up from behind the counter. He was tall and well built, wearing a clean white shirt and black pants. His dark eyes were serious as he studied the two girls.

"Can I help you?" he asked, his voice soft but deep.

"No, thank you. We must have wandered in here by mistake," Kara said, pulling on Elke's arm. "Let's go," she said to Elke in a warning tone.

"I want to look around."

Kara felt her knees grow weak. *What if a bunch of Jews came out of the back and seized her and Elke and they were unable to escape? No one knew they were here, so no one would know where to look for them. What if this handsome man was only a front for a group of strange people who drank the blood of Christian babies and had tails.*

The man smiled at Kara. His eyes were warm, his smile was sincere it stretched from his eyes all across his face. She couldn't imagine him hurting anyone. Except for the skull cap on his head, he seemed so normal. Just like everyone else. Except, perhaps, he seemed kinder. Was it possible that she saw so much in a stranger, or was it only her imagination? Still, as she watched him through the corner of her eye, she decided that there was something about this man that held her attention. She walked behind a bookshelf and studied him through the openings above the books. He sat quietly on a stool reading. He seemed so much more mature than the boys she'd met at dances. She was certain that any one of them would have been showing off if two young girls came into their store. They certainly would not be engrossed in reading. In fact, she'd never met a boy who liked to read. She was sure they existed; they had just never crossed her path.

"Do you have any forbidden books?" Kara asked boldly. She wondered why she'd dared to ask such a question—what had possessed her.

"Forbidden books are forbidden," he said in a gentle but logical manner.

She nodded. "Yes, you're right. I'm sorry I asked. I don't know what got into me."

There was silence for a few moments, then he said, "Are you looking for something in particular?"

"A storybook, a novel, anything that isn't about how great our führer is or how wonderful Germany is," she said, again surprising herself with her bold honesty.

"Kara!" Elke said, "What is the matter with you. Watch what you say."

Suddenly Kara's face turned crimson. "Oh, I am sorry. I was just . . ."

"It's all right," he said warmly. "I like novels too." Then he added, "Wait here."

The man walked through a hallway that led to a door behind the shop, then he disappeared. When he returned, he was carrying a book. "My personal favorite. A forbidden one, I'm afraid. So, you'll have to take care not to get caught with it. But I think you'll enjoy it," he said. "It's called *The Time Machine*, by an author named H.G. Wells, an English author. It's about a man who builds a time machine that allows him to travel through time, back into history and forward into the future." He raised his eyebrows, then said, "Can you imagine being able to go back into the past, or even more exciting, to travel into the future?"

"I can't imagine what it would be like to travel outside of Germany. I've never been."

"Oh, you must go. There is a wonderful big world out there just waiting for you to see it. I have dreams of Paris, London . . . America," he said.

"Have you been?"

"I've been to Cologne, Munich, and Poland. But not America, not yet. That's where I really want to go. I've read a great deal about it."

She felt her face light up, and her eyes too. She found this man utterly fascinating.

"In this novel, the protagonist travels through the past, but he stops in the future, in a world unlike any we have ever seen . . ."

"It sounds wonderful." Kara was mesmerized by the very idea of such an amazing book. She couldn't wait to get home and start reading it. Then she looked into the young man's eyes. He was about two feet taller than her. "How much do I owe you?" Kara asked.

"Well, that's the problem. I can't sell it to you, because I would miss it. And I can't get another one because they have all been burned. But, how about this: how about if I lend it to you? But you'll have to promise me you'll return it."

"Of course I will," she said, hugging the book to her chest. "I'll bring it back to the store, just as soon as I finish reading it."

He smiled.

"We'd better go," Elke said, her voice curt. It sounded like a warning.

Kara nodded. "I'll return it. I promise," she said as she tucked the book into her handbag.

CHAPTER SIX

AFTER THE GIRLS LEFT, a woman came out from the back of the bookstore. "Nu, Abram, what are you doing talking to them?" The woman looked out the window and watched Kara and Elke as they ran to the bus stop. "And I heard you—you gave her a forbidden book?"

Abram nodded. "I'm sorry, Mother. It's just that she was a fellow reader."

"She was one of *them*, not one of us. That makes her an outsider. She doesn't belong here. You should have made her feel unwelcome so she and her friend would leave and never come back. Instead, you put yourself, me—and not only us—but everyone in our neighborhood at risk with this thoughtless behavior of yours. How do you know she isn't going to the police to turn you in for having forbidden books for sale here? All she has to do is show them the book and, *bam*, they'll come right here and arrest us. You know she can get a reward for turning you in."

"I don't believe she would do that. You didn't see her face. She was a nice girl."

"Abram, Abram, *zie nit kain nar*, don't be a fool. I know you're smarter than that. So far, the Nazis leave us alone here. We should be grateful and stay out of their way. You know as well as I do that they don't like Jews. They are looking for only the smallest excuse . . ."

"I still don't believe that girl who was just here would turn us in; she was just a young woman looking for books that she can read for pleasure."

"And let's suppose you're right, and she didn't come to turn us in. Let's for a moment believe that she did actually come here to find books. But if she is caught with a forbidden book, instead of facing the punishment herself, you can be sure she will be sending the police right back here to our store. And then that will be the end of all of us."

"She is smart; she'll keep the book hidden."

"Sometimes, I worry about you, Abram. You act like you have no *sechel*, you don't use your head. You don't even know this girl. Yes, she was blonde and, yes, she was pretty. But she is not one of us. If you looked a little closer, you would take notice that she was wearing that German folk costume. And she sure looked like a Nazi to me," his mother said. Then she shook her head and looked directly at her son. "I hope I am wrong. I hope this doesn't bring the wrath of hell down on our heads."

"I promise you; it will be all right, Mama," he said.

CHAPTER SEVEN

KARA HELD her handbag close to her chest. She imagined she could feel the book burning through it like a hot iron. *If I get caught with this book I will be in real trouble.* As the bus turned down the familiar streets of her neighborhood, she felt even more nervous. But once it stopped, and she and Elke got off, she breathed a sigh of relief. Elke and Kara walked for a short while together, then Elke turned off to the left, but before she departed, she said, "Don't worry, I won't tell anyone about the book. But you must promise me you'll never go back to that store. I didn't expect you to take a forbidden book home and promise a Jew boy that you would return it. That's dangerous, Kara. I don't want to be responsible for what could happen to you. Promise me you'll never go back."

"I promise," Kara lied. She felt guilty lying to Elke, but she thought it was best if Elke didn't know the truth. It would only cause her to feel guilty, and if she did, she might turn the Jewish boy in because she felt it was best for Kara.

"See you tonight at the Bund Deutscher Mädel meeting?" Elke asked.

"Yes, I'll be there."

Kara walked into her apartment and ran into her bedroom.

"Where are you going?" her mother asked. "I need your help. Frau Gersh dropped off a whole basket of laundry, and she needs it back by tomorrow. I can't possibly finish it myself." Anka was sitting on the floor beside her mother with a basket of dirty clothes in front of them. She was scrubbing a man's shirt on a washboard.

"I just want to change, and I'll be right back to help."

Her mother wiped the sweat and hair from her forehead. "Hurry, please. We have all of this wash to finish, and then we have to peel and boil some potatoes for dinner. And isn't that meeting of yours tonight? Your father insists that you attend. I don't know how he can demand that. We have so much to do here. You'll never make it."

Kara ran into the room she shared with her sister and shoved the book under the bed. Then she took off her clothes and changed into an old work dress. She ran out to the living room and sat down on the floor next to her sister and began to wash the clothes.

"Take these and hang them on the line outside," her mother said. "By the time you return, we'll have more ready."

"Yes, Mutti," Kara said.

She did as she was told, but all she could think about was the book . . . and the boy with the dark hair and soulful eyes.

After dinner, Kara and Anka cleaned up, and then Kara went to her meeting. Elke was there waiting for her. "I've been thinking about you all day. I wish I had never taken you to that bookstore. I saw the way you looked at that boy, and the way he looked at you."

Kara saw the worry in her friend's eyes. "Don't worry, please. I thought it all over, and I threw the book in a trash can on the way here tonight."

"You did?"

"Yes," Kara lied again. She had never been a liar. But she was worried about the Jewish boy who had trusted her.

"Did anyone see you?"

"No, no one was around. I just took it out of my handbag and threw it in the can. Then I came to the meeting. No one saw me."

"Good. I feel better," Elke said.

They learned to make strudel that night with apples and raisins.

It was delicious. And by the end of the evening, Kara could see that Elke had forgotten all about the book and the young man with the kippah, and she was relieved. As they walked home together, Elke talked about how glad she was that they were able to prepare these lovely dishes. "My parents could never afford all these ingredients," she said. "That's what I love about the Bund Deutscher Mädel; we get the best of everything."

"Yes, you're right," Kara said, putting her arm around her friend's shoulder.

When Kara got home, Anka was awake in her bed waiting for her sister. "How was your meeting?" Anka asked.

"Good, we made a strudel. Wasn't your meeting tonight too?"

"No, it was canceled. Frau Hahn is sick. So, I helped Mutti finish the wash for Frau Gersh."

"Is it all done?"

"Yes, all of it. Thank goodness."

"I'm sorry you had to do it all without me."

"It's all right. I didn't mind. You would do the same for me."

"You know I would," Kara said as she got undressed and washed up for bed. Then she put a chair in front of the door of their room and pulled the book out from under the bed.

"You have a new book?" Anka said in a whisper, but she was excited. Even though she was fifteen and Kara was seventeen, she still loved it when her sister read to her.

"I have a new book for us, but it's more than just a new book. It's a forbidden book."

"What is it?" Anka asked.

"It's a story about a man who builds a time machine and travels through time."

"Where did you get it?"

"Never mind," Kara said. "Stop asking so many questions, and sit down beside me and listen."

"All right," Anka said, smiling. "You still treat me like a child."

"That's because I am your older sister," Kara said, "and no matter how old we get, I'll always be two years older than you."

They both giggled softly.

And then Kara began to read. When she heard her mother's footsteps on the stairs, she stashed the book under the bed quickly, then turned off the light, and both girls climbed into bed. Their mother peeked into the room and glanced around. Once she was satisfied that the girls were sleeping, she closed the door quietly. Kara and Anka waited until they heard their father's loud snoring, then Kara got out of bed and lit a candle. Anka followed her. They sat down on the floor and placed the candle beside them. Kara read by candlelight until it was almost morning.

CHAPTER EIGHT

THE GIRLS WERE EXHAUSTED the next day, but they forced themselves to get out of bed and get ready to go to school. Kara found that she was so tired that day that she almost fell asleep when her science teacher was giving a lecture. It was so difficult to keep her eyes from closing and her head from finding its way onto her desk. But she got through the day. After school, Kara and Anka returned home. "I'm so exhausted," Anka whispered in Kara's ear. "It serves us right for staying up all night."

"Would you change it? Would you rather not read tonight?"

"You know better," Anka said. "As soon as we can, I want to find out what happens to the time traveler in that book."

But life did not stop simply because the girls were tired. There were chores to do, and more wash had come in during the day, which their mother needed their help with. They finished all that was expected of them. And both of them were glad when it came time to go to bed. They were weary, but as soon as they were alone in their room, they took the book out again, and Kara began to read. They were so engrossed in the story that at that moment it seemed worth the price of being tired all day. A week later when they read the last paragraph, Kara sighed and said, "I loved that book."

"Me too. I wonder why it was banned."

"So many wonderful books were burned when our führer took power. In my opinion, it was a mistake. But I wouldn't dare say a word to anyone but you about how I feel," Kara admitted to her sister, then she added, "I'll try to get more of these forbidden books. But you must make sure you never tell anyone that we are reading these. I know how you are when you are with your girlfriends. You chatter away sometimes without thinking. And, if anyone ever found out, we could get into a lot of trouble."

"I know. I'll be careful not to talk too much. I'll watch everything I say."

CHAPTER NINE

K ARA TOOK Elke's arm and led her into an alleyway. "You're my best friend. I know I can trust you," Kara said. "I have to take that book back to the bookstore in the Mitte and I don't want to go alone."

"I thought you threw it away. You lied to me!" Elke said.

"I lied because I didn't want you to get upset. I am just going to return it, and then I'll never go back to that area again."

"Kara, that wasn't fair of you. I never lie to you."

"I had to lie. I feel guilty about it. But I had to, or you would have made me get rid of the book before I could read it."

"Was it that important to you?" Elke was angry.

"It was. I wanted to read it. I am tired of being told what we can and can't read."

"You had better stop all of this right now. I made a mistake taking you to that store. I was just looking for something fun to do. Maybe even something a little dangerous. But I sure wasn't expecting you to take a book home with you. A forbidden book, no less. Are you crazy, Kara? Is any book worth the price you'll pay if you get caught? The price we might both have to pay?" Elke snorted, then shook her head. "Just throw the damn thing away in a trash can in town. No one will ever know you had it."

"I don't want to throw it away. It's a wonderful book," Kara said.

"Don't be a fool. It's a forbidden book. An illegal book," Elke reminded her. "You read it. You lied so that you could read it. Fine, but now get rid of it."

"I don't feel right about not returning it."

"You offered to pay for it, didn't you? That bookstore is owned by Jews. Don't worry about them. You owe them nothing. They're lucky you don't turn them in for having an illegal book. I'm telling you, just get rid of it."

"So, I am assuming you don't want to look around that store again."

"You're right. I was curious about what was there. But now that I have been, there is no need to return. And Kara, I'm telling you that there is no need for you to return either. I am not just telling you; I'm warning you as your best friend in the whole world. You must just get rid of the book."

"Oh, Elke. It just seems so wrong." Kara sighed.

"What will be wrong is what will happen to you if you are caught. And even worse, what might happen to me if you tell the authorities that I brought you to that bookstore. I'm scared. I don't want to get into trouble. You are taking this nonsense way too far."

"All right. I'll do as you say," Kara said. She could see that Elke was worried about her, so she agreed. But she had no plans of disposing such a literary treasure.

"You must promise me, or I am going to have to tell one of our Bund Deutscher Mädel leaders that you have that book. That's the only way I can clear myself of any danger."

"Elke! Are you serious? Would you really turn me in?"

"I don't want to. I won't if you promise me that you'll throw the book in the trash and forget about that store and that the Jew boy who you were clearly making eyes at."

Kara felt her face flush with anger. But she realized that Elke was serious, very serious. Even more terrifying was the fact that she could see in Elke's eyes just how afraid Elke was, and she remembered once, a few years ago, overhearing her father tell another army vet, "A man who is scared is the most dangerous animal. I learned that in the war." Her father's words rang through her memory, and she felt the sweat begin to bead under her arms and on her forehead, but she forced herself to smile. Then she promised Elke she would never return to the Mitte. She vowed that she would dispose of the book in a trash can far from her home, and once again Kara lied.

She despised herself for lying. She'd hoped that she could finally be honest with her friend. But she found that one lie had led to another, and now she was caught in a web. After school that day, Kara walked into the downtown area where she boarded a bus that would take her to the Jewish part of town. *The Time Machine* was wrapped in newspaper, and then tucked into her handbag.

It was different, scarier, to be walking through the Jewish sector of town alone. When she'd come with Elke, she'd been afraid, but at least she had not been alone. Now, as she walked at a quick pace toward the store, Kara began to think that perhaps she should have listened to Elke and thrown the book into the trash somewhere far away from her apartment.

But she had made a promise to that boy, that unusual and special boy, and she intended to keep it. After all, he'd been nice enough to loan her the book in the first place. He had looked into her eyes, and when he did, she felt like he'd looked into her soul. And then he must have seen something in her, because he'd taken a risk in trusting her with his secret book. She could easily have turned him in and gotten a reward for it too. He knew that. And because he had believed in her, believed that she would not betray him, she wanted to keep her promise and return his beloved book.

When she walked into the bookstore, the little bell overhead rang. A woman was sitting at the front counter. She was a pretty woman, still young, but not as young as Kara. *I wonder where he is,* Kara thought. The woman had the same dark eyes as the man had, but her hair was auburn and mostly covered by a dark scarf. She looked up at Kara, "Can I help you?" she said. But there was something off-putting in the woman's eyes.

Kara shook her head and turned away. "No, thank you," she said. Then she left the store quickly and began to walk as fast as she could toward the bus stop when she heard a male voice call out, "Wait, please, wait."

Kara turned around. It was him, the boy from the bookstore. "I brought it back," she said, her hands shaking as she clumsily took the book out of her handbag. "I promised you I would bring it back."

"Yes," he said, "thank you, but not here, not on the street. It's too dangerous. Put it in your handbag for now."

"Oh yes. That's true. You're so right. What was I thinking?" Kara said, feeling foolish and stuffing the book back into her handbag. She was glad that she'd wrapped it in newspaper, so no one had seen what it was. But then she glanced up to see that he was watching her intently. Kara felt as if she had lost herself in his gaze. *I am acting stupidly, because I'm not thinking straight. He has a sort of strange hold on me. I should find a way to give him this book, then get out of here. But I don't' want to.*

"I was in the back when you came into the store. I saw you leave, and I followed you." He sounded unsure of himself, a little insecure. "The woman who was sitting at the desk is my mother."

She nodded.

Then he added, "By the way, my name is Abram Ehrlich."

"Thank you for the book, Abram," she said.

"What's your name?"

"Kara Scholz."

"Nice to meet you, Kara."

"I would have given the book to your mother, but I didn't know if she knew that you had a forbidden book."

"It's all right. I'm glad you didn't give it to her. If you had, I'd have had no excuse to come out and talk to you."

She blushed. Then she giggled not knowing what to say next. "Well, your parents must love books as much as you do, or they wouldn't own a bookstore."

"My father was the book lover. He was a journalist. Brilliant, if I must say so myself. The bookstore was his dream. He always wanted to own one. My mother was the prettiest girl in his neighborhood, so he married her. But she has no interest in books. My father was my best friend, but he died at the close of last year. I miss him so much."

"I'm sorry."

"Yes, so am I. He was quite a man, always challenging me intellectually. He wasn't religious and never demanded that I read the Jewish texts like the other boys that I went to school with. My father introduced me to a whole world through books. The forbidden books that I have were his."

"You have more?"

"A few. Would you like to borrow another?"

She nodded. "I would."

"Wait here. I'll be right back."

Abram returned a few minutes later. Then he said, "Follow me," and he led Kara behind a building. No one was around.

"Can I give you *The Time Machine* now?" Kara asked.

"Yes, that's why I brought you here behind the building," he said. She handed him the book. He took it and then pulled a copy of *All Quiet on the Western Front* out of a pocket inside his jacket and handed it to her. "The book I am giving you today is about a young soldier during the Great War. It's very good. I think you'll like it."

She smiled. "I'll bring it back as soon as I finish it," she said, her heart pounding as she looked at him.

"I'll be waiting," he said as he tucked *The Time Machine* into the pocket inside his jacket and watched her walk away.

CHAPTER TEN

ABRAM EHRLICH KNEW he was a dreamer. Before his father, Kaniel, died, he'd teased Abram affectionately for living inside the books they both loved. Kaniel had fostered that love of literature, so he understood him, but his mother, Hoda, did not. Abram had never been satisfied with the mundane. He was discontented with the life that was expected of him, a life where he never ventured far away from the place he was born. He wanted more; he longed to travel and experience things on his own terms.

When his father had been alive, his parents had argued about him. When he was little, Abram attended public school. But as he grew older and developed problems, his mother insisted that Abram attend a religious school. Abram had wanted to continue in public school. But Hoda was so adamant about it that his father finally agreed. It cost them more money than they wanted to spend to send him to a yeshiva, and because of it, they were forced to live frugally.

But Abram could still remember his mother telling his father that she was worried, because he had planted seeds inside of Abram's head that were already causing problems as Abram was growing up. His mother was anxious because Abram refused to fit into the world he'd been born into. And she told his father that she thought Abram should be married as soon as possible. By the time he was fourteen, he'd already earned a reputation for ruining a local girl. It was a *shanda*, an embarrassment, Hoda said. Her son was not considered a good marriage prospect by the local women. He had a wandering eye and openly stared at the girls as they walked by with a look of desire on his face. Kaniel insisted that the other boys felt the same way. But Hoda would shake her head and say, "At least they try to hide it."

When Abram turned fourteen, he stopped attending synagogue with his mother and openly declared that he followed no religion and even had the audacity to question God's existence. This made the other people in their little circle look upon him with disdain. It was clear that he paid no attention to the rules that the others valued so dearly, and he couldn't have cared less what was expected of him.

While his friends were being introduced to their potential brides, he was rejecting every possible girl that was presented to him by a matchmaker. The idea of an arranged marriage left him cold. And not only that, but his future career was questionable.

His family owned a bookstore, and he told his parents and everyone else he knew that he had no plans of taking over the business. "That store is my father's dream. Not mine." He said arrogantly. Then added, "I love to read, but I can't imagine spending the rest of my life sitting in a shop all day. I want to live a full life. A life of adventure. I not only want to read about heroes, I want to be one." He longed to travel to Africa or China perhaps.

To his mother's chagrin, the neighbors talked about Abram. They said he was a little bit crazy. And the more he talked, the more his marriage prospects diminished. When Hoda's best friend, Lillian, came to tell her that Abram was openly staring at the women on the street and flirting shamelessly, she was ashamed.

"I only come to tell you this because everyone is talking," Lillian said, "and, of course, because you are my oldest and dearest friend, and you should know."

Hoda shook her head. "I can't control him, Lilly."

"Oy vey. I feel for you."

Abram adored women. But not the way that the holy books said they were to be adored. He found them fascinating, sexually tantalizing, and he thought about them constantly.

Hoda hoped that somehow Hashem would send the right girl Abram's way and she would straighten him out. He would finally marry and settle down. This was her dream. But that didn't happen. Instead, Abram got himself into trouble when he was only thirteen, the year of his bar mitzvah. Unlike any of his friends at the religious school where his mother had sent him, he had sex for the first time at thirteen.

Her name was Rivka. She was a pretty girl who was a year older than Abram. They'd met at a party at the synagogue where they'd been introduced by a mutual friend. At the time, Rivka's parents were searching for a suitable husband for her. She and Abram began talking. Then she began coming to the bookstore to see him. He was easy to talk to, unlike any of the other boys she'd met so far. Rivka told Abram that her father was trying to make a match for her. She confided in Abram that she was terrified to marry, but her father was insistent. He listened intently. He sympathized. She hinted that she wished he would try to talk to his father and ask his father to contact her family and offer Abram as a possible match for her.

He just smiled.

"I would love that," she said.

Abram never lied to Rivka. He never promised her that he would send his father to ask for her hand. He was kind to her and became her friend. The sex was her idea. She said that she wanted to share her first time with someone she wanted to be with rather than someone her family had decided on. "My father has agreed on a match with a much older, unattractive, but wealthy fellow. I dread a life with him. But my father will go mad if I say a word. He expects me to do what he wants."

"It's your life," Abram said. "You should make decisions based on that, not on what other people want from you. *You* deserve to live your life the way *you* want to live it."

"I have to do what my father wants, Abram. I was raised that way. My father will make the match, and things will progress from there. Perhaps if you would have asked for my hand, things would have been different."

"I'm not ready for marriage. I'm not ready to be bound to anyone for the rest of my life. It's not you, Rivka, It's me. I am not like the others in our community."

"But you could have made a match and then we could have waited for a couple of years before our wedding."

"I'm so sorry. I know that's what you wanted, but I can't do that for you," he said sincerely.

"If I told you a secret, would you promise not to ever tell anyone?" she confided.

"You know I would."

She looked around the bookstore to be sure no one was there. "Are we alone?"

"Yes, my mother is shopping. You can speak freely," he said.

Then trembling, she told him that she longed to know what it would be like to make love with someone other than the man her father had chosen. "I would like that man to be you," she said.

He felt his pulse quicken. "Are you sure?" he asked. "You won't be a virgin for your husband. How will he feel about it when there is no blood on the sheet?"

"I don't care. I don't want to spend the rest of my life wondering what I missed."

Abram locked the door and led her to his room in the apartment behind the bookstore. They had quick and clumsy sex. But even so, it was a wonderful experience for Abram. He liked Rivka, but the sex didn't change anything. And he would have been quite satisfied to congratulate her on her marriage. But Rivka was in love, and she was bursting with excitement.

Later that day, she saw her best friend, Devorah, and she couldn't control her desire to share all the details of her secret liaison. When Devorah heard what Rivka had done, she was appalled. She went home and told her parents, and then they insisted that she separated herself from Rivka.

The news traveled fast in their small community, and soon Abram's mother found out. At the time, his father, Kaniel, was still alive. Hoda was in tears when she told her husband what Abram had done. But Kaniel only shrugged. "What he did was only natural, Hoda. A boy his age is curious."

"Not in our world, Kaniel. He ruined that girl. I doubt her wedding will take place."

"I'll go and talk to the girl's father," Kaniel said.

"I don't know if you should. He will be angry, and rightfully so."

"I'll take care of it." Kaniel smiled at his pretty wife. "Have I told you today that you are the most beautiful woman I've ever seen?"

"Kaniel. Can't you please be serious? Our son is getting a bad reputation. He will never find a decent wife." She wrung her hands together.

But Kaniel took both of her hands in his and began to slowly kiss her palms. He felt her anger leave as she leaned against him. Kissing her neck and breathing hot air into her ear, he whispered, "Abram won't be home from school for another two hours . . ."

She melted into his arms as he led her into their bedroom.

The following day, Kaniel went to see his father-in-law. He told him the situation, explained what Abram had done. Hoda's father was well-to-do, and he gave his son-in-law some money to help his grandson. "Go and see the father Kaniel. Offer him this money to help pay for the girl's dowery. Then do whatever you have to do in order to find that boy a wife as soon as possible. Do you understand me? If you don't, that boy is bound for trouble."

"Thank you for the money," Kaniel said. But he knew he would never try to control his son. He secretly loved the fact that Abram didn't follow rules, that he was his own man. He loved his son's courage, and his lust for life.

Kaniel went to see Rivka's father, who was angry. But thankfully he didn't want to see his daughter married to Abram, and so he didn't demand that Abram propose. Instead, Rivka's father reluctantly accepted the money. And once again, as Kaniel had done so many times in Abram's life, Kaniel had found a way to get Abram out of a jam.

Rivka never married that older man. Three months later, she and her family moved away from the Mitte in Berlin. No one in their small circle knew where the family went.

CHAPTER ELEVEN

KANIEL UNDERSTOOD HIS SON. Abram's father saw a lot of himself in Abram. The year of his bar mitzvah, Abram told his father that he longed to travel and see the world and to experience different cultures. He admitted he couldn't imagine being satisfied living his entire life in a small Jewish community. Kaniel sympathized with his son. He knew how small and confining a community like this could be for a boy like Abram.

Before Kaniel had met Hoda and married her, he'd been in search of adventure. He left home early, had traveled around Europe and had numerous lovers, the more exotic the better. But when he got home, he found that his mother was very sick; she was dying. Kaniel was shaken. He had not known, and if he had not come home when he did, he would never have seen his mother alive again. This thought unnerved him.

On her deathbed, his mother made him promise that he would eventually return to live in Berlin permanently. She made him vow to marry a Jewish girl and have children. Kaniel loved his mother, and he hated to argue, so he agreed. But after her death, his father tried to find him a wife, and he refused everyone who had been introduced to him.

Then he returned to Berlin and got a job as a freelance journalist. By then he was almost thirty-eight. That was when he met Hoda. In his eyes, she was by far the prettiest girl in town. And to sugarcoat the deal, her father had money. Working as a freelance journalist, he hardly earned enough to support himself, let alone a wife. But he made a point of wooing his father-in-law, who found him charming and intelligent even if he had never attended a university.

Kaniel had read extensively and could hold a conversation on almost any subject. He had business savvy and was more than willing to share his ideas with Hoda's father when asked. Kaniel went to Hoda's home at least once a week to see her. He made sure to bring wine for her father and candy for her mother. He spoke softly, respectfully, and kindly to Hoda's entire family. So it came as no surprise to Kaniel when Hoda's father approached his father to discuss a possible match between Hoda and Kaniel. Kaniel had been waiting for this. He listened from his room and overheard the conversation.

"I have come to you about a match between your son and my daughter," Hoda's father said. "She is good girl. A kind girl. I realize that Kaniel is much older than Hoda. And I am sure you are wondering why I would agree to such a match. That is why there is something I must tell you. Hoda was engaged before, and the boy broke off the engagement when he learned that she had been severely burned in a cooking accident when she was child. I know you can't see the burns, because she is a good and modest woman. But her entire chest and left arm are scarred. I want you to tell Abram about this before he agrees to the match. I don't want him to propose to Hoda and then find out about her burns and break up with her. She cannot go through that again."

Kaniel's father looked at the other man. "You are a good papa," he said. "I will talk to my son."

After Hoda's father left, Kaniel's father asked him how he felt about marrying Hoda, after explaining that she'd been scarred in an accident.

Kaniel smiled. "I don't care about the burns. I like her. I like her very much. In fact, I think I love her," he said. And so the marriage had been arranged.

On their wedding night, Hoda had been an innocent virgin. She was afraid and trembling when Kaniel came to her bed. He was a man who had much experience wooing women, and he knew the right things to say and do to win her heart. He was a gentle and patient lover, concerned more with pleasing his wife than himself. Before long, Hoda found that she was in love with Kaniel. He made her laugh even when she felt sad. And he introduced her to books. "Women deserve to read, not only religious texts, but to read for fun. The world outside of your little religious community accepts women as equals," he declared.

"But I was raised by a very religious father, and I am afraid to read these books. Besides, in our world, men don't even read these books."

"Well, don't you believe that a woman should listen to her husband?"

"Yes, of course."

"Then . . ." He smiled. "I demand that you read these books. You know why?"

"Why?"

"Because you will enjoy them. And I want you to be happy."

Oh, how she loved him. And the longer they were together, the more that love between them grew. Hoda felt that she was the most blessed and fortunate woman in the world. And then three years later, Hashem blessed their union, and Abram, their healthy baby boy, was born.

Kaniel worked writing articles for the local paper, but he didn't earn much. So his father-in-law, upon seeing how happy his daughter and his son-in-law were together, decided to give Kaniel money to open a bookstore. It was supposed to be a shop that sold only religious texts, but anyone who knew Kaniel, knew that he provided not only religious books, but he also had plenty of novels and poetry books.

Time passed, and Hoda's mother passed away. Kaniel did what he could to help Hoda cope with the pain. After losing his wife,

Hoda's father visited the couple often. He would come to play with his grandson, whom he adored, and stay for dinner.

Kaniel enjoyed the bookstore and adored Hoda. His son was the light of his life. He saw the future, his legacy, in little Abram. And he taught the boy everything he could, even to read at a very early age.

The years passed, gently like the flow of a river. It wasn't that Kaniel was dissatisfied with his life, but sometimes, an old longing would creep up inside of him. A yearning for something more exciting, a trip to an exotic land, or a love affair with a forbidden woman. The thoughts frightened him, and he stifled them because he loved Hoda, and he knew that he would never find as good a wife as her or as generous a father-in-law as he had right now.

Then one afternoon, he was returning from a meeting with a local author he thought was a brilliant writer. As he walked toward home, he felt flushed and nauseated. He was so sick that he had to stop and vomit behind a building. He'd eaten lunch at a local pub, and he blamed the food for his feeling poorly. But that night he didn't get better. And he didn't get better the following day. In fact, he felt worse. Kaniel told Hoda that he was so dizzy and nauseated that he could hardly stand up. She was overcome with worry.

Hoda and Abram, who was now a young man, had helped Kaniel into bed. He lay there for a few minutes, but then his body trembled, and he vomited profusely while Hoda held a bucket for him. She wiped his forehead with a wet cloth and sent Abram to fetch a doctor. But by the time Abram returned, Kaniel was dead.

Abram wept. He sobbed like a lost child. Losing his father was the hardest thing he'd ever faced. He loved his mother, but his father understood him better than anyone in the world. He was like the other half of Abram's soul. They could sit together in silence and know what the other was thinking.

Losing his father had left an empty, dark hole in Abram's heart. But even so, Abram's curiosity and his need to experience all things life had to offer did not end with the loss of his father. The only difference was, now Abram no longer had a net to catch him as he walked on a tightwire through life.

CHAPTER TWELVE

ABRAM THOUGHT about the girl with the blonde braids all day long. When his mother arrived home from shopping for food, she found him in the bookstore, reading. She put her basket of vegetables down on the counter and sat beside him. Then she touched his hand. "It's time you should settle down, Abram," she told him. "You don't have to move out of here. You and your wife can live here with me. I will give you the large room, and I'll move into your room. My papa will help to make a match for you. But my papa is getting older, and with your father gone, you should let your zede help you while he is still alive."

"I'm not ready, Mother. I don't want to marry just yet. Besides, I haven't met anyone with whom I would want to spend my life."

"That's because you don't give any of the girls around here a chance. You're always looking for someone or something that is different and unusual. I understand that you are a man, and perhaps it's all right for you to have gone away from home to try new things. But now that your father has passed away, it is time for you to marry. It is important that you find a nice Jewish girl who shares your culture and your way of life. In the long run, a girl like this will make a better life partner for you," Hoda said, frowning.

"I love you, Mother, I truly do. But I am not ready for a wife and children. I would not make a good husband or father. I would do the poor girl an injustice. I can't trust myself not to get an urge to travel again and that would mean leaving her, and maybe a child behind." Hoda sighed as he kissed her on the top of her head. "I'll put these vegetables away for you if you 'd like. You can stay here and watch the store," he said.

"No, I have to put up a pot of soup," she said, standing up and stretching. "I'd better hurry, or it won't be ready for dinner. You stay here and watch the store." Then she saw the book he was reading. "*A Farewell to Arms?*" She shook her head. "If you are going to read forbidden books, you should be reading them in the privacy of your room, not in the front of the store. All we need is for the police to come in here for some reason and see this. We would have trouble. Trouble we don't need."

"You're right, Mother," he said, shoving the book under the counter.

She shook her head and walked through the door in the back of the store, and to the apartment behind it.

Abram took the book back out from under the counter and held it for a moment. He knew his mother was right about reading forbidden books out in the open. But he wanted to finish this one before loaning it to Kara.

"Kara," he whispered her name and felt his body prickle with excitement. She was pretty; she loved to read, and her smile lit up the room. He was intrigued by her traditional German folk costume and her braided hair, the color of winter wheat. He envisioned her bright blue eyes looking up at him when he kissed her, and the romantic in him swelled with desire for more than just a mere kiss. He imagined her lying beneath him, naked, outside in the sunlight. Her hair would be like a golden flame lit by the rays of the sun. Desire made him anxious to see her again.

It was almost three weeks before Kara returned with the book. Abram was dusting the bookshelves when she arrived.

"Hello," she said, looking down at her shoes.

She's shy. How charming, he thought. And he liked her even more for the tender blush in her cheeks.

"Did you like it?" he asked. "The book, I mean?"

"I did. I read it to my sister. It was very sad. We both cried."

"It's a sad one. But it has an important message."

She handed him the worn copy of *All Quiet on the Western Front.* He shoved it under the counter. Then he said, "Wait here. I have another one for you if you would like it."

"I would," she said enthusiastically.

He smiled, and when she smiled back at him, he felt his heart flutter. "I'll be back in a moment," he said. Then he went through the door into his apartment. His mother was in the kitchen chopping carrots.

"Where are you going, Abram? Who's watching the store?"

"I'm just going to get something. I'll be back in the store in a second," he said.

"You want I should go and watch the store until you get back?" his mother asked.

"No!" he said, sounding more abrupt than he'd planned. "I won't be that long."

She didn't look up from the dough she was kneading. She just nodded, and Abram breathed a sigh of relief that his mother didn't notice his tone of voice. Sometimes, Abram felt that his mother could be ruthless like a bloodhound or a detective when it came to him. And if she had noticed his quick reaction to her question, she would have definitely put down her cooking and gone into the store to see what he was hiding from her.

But today he had been lucky. Perhaps her mind was elsewhere. He didn't know for certain, but he was glad she wasn't giving him her full attention. He ran to his room and quickly pulled the book from behind the shoes in his closet where he'd been hiding it. Then he headed back through the kitchen to the store.

"What is that? Another forbidden book?" his mother called after him. "Abram, you are going to get us in trouble. I wish you would get rid of those books. They are just not worth the problems that they could cause us." She sighed, but she didn't go after him. Then under her breath she said, "I don't know what I am going to do with that boy."

Abram turned to look, and he was glad his mother wasn't following him. Kara stood waiting at the counter patiently. He looked at her. How lovely she was with that hair that was even whiter than gold. And how charming her dirndl skirt fitted her slender waist and her little white blouse embroidered with red and green fitted her bodice.

Abram handed Kara the book *A Farewell to Arms*. She read the title that was written on the spine of the old book.

"Yes, it's by an American author. It's a war story, but it also has a beautiful romance."

She blushed as she took the book, and as she did, his hand brushed hers. He saw her tremble, and his hand felt hot where their fingers had touched.

"I think you'll like it," he added. "I did."

She smiled. "I can't wait to read it to my sister."

"How old is your sister? I mean this is not a book for a child."

"Oh, she's a teenager. But I have been reading to her since she was just a little girl. We enjoy our reading time together."

He nodded. "Reading is always good, and it's always nice to have someone read to you."

She let a small smile creep over her lips as she looked at the book in her hands.

"I have an idea," he said, then whispering, he added, "Why don't we arrange to meet at the park in a few weeks, so you can return the book. My mother is here at the shop most of the time, and she is always listening. If we meet at the park, we can have a few minutes to discuss the book."

She looked up and their eyes locked. He thought he heard her breath catch in her throat. Then she said, "The park? Which park?"

"The one right around the corner from here? Would that be all right? I mean do you know where it is?"

She nodded. "I know exactly where it is. I see it when I get off the bus. It's right on the left side of the street as I walk from the bus stop to your store."

"Yes, that's right. So, you'll meet me there?"

She nodded. "I will."

"How long do you think it will take you to finish the book?"

"Two weeks, would that be all right?"

He nodded. "Sure. Let's meet at the park exactly two weeks from today. Is six in the evening all right?"

"It is a little late. But since it stays light outside until seven, it should be all right. We can talk for about a half hour, then I can catch a bus and head back home."

"I hope you like the book," he said, gazing into her eyes.

She looked away and nodded. "I'm sure I will."

"Abram?" Abram's mother called out from the apartment behind the store. "Who's there? Who is that in the store whispering with you?"

"I'd better go," Kara said, her hand trembling as she held the book.

He nodded. "Two weeks from today?"

"I'll be there," she said and left.

Hoda Ehrlich walked into the store and looked around. There was no one there. Then she looked out the window and saw the girl in the traditional German outfit walking away. "Abram"—she looked at him, and her face was red with anger—"stay away from that girl. You act like such a *nar*, a real fool. If you keep on with her, you are going to get into trouble. Mark my words."

"Don't worry so much, Mother."

She shook her head and went back into the kitchen of the apartment.

CHAPTER THIRTEEN

As KARA WALKED to the bus stop, she thought she felt the eyes of everyone she passed scrutinizing her. *I don't belong here,* she thought. *These people don't want me here.* She was sure they were staring at her with dark, brooding eyes. And she felt as if they were dissecting her to see if she were made of the same flesh and blood that they were.

She thought about all of the lessons she'd been taught about Jews, not only lessons from the Bund Deutscher Mädel, but lessons from her parents, and from school. It had been drilled into her brain since she was little that Jews were different. That they weren't made of flesh and blood, but that they were some evil and magical group of subhumans, who posed a serious danger to the Aryan race.

Yet when she thought about Abram, she felt reckless and excited. He was interesting because he was different from the other boys she met. He was soft spoken and well read. And he spoke to her as if she were his equal, not a brood mare born to bear him children. But most importantly, he seemed to be very different from her father, who she was certain would have beaten her until she couldn't walk if he'd known that she was going to this Jewish bookstore.

Kara stood on the corner waiting for the bus and thought about her father. *He has never read a book in his life. In fact, I believe he can hardly read at all. He is a big, ignorant lout who rules our home because it's a house filled with women. He rules us through terror. I don't want to marry a man like him. If I ever marry at all, I want a man as different from him as can be.*

Even so, that night when she took the book out and began to read to her sister, she decided it was best that she not tell Anka she was meeting with a Jewish boy alone in the park to return the book. When Anka asked where she'd gotten the book, she told her that she and Elke had gone to a store in the Jewish sector of town. Anka gasped. "Weren't you afraid?"

"It was all right. I just bought the book and left."

"It's dangerous, Kara; these books are dangerous too."

"I know, but don't you love reading them? This one is so good."

"Yes, it is." Anka gave her sister a nudge. Then Kara started tickling Anka, and they both started giggling. "Just be careful if you go back there. Promise me?" Anka said.

"Of course, I will," Kara said, but she never mentioned Abram.

CHAPTER FOURTEEN

THE DAYS PASSED SLOWLY for Abram. He was bored to tears in the store, and he would have left Berlin in search of another adventure, even though his mother would have been forced to run the store alone, had it not been for the German girl. *I am selfish. I promised my father on his deathbed that I would take care of Mother*, he thought. *I know my mother needs me, but I hate it here, sitting in the store, morning until night. Every day is the same. Not only that, but every girl my mother wants me to meet bores me. All of them want to get married to a Jewish boy from a good family and have babies. That's all they care about. And although I am not an ideal prospect, some girls will put up with me because of my mother's spotless reputation and grandfather's money. If it weren't for Kara, I couldn't bear another month here in this tiny bookstore in the Mitte in Berlin. But sweet and beautiful Kara adds the excitement that I have been lacking. Thoughts of her fill my otherwise empty hours and I don't resent my mother as much for holding me back from traveling.*

Abram had not needed to mark a calendar to remind him of his meeting date with Kara. It was burned into his memory like a brand. It seemed there was nothing else of interest to him in his world, so he counted every minute that passed as a minute he was closer to the meeting. When the time finally came to meet Kara, his mother wanted to know where he was going. He told her that he was going to talk to someone about buying some hard-to-come-by, first-edition books.

"Abram, we hardly have enough money to survive. We don't need more books. We need to sell the ones we have," Hoda said as Abram prepared to leave.

"I just want to see what he has. I won't buy anything until I talk to you. Would that be all right?" Abram knew his mother would not suspect anything, and she would agree to those terms.

"All right. Go on and see what he is selling, but you promise me you won't buy without my approval?"

"I promise, Mother," Abram said as he smiled and left.

He was tall and handsome with dark hair and dark eyes. Abram's skin was light in color. His features were strong and even. His hair was cut short, and he wore no *payot* or beard. And had it not been for the yarmulke, no one would have known he was Jewish.

His father, Kaniel, had never denied that he was Jewish, but he had never practiced either. And although Abram's mother had taken her son to shul a few times trying to indoctrinate him into their religion, Abram had followed his father's lead. Abram was a man who longed to learn about different cultures but had little interest in discovering the beauty that lay within his own.

The sun was just beginning to set, and the sky was already turning to a watercolor painting of tangerine mixed with raspberry, as the golden orb of the sun beamed her final rays of the day onto the earth.

Abram sat on a bench at the park and waited. He'd brought another book tucked under his shirt. This time it was a children's book. He wondered if she would like it or if she would find it too childish. He thumbed through the worn pages and felt sentimental. His mother had read this book to him when he was young. It was a touching story of a baby deer whose mother was killed by hunters.

Abram was gazing at the sky watching the colors change, then he looked in front of him, and there she was.

"How did you like the book?" he asked.

"It was wonderful. I've never read anything like it."

"Yes, I quite agree. I love Hemingway too."

"It was so romantic. My sister and I could hardly put it down to go to sleep. One night we stayed up so late reading that we could hardly function the next day."

Abram smiled. Then he said, "I brought you another forbidden book, but this one is a children's story. I don't know if you'll like it." He handed her the copy of *Bambi*. "It's the story of a little deer. I know that might sound boring, but believe me, it's not. It's such a touching, meaningful story that it will make you cry."

"Oh?" she said, taking the book.

"Why don't we meet here in a week, and if you don't like it, I'll bring you another book."

"All right," she said, giving him the well-worn copy of *A Farewell to Arms* and taking *Bambi*. Then she turned to go.

"Kara . . ." he said.

"Yes . . ." She hesitated.

"Do you have to leave right away? Can you stay for a few minutes and talk?"

She was nervous but she nodded. "I can stay for a little while, but it will be dark soon."

Kara sat down at the end of the bench. She didn't look at Abram; instead she looked at the ground.

"I don't mean to be bold, but I would love to know more about you," he said. Then he added quickly, "Only so I can choose books I know you will like."

She smiled. "What do you want to know?"

"Well, what kind of books do you like?"

"Fascinating stories of all kinds. I've loved to read all of my life," she answered.

"Have you ever wanted to travel? To see the world outside of Berlin?"

"You mean like Munich?" she asked.

He smiled, and when he did, she caught a glimpse of him and thought he was terribly handsome.

"Yes, like Munich. But also, like America, or China, or even Africa."

"I've never thought about it."

"How about France? Or Poland? Italy? Maybe even Canada."

She giggled. "I never thought it was possible for me to go so far away from home."

"Poland's not far," he said, "France isn't either. Nor Switzerland or Italy."

"They are for me. A girl from my background would be lucky to ever get to visit Munich."

"I think you are a girl with an adventurous soul, like mine," he said. "I believe you would love to travel the world, at my side."

The breath caught in her throat. This was a life she'd only read about in books, not a life she had ever thought could be a reality for her. She didn't know what to say, so she just smiled.

"You're blushing," he said, and then he reached up and touched her face. "You're always beautiful, but even more so when you blush." Kara felt his fingers on her cheek, and her skin turned warm and tingled. She looked away.

"Don't look away from me," he said. "Please, like I said, you're so beautiful . . ."

"Beautiful?" she repeated as if he were speaking in a foreign language. "Me? I'm not beautiful."

"Oh, yes you are. Do you know that when you blush, your skin turns the color of blush roses?"

She shook her head. She was at a loss for words.

"Have you ever seen a blush rose?"

"I can't say that I have."

"It's a soft shade between cream color and baby pink. It's delicate, but stunning, just like you."

No one had ever said things like this to her. In fact, she'd never heard a boy talk like this in real life, only in books. She was fascinated and frightened at the same time. Her body trembled; her feet seemed to have a mind of their own. They wanted to get up and run, but her heart—her heart was in control, and her heart longed to hear more of what he had to say.

"I should probably go," she said nervously. But she didn't stand up. Her heart wouldn't let her. "It is getting late."

"I would like to escort you home," he said. "A young woman should not travel alone when it's getting dark."

"You mustn't." She shook her head, knowing the danger it would pose to him, but at the same time being charmed by his chivalry.

"Because I am a Jew?" He smiled wryly. "You don't want to be seen with me?"

"It's not that. I am not ashamed to be seen with you. Not at all, Abram. I am afraid for you . . . and for me."

"I'm not. I'm not afraid of a bunch of hooligans. I can fight," he said.

"I'm sure you can. But it's not just the street thugs that worry me. It's the law. You are Jewish, and I am Gentile. It's against the law for us to be seen together. So, please, I am begging you, don't try to go with me."

"If that's what you want, I won't. But I would really feel better if I could make sure you got home safely."

"You are quite the gentleman, and I am impressed. You don't find many of those anymore. But, even so, it's just not a good idea for either of us. Will you just respect my wishes, please?"

"Yes, whatever you would like," he answered.

Kara nodded. "Thank you." Then she forced herself to stand up and get ready to leave.

"Will you meet me back here next week? Please."

She nodded.

"Same time?"

Again, she nodded. Then she began to walk away very quickly. Her heart was pounding. She felt lightheaded, excited, reckless, and uncertain.

"Kara," he called out her name.

She stopped in her tracks and turned. *Oh, please don't try to follow me. You promised,* she thought.

He ran toward her. She felt like running into his arms and kissing him like a girl in a romance novel. But she was glued to the ground. A voice in her head kept repeating, *This is dangerous, run, go home go back to what is familiar.* She almost listened, but then there he was standing at her side.

"You forgot this." He handed her the book.

She let out a short laugh. "I did," she said, taking the book and looking into his eyes. Then he leaned down and kissed her. She felt the warmth of his lips on hers, and a hot tingle ran through her like an electric current. She looked down. But he lifted her head and looked into her eyes. "I'll tell you again," he said. "You really are beautiful."

Kara could not concentrate. Her mind was whirling. She was dizzy with desire and excitement, but also with fear. *Abram is a Jew,* she reminded herself as she stared into his dark eyes. *This kiss is forbidden. This book in my hand is forbidden.*

Ever so tenderly, he kissed her again. He eased his tongue into her mouth. She knew that if she stayed for even another minute she would be lost. She might never be able to leave. "I must go. It's almost dark," she said, pushing him away from her so that she could not feel the heat of his body near hers.

"I'm sorry. Of course, you must go. Are you sure I can't accompany you?"

"Yes, I am sure," she said firmly.

"I hope I didn't offend you, by kissing you. If I did, I am sorry. I hope you can forgive me. You see, it's just that your beauty has unnerved me. You are like an angel with the wind gently blowing your hair."

She didn't answer. She couldn't answer. Her voice would not come. So she tucked the book into her bag and ran toward the bus stop, leaving him to watch her go.

CHAPTER FIFTEEN

THE NEW BOOK that Abram had given to Kara was a children's book, but it was written so well that both Kara and her sister wept when the mother deer was shot.

"Where are you getting these wonderful books?" Anka asked. "Please don't tell me that you are still going to a Jew bookstore."

Kara cringed when she heard her sister say the offensive words, but she couldn't let on about her feelings and about Abram. It would be dangerous for Anka to know any more than she already did. "I go to a special library. I don't know if I am going to go there anymore."

"Is it a Jew library?"

"No, it's a secret library."

"Is it in the Jew part of town?"

"Why are you so obsessed with Jewish people?" Kara asked.

"I just wondered. I mean . . . I think that Jews would be the only people who would have the nerve to break the laws."

"Well, it's not a Jewish library. It's a secret library, and I'm not going there anymore."

"But why?"

"These books are forbidden, Anka," Kara said sternly. "We shouldn't be reading them. If we get caught . . ."

"Fine," Anka said, her voice angry as she crossed her arms over her chest. "That's just fine."

"You're angry."

"I like the books. I don't want to read *Mein Kampf,* or some travel book about how wonderful Germany is! I'd rather just stop reading books altogether than read those. Anyway, these reading hours we shared were nothing but a childhood thing that we did. And needless to say, we are no longer children."

"Anka, please don't be upset with me. I love our nightly reading sessions. I am just afraid that we will get caught," Kara offered, her voice gentle. The truth was she didn't want Anka asking any more questions. And even more importantly, she didn't want Anka to learn the truth.

"I know. I just don't understand why everything is so forbidden. How can a story about a baby deer hurt Adolf Hitler? Perhaps I should ask the leader of my Bund Deutscher Mädel group."

Kara felt the fear shoot through her spine like a lightning bolt. "No, Anka, you most definitely must not ask! We must be sure that no one ever finds out that we read these books. You must not forget that."

"You're right. For a moment I thought that maybe if I talked to her reasonably, she would be on our side."

Kara looked at her innocent sister, and she knew she'd made the right decision to stop the nightly readings. Anka trusted the world too much, and she believed that the Nazis could be reasoned with. Kara knew better.

"Anka, listen to me. This is important. The leaders of the Hitler Youth are rigid in their beliefs. Now you mustn't forget that, not ever. You and I have both agreed that when we go to meetings, we enjoy all the sports, and we love learning how to cook and sew, but we can't ever fully trust anyone there, and we must never tell them that we read banned books."

"Yes, of course, you're right, Kara. I just hate giving up our reading time. But I know it's probably best if you stop going to that library and if you don't bring home any more of these books."

Kara smiled. "But . . . we still have to finish this one." Her eyes twinkled.

"Yes, let's save the next chapter for tomorrow night. I want it to last as long as possible," Anka said wistfully.

"I agree," Kara answered.

They blew out the candle and got into bed. Kara thought Anka had fallen asleep, because her breathing had become slow and steady. But then Anka asked, "Do you believe all of the stuff they tell us in the Bund Deutscher Mädel? I mean all of it?"

"No, do you?"

"Well"—Anka hesitated for a moment—"I can't believe them about everything, because they are wrong about books. So, how can they be right about everything else?"

"Do you think they are right about the Jews," Kara asked carefully. She thought of Abram, of his eyes, of his lips pressed against hers.

"Hmmm," Anka said, "I have to believe that they are telling us the truth. Dr. Goebbels is constantly reminding us that Jews are dangerous. We hear it at school too. And Mutti and Vater are always warning us about them. I guess the truth is that Jews are magical, like witches or sorcerers, and once they get you into their clutches, you're done for. A book is one thing, but a real, live, living monster is another. I think it's best to stay as far away from Jews as possible. I believe what they say when they tell us that Jews are treacherous," Anka said. Then she added, "Why do you ask? Do you know any?"

"No, not really," Kara said.

"I would keep it that way if I were you," Anka said.

CHAPTER SIXTEEN

ABRAM WAITED in the park on the day he was to meet Kara, but she didn't come, and he was devastated. He chastised himself for pushing her too fast as he returned to his apartment. *What was I thinking? I had no right to kiss her. Who did I think I was? The truth is, I wasn't thinking. I wasn't thinking at all. She was so pretty with the wisps of hair that had come undone from her braids blowing in the wind. And when she looked at me with those azure-colored eyes, I just melted. I should never have lost control like that. She will never come back here again, and I can't blame her. I was disrespectful.*

When Abram returned to the apartment, his mother was waiting for him. "Where have you been going when you go out after dinner? You went out tonight, and you did the same thing a week ago," she said, "Abram, I have a terrible feeling that you are doing something you shouldn't be doing. I think you're looking for trouble."

"I just go walking, Mother. It helps me think."

"What do you have to think about?"

"I miss Father. Sometimes I like to go out and walk and think about him," he said. *That will shut her up,* he thought. *She won't ask me any more questions. But the truth is, I do miss my father. We could have talked about my feelings for Kara. My father would have understood. He always understood me, but I can't talk to my mother about Kara. I know she would tell me that it was best if I never saw Kara again. And maybe she would be right, but I can't stop thinking about her.*

Abram was right. Once he told his mother that he needed to walk because he was missing his father, she didn't ask him any further questions about it. For a few moments she was quiet, then she said, "You didn't eat any of your dinner tonight before you left. You want I should warm up a bowl of soup for you?"

"I'm all right," he said. "Just tired. I am going to bed."

She nodded, then in a soft voice she whispered, "I miss him too, Abram."

Once he was alone in his room. He threw himself on his bed. *Why was I such a putz? I pushed Kara too fast and now she's gone*, he thought. *Then he sat up and looked out the window. The stores were all closed. It was dark. Everyone had gone home for the night in this little neighborhood.* Abram sighed out loud. *I wish my father was here. More than anything, I wish I could talk to him. He'd probably say that this is for the best. Why tempt fate? He'd tell me that there are a million girls in the world. What makes this one so special? Because she likes to read? Because she is forbidden? Is it worth the effort? Is it worth the possible danger? It doesn't matter; I can't get her off my mind. But now the choice is hers. She will either return, or not, because even if I tried to go and look for her, I probably couldn't find her anyway.*

CHAPTER SEVENTEEN

DAVINA COOPERMAN WAS A QUIET GIRL, tall and slender, with golden-brown, long hair the color of maple syrup mixed with honey. Her hair was her best feature, but she wore it combed back severely away from her face and knotted into a tight bun. Saul Cooperman, her father, and Abram's father had been friends. Herr Cooperman was a scientist by trade, but he had a layman's interest in philosophy, and he and Kaniel Ehrlich liked to sit and drink schnapps and ponder the theories they'd read. So Abram and Davina had known each other since they were children.

Although Davina's mother was Jewish, her father was an atheist, and like Abram, she had grown up with no attachment to any religion. And because they were very much alike in that they didn't attend Shabbat services, Davina thought that she and Abram seemed to be a good fit. In fact, she had grown up believing that someday she and Abram would be betrothed. However, two years ago, when Herr Cooperman had gone to talk to Kaniel Ehrlich about a possible match between their children, Abram had rejected the idea.

"You are too young to marry now," Kaniel had told his son. "We would just set the arrangement, then you and Davina could marry later, when you are older and have finished your education."

"I don't want to marry Davina, Father. She's more like a sister to me than a possible wife. I want something more. I can't sign my life away yet. I haven't seen enough of the world to willingly agree to a match with anyone."

Kaniel, who had always indulged his son because he loved Abram more than life itself, said, "I'll explain how you feel to Saul Cooperman, in a nice way."

When she got the news that Abram had rejected the match, Davina had been hurt and confused. But she had been too embarrassed to go and talk to Abram about how she felt. So, from that time on, whenever she saw Abram in town, she said hello politely, but she did not spend time speaking with him. If he tried to start a conversation, she would excuse herself and walk away. As soon as she could, she would rush to get home where she could hide herself in her room. The hurt and shame she felt at being rejected made her withdraw into herself. But when Abram's father died, her mother insisted they attend the shiva. Her father, still too angry at Abram, refused to go.

"I'm so sorry for your loss, Hoda," Davina's mother said, hugging Abram's mother. Abram sat beside his mother, and they both sat on wooden boxes. He stared at the floor.

"I'm sorry for your loss," Davina said. Abram looked up at her. When Davina saw the pain in Abram's face, she wanted to take him in her arms and comfort him. It was at that moment as she looked at Abram, who was in his stocking feet, wearing all black, a piece of torn fabric on the lapel of his jacket, that she realized she loved him.

"I really am. I'm so sorry, Abram," she repeated. "If there's anything you need . . ."

He nodded. But he didn't speak.

Davina could see that he'd been crying. She knew he was a wild boy, a *vilde chaye*; at least that is what her mother called him. But now as she studied him, his dark eyes so filled with pain, his tall frame hunched over, she felt her heart swell with a need to comfort and protect him.

"I'm serious, Abram; if there is anything you need . . . anything I can do for you and your mother?"

He shook his head. "Thank you for asking."

She wanted to say a million things. She wanted to blurt out the words her heart longed to say. But, of course, this wasn't the right time, and even if it had been, she didn't have the courage. So she walked away.

Weeks, and then months, passed. During this time, Davina sometimes saw Abram in town. She would smile or wave; he would return the gesture. On a few occasions, she went into the bookstore to purchase a book or two. Hoda was always kind and welcoming to her. And Abram always seemed eager to help her. She loved that he was smart and worldly and that he knew which books to suggest. When she looked into his eyes, she still felt that sweet desire to be his, to live the rest of her life beside him.

So, once again, Davina went to her father and asked him to approach Abram about a match.

"He already said no. I don't want to put you through that again," her father told her gently.

"He might have been too young. He's two years older now."

"I have been watching you, and you don't seem interested in anyone else," her father said. "That's not good, Davina. Now, if it were up to me, I would tell you to further your education. I would send you to study at a university. But these Nazis have made it so Jews can't get an education in Germany." He frowned. "You have a brilliant mind. But your mother says that because of the circumstances in the country right now, it would be best if you found a nice boy and got married. What do you want? I mean . . . besides Abram?"

Davina couldn't bear the thought of marrying someone she didn't love. "Father," she said, "do you think it would be possible for me to go to university in another country? Don't you have a professor friend at Oxford?"

She saw his eyes light up, and she knew that he had not considered this idea before. "So I do," he said. "I'll get in touch with him. I'll see if he can't pull a few strings." Her father smiled at her.

CHAPTER EIGHTEEN

WEEKS PASSED, and Kara did not return to the bookstore. Abram had all but given up on the idea of ever seeing her again. He was growing restless with the mundane life of living with his mother and working at the bookstore, so he began to dream of faraway places and new adventures. He had found and read his father's private journals after his father died, and he longed for the adventures his father had lived. He thought about his father's affair with the girl in France and became obsessed with the idea of her.

He recalled his father writing about standing at the water's edge holding a beautiful woman in his arms while a gentle breeze blew. Abram imagined what it must have been like to be so young and free as he thought of his father listening to the girl's soft voice whispering gently in his ear. His father was not just his father; he was a man, a man named Kaniel who had tasted life. He'd tasted the salt from the ocean on his lips. Abram yearned to taste life; he longed to see the ocean, to experience all of that and more.

When he read about how his father's cousin had cursed him for leaving a poor girl in Poland with a broken heart and a bad reputation, Abram felt sorry for the girl, yet the admiration he felt for his father remained unscathed. After Kaniel left Poland in the heat of the scandal, his cousin had sent him a letter in which he cursed him and told him that he was no longer welcome in Poland. Abram read the letter because Kaniel kept it locked away inside of his journal. And after reading it, Abram felt fairly certain that he would not be welcome at that cousin's home either.

But, there is always Paris. I would love to see Paris. I wish I had someone to stay with, Abram thought, because he had no money to rent a flat on his own. He even considered trying to speak to the local rabbi about finding him someone to stay with in France. He would have to lie and tell the rabbi that he needed to go to Paris in order to further his education. If the rabbi agreed to help him, he might find someone willing to put him up. Then, he thought, he could find work and a place of his own. The idea appealed to him. There was only one problem. Abram had only attended shul once or twice. He didn't even know the rabbi's name. He'd heard that the rabbis were there to offer words of wisdom and assistance to those in need. Still, it would be difficult to go and ask a stranger to help him.

As Abram was contemplating his predicament, Kara walked into the store. She looked different. Her head was down as she walked up to the counter.

"I am sorry I missed our meeting," she said in a small voice. "I brought your book back."

Abram was glad that his mother was out shopping for chicken feet and some vegetables to make soup that night. "It's all right," he said gently.

Then she looked up at him, and he could see that she had a large purple and yellow bruise over one of her eyes; her nose was crusted with blood, and she was crying. He gasped.

"What happened to you?" he asked.

She shrugged. "I'm all right." Kara hesitated, then she added quickly, "I'm sorry, but I have to go."

"No, please. Don't go. Tell me what happened."

"I can't."

"You can. You can talk to me. I promise you I won't tell anyone anything you tell me." His heart hurt for her.

"I . . . my . . ." She shook her head. "I really must go."

He reached out and gently put his hand on her arm "Would you like another book?" he offered, trying to make her stay.

"No, thank you. I think it's best that I stop reading these forbidden books."

"Please, tell me. What happened?"

She looked down at her shoes, then she said, "My father."

"Your father did this to you?"

She nodded.

"Why?"

"Because he's a bastard, that's why." The words sounded so foreign coming from her lips. She'd always been so quiet and demure.

"Can you tell me why?"

"He was beating my mother, and I got in the way. That's why. I hate him. I've always hated him."

Outside, a bird called to its mate.

"Please, come, sit down. Let me make you some tea," Abram said, knowing his mother would be livid if she found out that he invited Kara into the apartment where he and his mother lived behind the store. And at any moment his mother would return. In his imagination, he could see her face red with anger as she looked at him. Hoda would be appalled that her son had brought a shiksa into their home. But right now, Abram didn't care.

Kara seemed to know what he was thinking. "What about your family? What will they say?"

"It's just my mother and me. She's out shopping right now. So, we would be alone."

Kara looked at him. "I should go," she said.

"Please . . ." he begged.

She nodded. "All right."

Kara followed Abram into the back of the store and then into a nice-sized, very clean, and organized kitchen.

"Please," he said as he filled a kettle with water and put it on the stove, "sit down."

Kara sat down in a chair across the kitchen table from Abram.

There was an awkward silence for a few seconds. Then she said, "I wasn't ever going to come back here."

"Why?" he asked, leaning forward to be as close to her as he could. Taking her hand, he said, "Did I offend you?"

She shook her head and swallowed hard. "It's not that. It's just . . ."

"It's just what? Please tell me?"

"I am a Gentile. You are Jewish. There is no place for us in Nazi Germany." Then she hesitated. "This is bigger than you and me, Abram. It's bigger than our storybooks."

"But . . ."

Kara raised her hand to silence him. "In another time or another place, we might have had a chance to see where our attraction to each other might lead. But here and now? It could only lead to misery . . . to trouble for both of us, and maybe for those we love too." She nodded her head; her eyes were glossed over with tears. Then she went on. "You see, I knew when you kissed me that if I returned here and you kissed me just one more time, I would be lost. I wouldn't care what the rest of the world thought. I would throw caution to the wind, and I would have to come back and kissed you again . . . and again."

He sighed. "And . . . here you are. Finally, you realized you feel the same way I do . . ."

"Yes, I feel the same way you do. But that's not why I returned. I returned because I had to tell you all of this. I was afraid I'd left you wondering. I was afraid I'd hurt you."

"You did," he said. "I was devastated that you were gone. I was even thinking about leaving Germany."

"It's hard to believe, because we only met a handful of times and only for a few short minutes, but . . ."

"Yes, I know. It's a miracle. But I feel it too," Abram said. Then he stood up. He walked over to her and took her hand, gently pulling her out of her chair. Then he put his arms around her and kissed her again.

She melted like ice cream in the sun on a summer afternoon. He held her tightly in his arms for a few moments. Then he led her into his room. They began to kiss passionately when he heard his mother call to him.

"Abram, are you all right?" She was knocking on the bathroom door. When he didn't answer, she opened the door, and upon seeing that the bathroom was empty, she yelled, "Abram, where are you? You left the store open and unattended? What is the matter with you?"

Quickly he jumped up and locked his door. Then he put his finger over his lips telling Kara to keep silent. In seconds, his mother was knocking. "Abram? What are you doing in here? You left the whole store open?"

"I wasn't feeling well, Mother. I am resting. I am sorry."

"What is it? What's wrong? You must be very sick to have forgotten to lock the door to the shop." His mother turned the knob on the door to Abram's room. "Why have you locked this door? What is going on here, Abram?"

"I don't feel well. I need to rest. Please let me be, Mother."

"You left a kettle of water boiling on the stove. Abram, this isn't like you. I'm worried. Please let me in."

"Just let me sleep, Mother. Please."

"I think I should maybe get the doctor. This is unlike you. What is it that you are feeling? Is it your stomach? Is it a headache? Maybe a cold? Please, talk to me."

"I am begging you to just give me a few minutes. I am fine physically. I had an emotional experience. I will talk to you when I can. Right now, I need a few minutes. Please just respect that, will you?"

Finally, Hoda conceded. "All right," she said. They heard her footsteps going away from the door.

Kara whispered, "How am I going to get out of here?"

"I'll show you." He winked. "You can get out through the window. Watch." He opened the window and climbed outside. They stood behind the building in an alley.

She giggled softly and followed him.

"Will you come back again? Won't you please promise me that you will come back again?" he begged. "I don't want to say goodbye."

"Yes, I will come back. But should I come to the store, or shall we meet at the park?"

He kissed her. "Let's meet at the park. We can talk more freely there. Can you come later tonight?"

"Yes, I will come. It will serve my father right when I am not home by nightfall."

"What time?"

"Is six too early?"

"I'll be there," he said.

CHAPTER NINETEEN

AFTER KARA LEFT ABRAM, she wandered the streets for a short while, but she felt out of place. It seemed that everyone was casting sideways glances at her with her golden braids and German folk dress. So she walked over to the park. It was early. Abram wouldn't be there for hours. Kara sat down on a bench. She wished she'd asked Abram for a book. It would be wonderful to have something to read while she waited. She pondered the idea, but, of course, she couldn't read one of the forbidden books out in the open like this. She would have to read something approved by the government, and the truth was, she'd rather not read at all. She hated being told what she could and could not read.

But, even with all the unhappiness Kara felt about her family and the government, she couldn't help but notice that it was a beautiful day. The sun shone like a giant ball of golden heat, and it seemed to be beaming rays directly toward her, which poured hope into her youthful blood. She stood up and walked over to a patch of dandelions under a tree. The bright yellow heads against the rays of the golden sun were so beautiful that she felt a wave of deep emotion come over her. Kara sat down and gently touched the head of a dandelion. It felt soft and perfect under her fingers. She remembered how she and Anka had made crowns out of the dandelions when they were children. In her mind's eye she saw Anka, a child of four or five, running through a field with a dandelion in her hand blowing tiny yellow petals into the wind.

Then—it was very sudden—but her tears came in a wave of hysterical anger. She wailed and was filled with rage, pounding her fists on the ground. But when she hurt her hand, she stopped and lay down, curling her body into a little ball and sobbing softly. *How could my father do the things he has done to me? I tried to blame it on the alcohol. I wanted to believe it was the alcohol and not him. But when he turned his horrible attentions on my little sister, I had to stop him. I couldn't let him do that to her. I couldn't. I knew he would beat me. I knew it would be bad.* She gently touched the bruises on her face.

Damn my mutti. There is no excuse for her reaction when I told her. She called me a liar. She said I was trying to cause trouble. I hate her for that. I don't know why she refuses to leave him. She makes a million excuses for him. Is it possible that she loves him? But how could she love a man like him, who hurts her children, and beats her so badly that I think one day he might kill her. And to think that bastard, who calls himself my father, has the nerve to demand that if I ever marry, the man should be a good German, like him. He may be a good German, but he's a lousy father and husband, and if I had to marry a man like him, I would never want to marry anyone.

She hadn't slept at all the previous night and she was tired. But yesterday had been so explosive that she had not been able to close her eyes. Now as she lay under the tree, it all came back to her. She'd been scrubbing a large load of wash with her mother when she heard her sister whimpering. Kara turned to her mother, who pretended not to hear.

"Mutti, Anka is crying," she said, stunned. She knew what was happening, but she didn't want to believe it for a moment. Then when Anka continued to moan, Kara shivered. *He's doing to her what he has done to me.* "Mutti," she repeated in a more desperate voice, "Anka is crying."

Her mother nodded. And at that moment, Kara knew that her

mother had known of her father's abusive behavior a long time, and she'd chosen to ignore it.

"Mutti, he is touching her. Vater is touching Anka. I know, because he did it to me. He forced himself on me, Mutti."

"You're a liar," her mother said in a deep growl, a warning tone like an animal that had been cornered.

Kara stared at her for a moment. Then she heard Anka moan again, "Please don't, Vater," Anka said.

Kara knew what it felt like to have that horrible man's dirty hands traveling like snakes over her body. She knew what the smell of his foul breath in her face was like. And she wondered how long he'd been forcing himself on Anka. The idea made her sick. She refused to sit by like her mother and do nothing. Terrified of what her father would do to her, but unable to bear her sister's suffering, she got up and walked into her parents' room. It was exactly as it had been when he had done this to her. Even so, what she saw unnerved her. Her father was naked from the waist down. Anka's blouse was unbuttoned, her face red from crying.

"Vater. Stop it. Stop it right now!" In defending her sister, Kara found the courage that she had never had to defend herself.

"Get out of here," he warned.

"I won't," she said, trembling with fear. "Leave her alone!"

He stood up. She couldn't bear to look at him.

"Leave her alone. It's bad enough that you . . ."

"Shut your filthy mouth," he said, then he hit her hard across the face. The room went dark for a moment. Pain shot through her cheek.

"Get out of here," Kara commanded her sister. "Hurry! Run! Go into our room and lock the door. Put as much furniture in front of the door as you can."

"You're bleeding," Anka said.

"Go, go now," Kara demanded.

Anka got up and ran.

Kara's father grabbed her by the shoulders. Then he beat her until his anger left him out of breath and exhausted. Once he was spent, he put on his pants. Then he walked out of the room. She heard him taking money out of her mother's savings box in the living room.

"We need that money for rent," her mother said in a pitiful voice.

"Shut up," her father barked.

Then Kara heard the door slam, and she knew her father was gone.

That night she read the rest of the book Abram had given her to Anka as Anka lay on her bed. After Kara had finished reading, Anka said, "I'm afraid of Vater. He was horrible today."

"I know," Kara said, touching her sister's hair. "Is this the first time he's done that to you?"

"Yes," Anka said, "it was horrible, Kara."

"I know, sweetheart. I know."

"I want to get married as soon as possible. I would marry anyone just to get out of here," Anka whispered so her mother would not hear. "He will be home soon, and I am so afraid he will break down the door and come in here."

"Let's put a chair by the door. No, better yet, let's put the bed in front of the door," Kara said. "Will you help me?"

"Of course."

It was hard because the bed was heavy. But together they pushed it until it blocked the doorway.

"He won't be able to get in here tonight," Kara said. "We'll have to move the bed in the morning."

Anka nodded, then she climbed into her sister's bed and put her head on Kara's shoulder. "I don't think I can sleep."

"It's all right. Just lie here."

Anka finally fell asleep sometime after midnight. Kara knew her sister was asleep by the gentle rise and fall of her breathing. Her arm ached where Anka lay on it, but she dared not move it and disturb her sister. So she listened to her heartbeat mingled with Anka's breathing until she heard her father come home sometime in the wee hours of the morning. Kara felt her heart begin to pound with fear as she heard his footsteps on the floor outside their room. But he didn't try to enter. Instead, she heard him open the bathroom door. He stayed there for a while, then she heard him open the door to the room he shared with their mother. About a half hour later she heard his loud snoring. And she breathed a sigh of relief.

CHAPTER TWENTY

ANKA WAS PRETTY. Both sisters were beautiful, and their coloring was especially prized by Aryan standards. They had light hair and deep-blue eyes. Kara was tall and slender like their mother, while Anka, petite with full, round breasts and shapely legs, took after the women on their father's side of the family. The girls had high cheekbones and straight noses. But of the two sisters, Anka was the more vivacious. She was always ready to smile. Her laughter was contagious, and most of the boys in school would have given anything for a date with her.

But the following day when she went to school, she wasn't herself. She was withdrawn and unable to concentrate during the teacher's lectures. She sat in class biting her nails and remembering the horrors of the day before. It was impossible to erase the look on her father's face as he stood over her about to do something that would have ruined her life. She thought of her sister, Kara, and how their father had beaten her. She remembered the sound of the slap as he hit Kara across the face, and Anka trembled. *It was all my fault. Kara suffered for me.*

Her guilt was overwhelming her. And it was only because of this that a boy like Ludwig Brunner, a shy, introverted boy, found the courage to speak to her. He was two years older than Anka and would be graduating that spring. The students had little use for him as he was not very good in sports. But the teachers all liked him, and they let it be known that Ludwig was smart, and he'd received a scholarship to attend the university in Berlin come autumn where he would study architecture. Although Ludwig wasn't a handsome boy, he was perceptive. And on that fateful day, when his eyes fell upon Anka Scholz, as she sat at the lunch table in the cafeteria, he knew she needed a friend.

"Is it all right if I sit here?" Ludwig asked in the most charming voice he could muster.

She nodded. Anka had known him since they were young children. Although they had hardly ever spoken to each other, she always found Ludwig to be nonthreatening.

He sat down across from her and spread his lunch out in front of him. "I have some cookies my mother baked. Would you like one?" he asked.

"No, thank you," Anka replied.

"Do you feel all right? You've hardly eaten a thing."

"I'm all right," she said, but the tenderness in his voice made the tears well up in the backs of her eyes.

"You don't look all right. You look upset. Can I help?"

She shrugged. He was nice. Quiet and kind. Different from her father. So very different from her father. And everyone knew his family had money, and that his father held a good position in the Nazi Party. But in all the years she'd known him, she'd never considered him as a potential boyfriend. At least not until now. Not until this very moment.

She studied him, looked into his eyes. *He couldn't be interested in me as a wife. A boy like him, who is going to the university, will probably marry a wealthy girl who comes from the same sort of background as he does.* Then she said, "I'll be all right. I'm not feeling well."

"I'm sorry to hear that. Nothing serious, I hope. Can I walk you home? Carry your books, perhaps?"

She shook her head. "No, thank you."

"What is it that is bothering you?" he said, then he added in a small voice, "May I be so bold as to ask?"

"Headache," she said. "It's nothing really, just the weather."

"Yes, it's been very humid. Humidity sometimes affects me that way." He smiled. And although he wasn't attractive in the classic sense, she found his face to be appealing. His eyes were warm and filled with concern. His glasses and high forehead gave him the look of intelligence. They ate quietly, neither of them speaking. Ludwig was eating carefully, making sure to only take small bites of his sandwich.

"Please try these cookies. If you don't like them, you can throw them away," he said, putting a cookie on a napkin in front of her.

She mustered a half-hearted smile, then began nibbling on the cookie. It was hard to eat, hard to swallow the way she was feeling. When the time came to return to class, Anka stood up. "Thank you for the cookie," she said.

He smiled. Then she picked up her books and the remains of her lunch and turned to leave. Quickly he stood up and rushed after her. "Perhaps you would like to have dinner at my home on Sunday?"

"Oh," she exclaimed, surprised at his request. It seemed to come out of nowhere. And after he'd said it, he looked at her embarrassed.

"I guess I overstepped my boundaries," he said sheepishly.

"No . . . not at all." Now that he'd asked her to his home, she seriously considered him as a possible husband. *Perhaps I was wrong. Perhaps he does like me in that way. Could this be what I've been waiting for? A way to get away from my father and my parents' home?* The idea gave her hope, and a feeling of promise. Then she added, "In fact, I would love to have dinner at your home on Sunday."

"I'll pick you up at your parents' apartment at two in the afternoon. We usually eat at about three. Would that be all right with you?"

She nodded.

"Thank you," he said, excited, and the excitement made him clumsy. He went back to the table to gather his lunch and pick up his books, but things kept falling out of his hands. Anka stood there not knowing whether to help him or not. She didn't want to embarrass him. But when all of his books fell on the floor, she bent down to help him pick them up. He bent down too. His face was as red as a ripe strawberry. As he awkwardly gathered his books, his glasses slid off and fell to the ground. He picked them up quickly and then held them to the light to check them for cracks.

"Are they broken?" Anka asked.

"No." He nodded. "They're fine." Ludwig smiled a big smile, and she thought that he was sort of attractive. Then he added, "Today is my lucky day . . . maybe the luckiest day of my life. In so many ways."

CHAPTER TWENTY-ONE

KARA FELL asleep under the tree in the park. It was growing dark when she was awakened by Abram who sat down beside her and quietly called her name, "Kara, wake up."

"Abram." She sat up quickly. "I must have dozed off."

"You look lovely when you sleep," he said boldly. Kara felt the blush rise in her cheeks, but it was already growing dark, and she was glad he couldn't see it.

"How lovely can I possibly look with bruises on my face?" she said.

"I'm so sorry. No man should ever hit a woman. It's wrong."

"Yes, well, maybe in your world. But in mine . . ."

"In any world," he said.

"Jews don't ever hit their daughters or wives?"

"They're not supposed to. That doesn't mean that they don't. There are good and bad people in every group."

"Your father never hit your mother?"

"No . . . never." He shook his head. "My father was the kind of man who cherished his wife and his family. He often told me that he was honored that a woman as beautiful as my mother married him. And he was even more honored that she fell in love with him."

"She married him first, and then she fell in love with him? That's odd."

"Arranged marriages are common amongst our people. But that's the old way. Not everyone has an arranged marriage. The world has changed, and there are so many different sects of Jews, that it would take me all day to tell you about all of them. But in answer to your question, my parents' marriage was arranged. My father saw my mother, and he was awestruck by her beauty. So, he sent his own father to arrange a match. The match was presented to my mother who agreed to marry my father. And then, he told me, after they were wed, he treated her like a queen, and she fell in love with him. He said he loved her from the first time he saw her."

Kara listened to the story of Abram's parents, and it sounded so romantic that her heart swelled with longing. She wanted a man like that in her life. A man who would see her value. A man who would treat her well and win her love. Her father had never treated any of the women in his family like they were worth a thing to him.

"Do you have to get home?" he asked.

"I'm not going," she said, "I don't care that it's dark. I am not going back there. At least not yet. My sister is at a sleepover from her Bund Deutscher Mädel group. So, as long as she is all right, I don't need to go home."

"Bund Deutscher Mädel? You mean the Nazi youth group?" he asked.

"Yes, we're required to attend."

He shook his head, but he didn't ask anything more.

The night settled over them like a blanket. She leaned over and kissed him. He held her in his arms. There was no one out on the streets. The park was empty except for the song of the gentle wind whispering through the trees. They kissed again. He took off his shirt and told her to lay her head on it. She did. Then he lay down beside her. It was Friday night, Shabbat, so the streets were empty with no one around. Everyone was at home sharing candlelit Shabbos dinner with their families. The only sound was the wind as it rushed through the leaves and the soft rhythm of their beating hearts. Abram leaned over and kissed Kara. She put her arms around his neck, and they made love.

Once they'd finished, they both lay on their backs looking up at the stars. He heard her weeping and held her tightly. "Are you all right?" he asked. "I'm sorry. I didn't mean to do something that you didn't want to do," he said.

"It's not that."

"Then what is it? Did I hurt you?"

"No."

"Was this your first time?"

She didn't answer.

"Kara. Please talk to me." Abram felt a strong sense of tenderness come over him. He'd been with women before. He'd even been with virgins, but this had not felt like making love to a virgin. Even so, he saw an innocence in her that he'd never seen in any girl before. A sort of tragically beautiful innocence.

"This is the first time a man has ever touched me with my permission."

"You were raped?" he said, stunned. The thought of someone hurting this delicate person made him feel sick to his stomach.

"Rape? I don't know if it was rape. I suppose you could call it that."

"If a man takes you against your will, it's rape," he said firmly, but gently.

"Well, that's what he did, then."

"Did you tell your parents?"

She let out a harsh laugh. And thought of her father's face as he forced himself on her.

He didn't understand, so he kept silent. She said nothing more, so he stroked her hair and tried to comfort her. For a half hour they lay under the tree. His arms encircling her. Her head on his shoulder.

"It's really late. Won't your parents be worried about you?" he whispered in her ear.

"I don't care," she said.

"We can't stay here in the park all night."

"You go home. You don't have to stay with me. But I am not going anywhere," she said with conviction.

"No, I would never leave you alone in the dark here," he said. "Why don't you come back to my apartment. I'll sneak you in through the window, and then you can go home in the morning?"

"What if your mother finds out?"

"We'll worry about that when it happens," he said, kissing her again.

CHAPTER TWENTY-TWO

ABRAM HELPED Kara through the window to his room. Once they were inside, they lay on his bed together. She curled into his arms and fell asleep quickly. He watched her as she slept. Never before had he felt such a strong need to protect someone. There was something in her delicate features, in her graceful slender fingers, in the gentle curve of her cheek, that was so tender that he thought he might be falling in love. *Is this what it's like to love someone?* he thought. *I hardly know this girl, and I must admit she wasn't the best lover I've ever had, but there is just something about her. She is so soft and vulnerable that I want to keep her safe from the world. I wish I could hold her in my arms forever.*

CHAPTER TWENTY-THREE

WHEN KARA RETURNED HOME the following afternoon, she sneaked into her room. Anka was sitting on the bed waiting for her. Her eyes were red, and her face was stained from tears.

"Where were you all night? When I got home from my sleep-over, Mutti was frantic. She said you didn't come home all night. So, I had to make up a lie to Mutti. I told her you were staying at Elke's. I said you two had a project to do for the Bund Deutscher Mädel. But I was scared, Kara—I thought something happened to you."

"I am sorry, I really am."

"So, where were you?"

"I met someone."

"You what?"

"I said, I met someone."

"And you stayed out all night with them? Was it a boy? Kara, have you gone mad?"

Kara shrugged.

"Who is he?"

Kara studied her sister. She loved Anka with all her heart, but she knew Anka would never approve of her relationship with Abram. After all, he was a Jew, and any relations between Jews and

Aryans were forbidden by law and they both knew it. Everyone knew it. If she told Anka about Abram, Anka would beg her to break it off. That was the last thing in the world Kara wanted.

She had never felt so right about anything before this. Abram was the kind of man who lived in her dreams, and in her books. They had the same interests. He loved to read, and he longed to go to faraway places and take her with him. She'd always enjoyed reading, and she'd always wondered what it would be like to see the world. Abram was tender and gentle with her. His voice was so calm and understanding. And he had a way of touching her and looking into her eyes that made her feel like she was important, like she was loved.

"Just a boy from school," Kara lied. She hated lying to Anka, and as soon as the words left her lips, she felt guilty.

"You are going to get yourself a bad reputation," Anka said, "staying out all night with a boy. Kara, what are you doing?"

"Yes, well, I must admit you're right. But I don't care. If everyone in the neighborhood knew that Vati is an alcoholic who forces himself on his daughters for fun, and Mutti is a long-suffering woman who looks the other way, we would already have quite the reputation, now, wouldn't we?" Her tone was sarcastic.

"Mutti is afraid of him," Anka said.

"I am afraid of him too. He's bigger and stronger than we are. So he thinks he can do as he likes. But I still spit in his face," Kara said. Then in a soft voice, she asked, "He hasn't touched you again, has he?"

"He tried, as you know. But no. He hasn't."

"Good. I never want him to touch you. I'd rather die than let that happen."

"But he's done it to you. I know he has. And I was always too afraid to try to stop him. But I heard you crying many nights. I wanted to help you, but I was a coward. Like Mutti," Anka said as she ran over to her sister and captured Kara in an embrace. "He would have done the same to me if you hadn't stopped him. You have the courage we lack. That's no excuse, I know. I don't know if you can ever forgive me."

"Of course I forgive you. You were just a child. But Mutti? She should have done something."

"Look at you. I know you were afraid, but you protected me anyway. And now you have a black eye to show for it. I feel so guilty." Anka gently touched the purple bruise around Kara's eye.

"Don't feel guilty. It was my choice."

The two sisters sat down on the bed. A few moments passed before Anka said, "I have to get out of here. I have to get away from Vater. So, I made a date on Sunday with Ludwig Brunner. His family is very influential in the Nazi Party. I am hoping to marry him."

"What? Ludwig Brunner? You are serious about this? You want to get that close to the Nazi Party?"

"I want to get out of here, Kara. I have to get out of here. Away from Vati and his violent outbursts. Away from Mutti and her constant crying. If I marry Ludwig, I'll have a home and husband. His family has money. I don't care about politics. I'll agree with whatever he says. But I'll have a good life. What more is there?"

"Love . . ." Kara said.

"Only in books." Anka shook her head. "In the real world, in the world we live in, having enough to eat and a warm bed to sleep in, as well as a safe place to rest your eyes is everything."

As Kara turned away from her sister, she caught a glimpse of herself in the mirror. Her black eye, her bruised cheek. The deep look of desperation on her face. "Yes, I suppose you might be right," she said.

"Anka . . ." Mutti called, "I just got another bushel of laundry. I need you to peel potatoes for dinner. Is Kara back yet?"

Anka looked at Kara. Kara nodded. "Tell her yes."

"She's here, Mutti."

"Then get down here right away. I need your help."

Kara nodded and followed her sister into the kitchen.

CHAPTER TWENTY-FOUR

ON SUNDAY MORNING, Kara helped Anka get ready for her dinner at Ludwig's home. Kara loaned Anka her prettiest, most colorful dirndl skirt. Anka had scrubbed her best white blouse until it was spotless. Now Kara carefully braided Anka's blonde curls into a perfect twist that coiled around her head.

"You don't have to do this," Kara reminded her sister. "You don't have to marry a man you don't love."

"I'm not worried about whether I love him or not. I am just hoping he'll want to marry me. After all, our vater has soiled our family name by drinking in the taverns all night. And don't you think his parents know that Mutti has to take wash in to make ends meet? I will be lucky if they allow him to marry me."

"His father is a die-hard Nazi. Friends with Dr. Goebbels, I hear. You would be swept up into the party. And you would never be able to read another forbidden book. That's for sure."

Anka shrugged. "At least I would be far away from Vati and Mutti and the poverty that we live in. Ludwig isn't handsome, but he really isn't so bad."

"No, I suppose not," Kara said, thinking of Abram and then

thinking of what Ludwig and his family would say if they knew Kara was in love with a Jewish man. "Well, no matter what you decide to do about Ludwig, I must say you do look lovely tonight." Kara smiled.

CHAPTER TWENTY-FIVE

LUDWIG ARRIVED EXACTLY ON TIME. When he saw Anka, his face lit up. "You look lovely this afternoon. Like a sunflower. Did you know that the sunflower is the official flower of the party?" he said, then not waiting for an answer, he continued, "My parents are going to love you."

She smiled.

Anka and Ludwig arrived at his parents' home a little before two. Fredrick, Ludwig's father, was sitting in a large comfortable chair in the living room reading last night's edition of *Der Angriff*, the newspaper that Dr. Goebbels produced in Berlin. His mother was in the kitchen preparing dinner.

"This is Anka, the girl I told you about, Vater," Ludwig said a little nervously. Anka could see by the way he spoke to his father that Ludwig was afraid of him. She wondered if Fredrick struck his son and his wife the way her own father took his frustrations out on their family.

Fredrick Brunner looked up from the paper he'd been reading and studied the girl in front of him. "Pretty enough," he said under his breath. "Aren't you Anka Scholz? Artur and Heidi's youngest?"

"Yes, Herr Brunner," Anka said, wishing she'd had enough

money to buy the ingredients to bake something to bring to this dinner. She'd come empty handed and she was feeling out of place.

"Yes, Son, she's pretty enough," Herr Brunner said, "but still, she's not from a good family."

Anka's mouth fell open. She felt her face grow hot. She wanted to leave, to run out the door. But Ludwig held her arm. "It's all right," he whispered. "He says things like that sometimes. Don't pay him any attention. Please . . . come, sit down," he said.

Anka did as Ludwig instructed. She stared at her plate, unable to meet Herr Brunner's gaze.

Then the meal was served. Although it was not particularly elaborate, it was far more extensive than Anka ever had at home. At the Scholz home, they ate potato soup or vegetable stew. Most days they had bread, but the servings were small. Still, they were glad to have the little they had. Here at Ludwig's home, there was a small serving of chicken, along with some fresh vegetables and enough bread to go around. There was even a dish with a dollop of butter in it. But there was so much tension in the atmosphere that she could hardly enjoy the food.

"So, Anka, the last time I saw your parents, your father was just returning from the war. What does your father do now?" Herr Brunner asked as he took a bite of bread.

Anka was certain that Herr Brunner already knew that her father was an unemployed drunk. But he wanted to see what she would say if he asked her this question. She almost choked on her water, but she looked at Herr Brunner and said, "As you know, my father is a war veteran. He fought bravely for our country. And he was wounded. It left him unable to work." It was not completely true. Her father was wounded, but not so badly that he couldn't find a job. He had been wounded to the point of being unable to work, but the scars he bore were mental, not physical.

"And your mutter? She is a hausfrau?"

"Yes," Anka answered.

"Hmmm. That's rather curious. I thought I had heard that there were a few families who employ your mother to do their wash for them."

Anka's hands were trembling. The delicious food was wasted on her: she couldn't eat. Instead, she stared at Herr Brunner and said nothing.

"Well, is it true?" he asked casually.

"Yes." Tears threatened the backs of Anka's eyes. She wanted to say, *If you already knew that my mother was working taking in wash, then why did you feel the need to embarrass me by asking.* But she said nothing. Her mouth was dry. She couldn't speak. She wanted to get up and run away from this table, from this house, from these heartless people.

"A washerwoman, Ludwig?"

"Please stop, Father," Ludwig said.

"You've outdone yourself this time, Son. You've embarrassed me and shamed yourself." He shook his head. "Why do you insist on choosing a girl from a disreputable family? This isn't the first time you've shamed us. The girl you brought home last time was a Pole. An intellectual, you said"—he shook his head again—"a girl I wouldn't be seen with. Well, at least . . . I must admit that this one is prettier than the last."

"It could be worse, Fredrick," Ludwig's mother said. "She could be a Jew. She's a good German. And she is very pretty."

"Please, Gertrude. Don't give this boy any ideas."

"She's not only pretty, but she knows her place," Gertrude said, "I can see what our son sees in her."

Anka couldn't believe that they were talking about her so openly right in front of her.

Herr Brunner took a sip of wine, then he went on, "There is more to this." Then clearing his throat, he said, "When our son chooses a mate, he must consider his future. He must think about the position he will hold. As his father, I want to see him become successful. I want to see him rise in the party."

"I think I should go home," Anka whispered to Ludwig.

"No, please don't leave. Forgive my father. He isn't a tactful man. He is a bit of boor. He blames it on the fact that he's highly ambitious. But please remember this: you are not keeping company with him. You are keeping company with me."

Anka looked up into Ludwig's eyes, and for the first time since they'd started talking to each other on a romantic level, she saw that he had an inner strength in his quiet demeanor. And for the first time, she could say that she truly liked him. "All right," she said, "I'll stay."

After dinner, Anka got up to help Gertrude Brunner with the dishes. As they carried the platters back into the kitchen, Gertrude whispered, "Do you like my son, Anka?"

"Yes, I like Ludwig very much. He's smart and easy to talk to. And in a quiet way, he is very strong, and I find that strength comforting. But I don't think Herr Brunner cares for me."

"Don't worry too much about my husband. He'll come around," Gertrude said with a smile. "You are a pretty Aryan girl. You may not have the ideal family, but you have beautiful genetics. You would make a baby that would make our führer proud."

"Do you think your husband will really accept me if Ludwig and I get serious?"

"Of course he will," Gertrude said as she washed a dirty pan and then handed it to Anka to dry. "And . . . in case you don't realize it, my son is already serious about you." She winked at Anka. "You see, a mother knows her own child. And I can see in my Ludwig's eyes that he likes you very much."

Anka helped Gertrude Brunner to finish cleaning the kitchen and then to serve dessert while Ludwig sat at the table with his father drinking schnapps. They spoke in whispers which Anka couldn't hear. She wasn't sure what Ludwig had said to his father, but Herr Brunner didn't say another insulting word to Anka that evening.

CHAPTER TWENTY-SIX

It was the end of the workday for Josef Beck. The bell at the factory rang, and he gathered his lunch pail, said goodbye to his friends and foreman, and then walked quickly for three blocks until he came to his destination. *Today is the day,* he told himself as he huddled under the stairwell inside the apartment building and waited. The strong odor of sauerkraut filled his nostrils and told him that the women who lived in this building were preparing the evening meal for their families. Josef had been working on this plan for weeks, and each time he'd tried to put it into action he'd lost his nerve. But last night he lay awake forcing himself to find the courage to finally carry it out. He knew which apartment was hers. He'd already checked that out. And when the door to that flat opened, his heart leapt into his throat and began to beat wildly.

From where he stood, he could hear the man and woman who lived in that apartment arguing.

"I'm sick and tired of you, Heidi. I'm sick and tired of you and of these good-for-nothing daughters I have been cursed with. I'm going out, and you know what? I might just never come back. Did you hear me? I might never come back," Artur yelled, then he slammed the door.

Josef stayed hidden, watching as Artur left the building. After a few moments passed, Josef left his hiding place and followed slowly behind Artur Scholz, so as not to be noticed. He need not have worried; Artur was not paying attention. He walked three streets and then entered his favorite tavern. Josef waited outside, taking several deep, long breaths, and then he, too, entered the tavern. Pleased to see that the barstool beside Artur Scholz was unoccupied, Josef sat down. After he slid onto the barstool, a young man who was sitting to Josef's right gave him a nod. Josef returned the nod.

"I'll have a beer," Josef said to the bartender.

A radio blasted, and everyone recognized the voice of their führer as he gave a speech in his heightened emotional way. The room was quiet for a bar because everyone wanted to hear what their leader had to say. At first it was the usual stuff: Germany was being restored to her rightful place in the world, and the Aryan men and women who called Germany home could be proud of their country again. But then Adolf Hitler said something that made Josef listen more closely. Hitler said that he had designed an automobile, his Volkswagen, and he had a plan where every German family would be able to own one. There was a chorus of excited yesses from the men who sat at the bar, Artur and Josef included. But the young man who sat to Josef's right didn't cheer. He continued quietly sipping his schnapps.

Hitler ended his speech on a very strong note meant to excite his audience, and everyone at the bar drank to their führer's health. Then the radio volume was turned down.

Josef had wondered how he was going to start a conversation with Artur, and this speech was just what he needed to ignite the flame.

"An auto. Can you just imagine, owning an auto?" Josef said, turning to Artur.

"I can. I can see me driving along with a beautiful young woman, who looks like a film star, seated beside me," Artur said as he took a swig of his beer.

"Wouldn't that be something. I believe if anyone can do this for the German people, our führer can," Josef said.

"He has started doing good things already," Artur said.

"Yes, I know. I believe in our führer. I believe he will do what he promises."

"Of course he will. He's a good German who loves his people and his country. He fought in the war. He was a hero," Artur answered.

Then the man who was sitting on the other side of Josef said, "You two are fools. He's no hero. He's a madman, and you mark my words—he will drive our fatherland into ruin."

"How dare you," Josef said.

"You'll see. He's power hungry. He makes a lot of promises, but I don't trust him," the young man said.

"Treasonous bastard," Artur muttered.

Josef had wanted to befriend Artur. That was the purpose of this meeting. So, when Josef heard Artur's reaction to the young man, he knew that this was the opportunity he'd been waiting for. He turned to the man and punched him in the nose. Blood spurted in Josef's face, and the man, who hadn't been expecting such a blow, fell off his stool and onto the floor. The bartender, who was also the owner of the tavern, slammed his fist on the counter and said, "Stop that this instant! There will be no fighting in here. You louses will break something. And then who do you think has to pay for it?"

The young man got up, and without hesitation he punched Josef in the stomach. Josef doubled over. The young man thought the fight had ended, and he took his drink and went to move to the other side of the bar. But before he could get away, Josef punched him in the face again. his beer glass fell from his hand, breaking into pieces, and the man fell to the floor again. When he tried to stand up, he couldn't right himself. "Listen to me," he said as he turned to Artur. "You two have it all wrong." His face was bloody mess.

The man was still trying to get up. He grabbed the edge of the barstool, but Artur stopped him. Artur was still carrying the anger he felt toward his family, and he began to kick the man in the stomach.

"That's it. Get out of here, all three of you—before I call the police," the tavern owner said in a gruff voice. Then he turned to

Artur and indicated to Josef. "Scholz, you had better get your friend out of here right now, or I swear I'll never let either of you back in here again."

Artur took Josef's arm and led him outside.

"I'm sorry I got you kicked out. Listen, we can go somewhere else. I'll buy you a drink to make up for it," Josef suggested.

"Sure. There's another place that I know of. It's right down the street."

They walked to the other bar, went in, and sat down.

"Beer?" Josef asked.

"Sure," Artur said.

"Two beers," Josef ordered the bartender. Then Josef wiped the blood from his fist onto his black pants.

"I hate to hear those ungrateful bastards insult our führer."

"I think the man was a Jew altogether. He looked like one, didn't he?"

"Sure did. Ugly bastard. Those good-for-nothing Jews are trying to destroy us," Artur said.

They drank for a while, and although Josef had made friends with Artur, he was finding it difficult to approach the real reason he'd followed Artur in the first place. Then he had an idea. He waited for a moment, then he bravely announced, "Pretty girl over there, don't you think?" Josef indicated a woman who was sitting with another woman at a table eating.

"She's all right," Artur said, "nothing special. Are you married?"

"No," Josef said. *This is it. This is my opening. Carefully, proceed carefully.* "But I'd like to be. Have you heard about that new program that the government has put into effect? The one where they are giving low-cost government loans, to pure Aryan young couples for marrying and having a family."

"Money?" Artur looked up from his beer. "How much money?"

"Plenty. Enough to split between two fellows, if they had a mind to."

"But don't you have to pay it back?" Artur asked.

"Only if and when you can," Josef said.

"Two fellows? Why would two fellas split the money the government gives to a young couple?" Artur asked.

"Because the two fellas would be family. Like a father-in-law and husband," Josef said.

"But what kind of a man would agree to split the money with his father-in-law when he could keep it all for himself?"

"If the father-in-law and the fellow were friends . . ."

"Hmmm," Artur mused, "and would you happen to be that kind of man?"

"I would, if the girl's father and I got along well."

"That's very interesting," Artur said, "because I have a beautiful daughter. She's just the right age."

"Oh?" Josef said, but he thought, *Stay calm; don't let him know that this was your plan all along.*

"Would you be interested in meeting her? She can cook, and clean. She'd make you a good wife."

"Of course, and if she agrees to marry me, we could split the money."

"Yes, the money," Artur said as he emptied his glass.

"Why don't I buy you another beer and we'll drink to it," Josef said.

"I never turn down a beer." Artur smiled.

The bartender poured the amber liquid into two glasses.

They raised their glasses. "By the way, what's her name?" Josef asked.

"Kara. Kara Scholz."

"To Kara."

"To Kara, and to a long friendship with my new son-in-law," Artur said.

They drank.

"Why don't you come home with me right now. I'll introduce you to her tonight," Artur suggested. He'd been drinking all day and he was feeling pretty drunk.

"Do I look all right? I mean, I want to look good when I meet her. Besides, it's late too. Do you think she'll be awake?"

"It's only ten p.m. If she's not awake, I'll wake her up. And don't worry, you look fine. Besides, she will do as I say. If I say she marries you, she marries you."

"Let's go." Josef downed the rest of the beer in his glass, and the two men began walking toward Artur's apartment.

CHAPTER TWENTY-SEVEN

As they were walking, Artur realized that he was more than a little drunk. He leaned on Josef as he fumbled for the keys to his apartment.

"Damn, I don't know what I did with the keys," he muttered. Then he saw Kara enter the building. She was at the bottom of the stairs but heading up toward the apartment. "Kara, my dear," Artur said, slurring his words, "I have someone I want you to meet. This is Josef. Josef? I don't know your last name."

"Beck, Josef Beck."

"This is Josef Beck."

"Nice to meet you," Kara said, trying to push past the two drunken men to get inside.

"Josef Beck is going to be your husband," Artur said, smiling. "Go on, give her a whirl," he said to Josef.

"A whirl?" Josef said.

"A hug, a kiss, a feel, a squeeze. She's going to be your bride. Go on. Don't be a coward. I hate cowards," Artur said.

Josef's face was as red as a ripe strawberry. His hands were trembling, but he knew that if he wanted to maintain Artur's respect, he must appear to be brave, crude even. He pulled Kara into his arms roughly and pushed her against the wall, then he kissed her hard. She winced in pain and he let her go.

"Kiss her again, fool. Don't you like the way she looks?"

"Yes, she's very beautiful," Josef said, his breath catching in his throat.

"Well, show her you like her. Women like a strong man. They respond to power."

Josef grabbed Kara's arms and pulled her to him. He kissed her hard again. She pulled away, but he held her fast. Then she lifted her knee sharply into him. He released her as he let out a yelp. Before Josef could recover his grasp on Kara, she had opened the door and was inside, but not before her father had punched her in the face.

After Kara was inside, Artur turned to Josef. "Don't worry, she'll warm up to you. Give her a chance."

Josef nodded. "If you say so." He'd hated to be a brute, but he dared not be his clumsy, awkward self in front of Artur. He knew that if he was, he would lose the old man's respect.

"Don't get discouraged. There's a lot of money at stake here. We can make this work. I know my daughter. She'll do as I say and she'll like it, or else." Artur smiled. "Now, why don't you come over for dinner on Monday night? Hmmm? It'll give you a chance to get to know Kara."

"Sure. What time?"

"What time can you make it?"

"I get off work at seven."

"See you at seven thirty?" Artur smiled.

"I'll be here."

CHAPTER TWENTY-EIGHT

KARA RAN to her room and put a chair in front of the door. Then she threw herself on the bed and began to weep. She touched her eye. It hurt. It would be bruised again. *Why does my father always give me black eyes? It's as if my eyes are right where his punch always lands. What a bastard he is,* she thought. Kara was glad Anka was not at home to see her crying. She'd gone out for the evening with Ludwig. Kara needed to be alone.

Her entire body was shaking. Her father had gone too far this time. She wasn't sure why he had decided that he was going to force her to marry this man. But what she did know about her father was that when he gave his word to one of his drinking buddies, he kept his promise. It was strange because he never kept any promises he ever made to her or her mother.

She forced herself to stand up and take off her dress. There was blood from her nose on the front of it, and she knew from past experience how difficult it was to remove a bloodstain. For a moment she considered taking the dress into the bathroom and washing the stain, but she was spent. So, she wiped her face as best she could. Then she lay shivering under the covers. Soon Anka would be home. She didn't want to upset her sister, so she was glad that the room was dark and Anka wouldn't be able to see her bruises.

It seemed like a long time before Anka arrived. The bed was so cold, and Kara began to wish she had her sister to cuddle up to. Then she heard the front door to the apartment open and she knew Anka was home. Anka came into the bedroom quietly. She wasn't sure if Kara was asleep. She climbed into bed beside her sister and whispered, "Are you awake? I am so excited. I think things are going to go my way with Ludwig and his family. I think he'll marry me."

Kara wanted to share in her sister's joy, but she was miserable. Her face ached where her father had hit her, and she didn't feel like talking. So she pretended to be asleep.

CHAPTER TWENTY-NINE

LATE THE FOLLOWING afternoon before he left for the tavern, Kara's father knocked on the door to the room Kara and Anka shared. "Get out here, you filthy bitch," he said.

Kara didn't respond but sat on the bed trembling in fear. At the very least, Kara was glad that Anka wasn't there. She had gone to the market to buy food for Mutti. So Kara's father knew she was alone. Swallowing hard, Kara feared that her father was coming to do his awful business to her, and she felt the bile rise in her throat.

"Do you hear me?" he growled.

She still didn't answer, hoping he would go away but knowing he wouldn't.

"I know you're in there. Answer me, or I am going to kick this door in," Artur said.

The last thing Kara and Anka needed was for their room to be without a door; the door was the only protection she and Anka had from their father.

"What is it, Vater?" she said, knowing that if she didn't answer he would kick the door in.

"You want me to talk to you through the door? This is how you treat your father, you good-for-nothing ingrate."

"What do you want?" Kara was shaking.

"I want you to know that I expect you to be here on Monday night for dinner. Josef is coming. I'm sure you remember Josef from last night. I've decided that you will marry him, Kara, because they are giving low-cost government loans to newly married pure Aryan couples, and that's what you are, a pure Aryan, so we might as well get that money. Now, if you are stupid enough not to be here on Monday when Josef arrives, I will make you and your sister suffer. You understand me?"

She swallowed hard. "Yes, Vater," she said.

"Not just you, Kara, but you and your sister," he repeated in a threatening tone, putting the emphasis on the word sister. Then she heard the heels of his shoes hitting the floor as he walked away.

At least he's gone for now. At least he didn't try to put his hands all over me.

Anka returned at five that afternoon. She had a date for dinner and a film with Ludwig. She came into the bedroom, and the first thing she saw were the bruises on Kara's face and arms. "What happened?" she asked. "Did it happen this afternoon while I was gone?"

"No, it happened last night when I got home."

"How did I not see it?" Anka said, angry with herself.

"It's all right. I was asleep. Then you went to the market. It's all right, Anka."

"Oh, Kara. I am so afraid to get married and leave you here with him. I hate him so much."

"You have to do what is best for you, Anka. I want you to marry Ludwig, if that is what you want. Please don't worry about me. I'll be all right."

"I don't believe you."

"You must believe me."

"Maybe once we are married you can come and live with Ludwig and me."

"Aren't you going to be living with his parents?"

"Probably."

"Well then, let's see how that goes before we start thinking about me moving in with them too. Right now, please, don't worry about me. I'll be all right," Kara insisted. Then she smiled. "Don't you have a date tonight? You'd better hurry and get dressed. Ludwig will be here in a few minutes."

"Maybe I should call Ludwig and tell him I can't go out tonight."

"No, I insist that you go."

"Would you like to come along?" Anka suggested. "Ludwig won't mind."

"Absolutely not. Now get dressed."

"Are you sure you'll be all right if I go?"

"I'm sure," Kara said.

After Ludwig picked Anka up, Kara sat on the bed thinking about Abram. When she was with him, she had a feeling of well-being. It made no sense that he brought her such peace, considering how dangerous their relationship was. But Abram gave Kara a reason to look forward to waking up in the morning, and a reason to smile. For the first time in her entire life, she had hope. Hope that her life would not be like her mother's. She felt selfish and guilty because she knew that if she and Abram were discovered it would ruin Anka's chances with Ludwig's family, but she couldn't help herself.

Her parents were downstairs. Her father had just come in from the tavern, and she could hear them beginning to fight again. Kara sighed as she heard the same pathetic cries from her mother that she'd heard for as long as she could remember, and her father yelling in his drunken voice, angry for some small imaginary reason. Then she heard the crash of glass. This time it sounded like her father had begun breaking dishes. She could hear her mother begging him to stop. And then came the slap, and then another.

Kara felt her stomach knot up, and she knew she had to get out of the house.

Grabbing the small pad of paper that the girls kept in their room, Kara scribbled a quick note for her sister:

"Anka, I'll be home late. Please don't worry about me. And please, if Mutti or Vater ask, tell them I had to go to Elke's to work on a project for school."

She left the note on Anka's pillow, and then she crawled out the window.

It was already dark when she exited via the window. Nervously, she caught one of the last buses of the night and made her way to the Mitte. By the time she arrived, the streets were empty. It was becoming less frightening to walk down the streets and see the Jewish shops with the Star of David printed on the windows. *Are all of these people like Abram? Are they all kind and understanding? And if that's true, then why are we so afraid of them. Why does Dr. Goebbels warn us to be careful? Could I be wrong? Could there be some hidden secret about Abram and his people that I don't know? Is there something I will find out? I really hope not. I really hope that everyone is wrong about the Jews.*

When Kara arrived at the bookstore, she went around the back, through the alley, and directly to the window in Abram's bedroom. The shades had been pulled so she could not see inside. *What if his mother is in there? Or even worse, what if he doesn't want to see me? Maybe that's why he pulled the shade,* she thought. She considered turning around and heading back home. But then she thought, *I am here. I sneaked out of my house and came all this way. I am going to knock and take my chances.*

With her fingernail, she tapped lightly on the window. There was no answer. She tapped again a little louder. Then the shade moved, and she felt her stomach turn over with fear and excitement. Abram looked outside. She could tell by his mussed-up hair that he'd been asleep. But as soon as he saw her, his eyes lit up. Quickly he opened the window and whispered, "Kara . . . come in." The way his voice sounded deep and husky when he said her name, made her swoon with desire for him.

Abram helped Kara climb through the window. Then in a soft voice he whispered in her ear, "I was afraid that the other night we spent together was just a dream. I was afraid that somehow I would never see you again."

He pulled her to him and held her tightly.

"I'm here," she said. "I wish I could stay here forever in your arms. I hate my father. And I never want to go home." She kept her face turned away from him so he wouldn't see her bruises.

"I wish it too. Damn those laws to hell. Let's get married," he said.

Girls had tried to sell Abram on the idea of marriage in the past, and although he liked them, he'd never wanted to give up his freedom. *But this one . . . what is it about this one? If my father were still alive, he would say that it was the magnetism of the forbidden. Perhaps he would be right. But I have never felt this way before. It reminds me of the story of Carl and Anna. A beautiful forbidden love story, another book that the Nazis have stolen from us.*

She let out a soft, sad laugh. "I wish it were possible, but you and I could never marry. Not legally anyway. The laws forbid it."

"Let's not dwell on it now. Our time together is so short, and so precious." Then she turned to face him, and he saw the bruise on her face. He looked down and saw the bruises on her arms. Abram gasped. "What happened? Who did this to you?" he asked.

She shook her head, then she broke into tears. "I won't be coming to see you tomorrow. My father is having one of his friends over for dinner. He insists that I be at home." She hesitated for a few moments. Then she looked at Abram sadly and said, "He is demanding that I marry this man."

"Who is this man?" Abram asked.

"I don't know him. He's a young German fellow. My father brought him over the other night . . ."

"He hit you?"

"He was rough with me. Very rough."

"The bruises on your arms are from him?"

"Yes."

"And your eye too?"

"No, my father did that."

"Oh, Kara," Abram said as he gently touched her face. Then he leaned over and kissed the bruise. "Did this man force himself on you?"

"No, he didn't touch me that way. And I don't want him to. Not now, or ever."

"Come, lay in my arms and let me hold you," he said.

She took off her shoes and got into his bed. They lay wrapped up in each other. "Oh, Abram, I want another life. A different life. I can't marry this man. I won't. I wish there were some way I could escape from my father. I hate him. I am ashamed, but there have been times that I wished he would die. I know that's terrible, but I have. I can't bear my father's touch again. It is the vilest thing in the world," she said as the tears rolled down her cheeks. "You know, Abram, I have never told anyone about my father and what he does to me."

Abram held her tightly. "I am glad you feel safe enough with me to tell me. I wish I could go and kill him for doing that to you."

"You must not. You must promise me you won't. He's my father. If I were responsible for his death, I know I would spend eternity in hell."

"I thought you weren't religious."

"I'm not, but I know I would go to hell for something as serious as that. And you would too. Right now, I must find a way to get out of this marriage."

"You won't have to marry him. We'll find a way. I'll help."

She sat up suddenly and looked directly into his eyes. "My father has his mind set on this marriage. Do you know why?"

Abram shook his head.

"Not because he wants me to get married and start a family of my own. No, that's not it at all. It's because this boy who he has his mind set on, has promised to take out one of those low-cost loans that the government gives to young newlywed Aryan couples. And he promised that if my father would give him my hand, he would share the money with him. My father would do anything for money. You know why? Because money buys drink. And my father would drink that money up as fast as he could."

"How do they intend to pay it back?" Abram asked.

"Who knows? They are drinking buddies. All they can think of is today. And today, they want more money so they can buy more liquor."

"But you don't want to marry him, do you?"

"Absolutely not."

"Then don't. Marry me."

"I can't."

"Why? Why can't you?"

"Because I can't." She looked away from him.

Abram sat up and looked into Kara's eyes. "Maybe you don't want to marry a Jew," he said, his voice cracking. "Then maybe you should run away. I would hate to see you spend your life with someone you don't love."

She shook her head. "It's not that I don't want to marry you, Abram. I do. But I can't. The law won't let us get married."

"Well, maybe you can get a job, and give your father some money so that he leaves you alone. At least for now."

"A job? I can't do anything. I am not qualified to do anything."

"I can help you. I can teach you how to type, and how to take shorthand. I taught myself, and I must admit, I'm not bad at it." He smiled, then added "Once you learnt these things you can get a job, and maybe while I am teaching you, you will decide I am worthy of you, and we can live together and be married in the eyes of God."

"Oh, Abram . . ." she moaned.

"Well, how about if we just start with my teaching you typing and shorthand? How about that? You don't have to make any other decisions today." He squeezed her shoulder gently.

"You know shorthand? You can type?"

"Of course. And I would be happy to teach you."

"Abram . . ." she said, "I hope you know that I am not accepting your proposal only because of the law and the trouble it would cause both of us. But I know you are more than worthy of my hand, and of my love."

He was quiet. Then he lifted her face so that their eyes locked. "Did you say love?"

She nodded. "Yes, I think I am falling in love with you."

He kissed her and said, "I've never felt this way about anyone before."

They fell into each other's arms and made love. Once they'd finished, he said, "You must stay until it's light outside. It's dangerous for a girl to be out alone in the dark."

"I know," she said, "but I must leave at first light because I don't want my father to see that I am gone. So far, I've been lucky. My sister has been able to cover for me, but why tempt fate? I'll leave early and come back to start my lessons later tonight."

"I am going to tell my mother that you are paying me to teach you. That way we won't have to hide when you come over in the afternoon. Of course, we will have to hide when you come here at night."

"But won't she expect you to come up with some extra money?"

"Don't you worry about that. I'll take care of it," he said. "I'll tutor some children and earn a few extra marks. She'll be happy with that."

She kissed him. "Do you love me?" she asked.

"You mean you can't tell?" He smiled in the dark. "I do. I really do."

CHAPTER THIRTY

KARA LEANED over and whispered in Abram's ear, "I have to go home now. I left a note for Anka saying I would be home later tonight."

"I'll walk you," he said.

"No."

"It's dark, and I don't want you walking through the streets alone. I have never liked it when you did that. I insist on escorting you."

"Abram, all of my life men have told me what to do. For once, please respect my wishes. I don't want you to take me home." She looked at him.

He nodded. "I respect your wishes, but please be careful," he said as she slipped her dress back over her head.

"I will," Kara said as she climbed out the window.

As soon as she was gone, Abram jumped out of bed and threw on his clothes. Then he climbed out the window, leaving it open so he could get back in when he returned. And then he followed her. He stayed far behind so that she couldn't see him. It was very late, and the buses had already stopped running for the night. And even though it was a long walk back to her home, she walked all the way with him trailing behind her.

When she arrived at her flat, Abram noted the address. He watched her as she went inside. A light went on in one of the apartments. He assumed it was hers. Then he stood in the shadows on the sidewalk and waited until the light was extinguished. Taking a deep breath, he began walking home. And as he did, a plan began to form in his mind.

CHAPTER THIRTY-ONE

ANKA WAS angry when Kara entered their room. She lay awake in her bed.

"Vater came knocking on our door. He was looking for you," she said. "I told him that you had to go to Elke's house to do an assignment for school. Again! But eventually, if you keep this up, our parents are going to know that you're up to something," she said. Then she added, "I can't believe that you won't even tell me who the boy is. This all happened so suddenly. I never even knew you were interested in anyone."

"I met him recently," Kara said, careful not to tell her sister that the boy she'd fallen in love with was the same boy who had given her the forbidden books and that he was Jewish.

"Where? How?"

"At school. I am trying to get into a special tutoring class to learn to type and take shorthand."

Anka looked at her sister in disbelief. "When did you start to keep things from me? We've always told each other everything. All of a sudden you are acting like someone I don't even know."

"I am not keeping things from you. I would have told you everything, but there is nothing to tell. I like this boy. He likes me."

"And you are spending the night with him. That is something you should have told me. Who is he, Kara?"

"Stop questioning me. You're starting to sound like Vater," Kara said angrily.

Anka glared at her sister, then she got up and left the room. Kara heard the bathroom door close and she felt bad. *I wish I could tell her the truth. But it's better if she doesn't know.*

Kara wished she could hide in her room. The last thing she wanted was to face her father who might be awake and sitting in the kitchen. It was impossible to know what his mood might be. There were times when he was dead drunk and almost comatose. Other times he was almost jolly, and nothing seemed to bother him. But then there were those moments when he seemed to be possessed by a demon. During those horrible events, he might inflict blows on Kara, or her mother. Sometimes, if Kara was not quick enough to protect her, Anka would catch a punch in the stomach or a kick in the back of her legs as she ran to her bedroom, or out the back door.

The clock was ticking, and Kara knew if she didn't leave soon, she would be late for school. So she got dressed quickly and ran through the kitchen toward the door.

"You're in a hurry," her father said.

"I'll be late for school."

"You should maybe eat something?" her mother offered.

"I can't, I slept too late. I was studying."

"Were you, now?" Her father had that look in his eyes that made the tiny hairs on Kara's arms stand up.

"Yes, I have a project due."

"I see." He nodded. "Is that why you are gone so much these days?"

She wanted to say, *I am gone all the time because I can't stand your filthy hands all over me anymore. I can't stand to listen to you beating my mother or bear her constant whimpering and begging. And I can't endure the smell of alcohol and your sweaty, unwashed clothes and body that permeates this place.*

But she knew that she dared not speak those words. If she did, he might beat her to death. No one had ever stood up to him that

134

strongly, that honestly. So all she said was, "Yes. I have a school project due. I am working on it with Elke." But then she added quickly, "I also have some good news. I am taking an extra class at school. It is in the evening. I will be learning to type and take short-hand. Once I have finished the class, I will be able get a job and help the family out financially. We could use the extra money, don't you think so?" she lied.

She had to lie. If he thought she was going to be bringing in more money, money he could get his hands on for alcohol, then he would approve of the class and not cause her any more trouble when she was gone in the evening. Once she learned to type and take shorthand and she was earning money, Kara knew she would run as far away from her parents as she could. She would have loved to go and rent an apartment in the Mitte, where she could see Abram all the time. The only thing that bothered her about leaving was that she knew if she went to the Mitte, she would have to leave Anka behind. And if Anka decided to marry Ludwig, it would be best if she never told Anka where she was living.

"You would be bringing in extra money," her father mused out loud to himself and his mood seemed to lighten. "That's good. That would be very good," he said, nodding.

She smiled.

"How long will you need to study before you will be finished and ready to go to work?" her mother asked.

"About six months," Kara said.

"Six months?" her father said loudly. "Why so long?"

"I have to build up my speed at typing if I want to land a good position that pays well."

That seemed to satisfy him. He nodded as Kara walked out the door.

CHAPTER THIRTY-TWO

JOSEF ARRIVED ON TIME. He apologized to Frau Scholz for coming to dinner at her home still wearing his work clothes. "I just didn't have time to go home and change," he said.

She nodded. "Please sit down, I'll let my husband know you're here."

Artur came out of his room in his dirty undershirt and trousers. "Good to see you, Josef. Want a beer?"

"Sure."

Josef noticed the angry look Artur gave his wife when she set a pot of a watery carrot and potato soup, and a bit bread on the table for their dinner. But Josef didn't care what food was served. His dream was coming true. He was going to marry the girl of his dreams. He watched Kara, who sat across from him. She sipped her soup slowly and delicately as she tried to avoid his gaze. Josef decided that she was even more beautiful than he had originally thought the first time he saw her.

For a second, he remembered. It had been a warm summer day and he had just left work. As he'd walked by the park, he stopped to watch a group of Bund Deutscher Mädels in a relay race. When it was Kara's turn, he felt his mouth fall open. He'd never seen such a beautiful young woman. She was tall and blonde and slender. His dream girl in the flesh, standing right there in front of him. He was smitten. But he didn't know anything about her, and he had no idea how to meet her. He went home distraught. *I can't lose her,* he thought, *I have to find a way.*

Josef returned every day to that park, but the girls from the Bund Deutscher Mädel weren't there. Then one day over a week later, he saw her. The girls were finishing up another race. She was laughing and talking with another girl. He waited across the street until the girls said goodbye and left the park. That was when he followed her home. And it was just as she arrived at her flat that her father was walking out the door of the building. He overhead them talking.

Then the girl went inside, and he followed her father, who it turned out, was on his way to the tavern. Artur sat at the bar between two other men. He was trying to talk one of the men into buying him a beer when Josef entered. Josef sat alone in the back of the room watching the older man, and it wasn't long before he realized that the man was a drunk.

A few days later, Josef was listening to the radio when he heard about the loan program for Aryan couples just starting out. And then an idea began to form in his mind. If he could somehow befriend the girl's father and could also mention the loan, perhaps the old man might consider a marriage. Well, things had gone even better than he could ever have hoped for. Artur had loved the idea, and although Josef knew that his future father-in-law was a crude drunk, and mean-spirited man, the prize of marrying Kara was well worth putting up with the father.

Now as Josef stole a glance at Kara, a few strands of hair fell across her forehead. He felt his heart swell and thought with tenderness, *Don't worry, I'll be kind to you once your father has no more say in it. I'll make you happy. I'll make you like me.*

After dinner, Artur insisted that he and Heidi go for a walk so that Kara and Josef could have some time to get to know each other.

"But before we leave, I want you to promise me that you'll come back for dinner next Monday night," Artur said to Josef.

"Of course, I would love to come," he said. "This was a lovely dinner. Thank you for having me."

"Come on, Heidi, let's leave these two young people alone for a while," Artur said to his wife, and she obeyed.

"Your father told me that you are taking some kind of a class to teach you how to do secretarial work. I think it's good for a woman to have a job, even if she's married, at least until she has children," he said.

"When did my father tell you that?" Kara asked.

"When I first got here tonight, before you came out of your room."

She nodded.

"Do you enjoy typing?"

She shrugged.

"You don't like me much, do you?"

She shrugged again.

"Why? What could I do to change your mind?"

"My father is forcing this marriage. This is not my choice."

"Is it because I'm not handsome enough, or rich enough?"

"It's just that I don't feel that way about you. After all, Josef, I don't even know you."

"But you could get to know me."

"I just don't want to lead you on. The truth is I don't want to marry you."

He felt a wave of anger come over him. He'd worked so hard to get to her, and this was the way she treated him. "You could at least give me a chance," he said. "Your father is going to force you to marry me whether you like it or not."

Kara shook her head. "If I were a man, I wouldn't want to marry a girl who didn't want me. And make no mistake, Josef Beck, I don't want you. I don't like you. I don't like drinkers. And if I am forced to marry you, I'll make you miserable."

"Your father is right. He said you were a bitch, and you are a bitch. But I won't let that discourage me. I am going to marry you."

Then he whispered, "I'm going to feel what it feels like to have you lie naked underneath me. You are going to be mine."

She glared at him.

He stood up and took his hat and jacket from the coatrack. "Good night, Fraulein Scholz," he said.

CHAPTER THIRTY-THREE

JOSEF SLAMMED the door to the apartment and walked quickly down the stairs. He kicked a stone into the street as he stepped out the door of the building. *Damn girl*, he thought. He was fuming. *Who does she think she is? She's a nobody, the daughter of a drunk. At least I have a job. He doesn't even work. She comes from the bottom of the sewer. That food they served for dinner was slop, food for pigs. It was hardly edible.* He walked for a few more steps, then he thought, *I need a drink.* And as he headed toward the tavern, a man came up behind him.

"Hey, you," the man said. Josef could hear in the man's voice that he was very drunk. "I'm celebrating my wife's leaving me. Would you like to celebrate with me? I came home the other night and she was gone. Women!"

Josef didn't answer.

"Aww, come on, have a sip of my schnapps. It's a bottle of the good stuff," the man said.

Josef stopped. *Good schnapps is preferable to cheap beer.* "Sure. Why not."

The handsome young man handed Josef the bottle. "Women are no good," Josef said as he took a swig. "I'm sorry your wife left you."

"Yeah, me too."

Josef took another long swig. Then as he went to hand the bottle back to the other fellow, he felt a sharp pain in his stomach and a strong burning in his throat. White foam poured out from his lips. He gripped his neck as his windpipe closed and eyes bulged. Then he fell on the ground, and within a few moments, Josef was dead.

CHAPTER THIRTY-FOUR

ABRAM COULD HARDLY KEEP his hands from trembling as he checked Josef's pulse to make sure he was dead. *No pulse.* He took Josef's identification papers out of the breast pocket of his jacket and stuffed them into his own pocket. He quickly looked through all of Josef's other pockets to make sure that there was no further identification on the man's body. When Josef was found, no one would know who he was. He would appear to be just another drunk who died on the streets of Berlin.

Abram emptied the rest of the liquid and broke the bottle of schnapps on the ground. It had cost him a good sum for a bottle like that, but he knew that it had to be a bottle of good schnapps in order to lure his victim. Abram had bought the liquor that afternoon in the Mitte and laced it with rat poison. He'd been so terrified that someone would come by during the deed and he would be arrested for murder. Being a Jew would make his arrest even worse. But he had to do it for Kara. He had to protect her. He loved her so much that he was willing to kill for her.

Satisfied that there was no identification on the body and assured that the liquid from the bottle had already been absorbed into the cracks in the sidewalk, Abram left and hurried back toward the Mitte. On his way back, he threw all of Josef's identification into a canal. Then, careful not to be seen, he hid in the shadows, keeping watch behind him until he was safely back home.

CHAPTER THIRTY-FIVE

Kara longed to return to Abram that night after Josef left and her parents had gone to bed, but the look on Anka's face stopped her.

"Why don't we stay in together tonight and tell stories or read?" Anka said. "I miss spending time with you."

"I don't have a new book. I've stopped going to get those forbidden books. I told you I was going to stop. It was just too dangerous."

"So, we can read something old. I don't care. I just want to be with you, Kara. You are gone so much these days. And . . . soon I will be getting married. Then I won't live here anymore. And we won't be sharing this room the way we are now."

"How do you know that? You're not even engaged."

"Well, I was going to tell you . . . Ludwig asked me to marry him yesterday. I wanted to tell you about it all night last night, but you never came home."

Kara looked at her sister and smiled. "I'm so happy for you. This is what you wanted, isn't it?"

"Yes, I mean, I am not in love with him. But he cares for me. And more importantly, he has the means to take care of me, and I won't have to live with our parents anymore. The only thing is . . .

I'll miss you. I'll miss sharing a room with you and reading and talking all night."

Kara hugged her sister. "I am glad you're getting out of here. It's for the best. We'll see each other."

"But it won't be the same. We won't share our room and read or tell stories until late into the night."

"I know. And I will miss you too. But quite frankly, I will be glad that you are far away from our vater."

"You have always protected me from him. It's always been you who has faced his violent temper."

Kara nodded.

"And you stopped him when he tried to touch me . . ."

Again, she nodded, this time closing her eyes holding back tears.

"He's done that to you, hasn't he?"

"Anka, it doesn't matter. Just get married and get out of this house," Kara said.

CHAPTER THIRTY-SIX

ABRAM BEGAN TEACHING KARA SHORTHAND. Out of thick paper, he created a keyboard for her to use at home to learn the placement of the letters as they would appear on the typewriter. She practiced at night while Anka was out with Ludwig, and each time she and Abram were together, they spent at least an hour working on her lessons.

When Anka was at home, she asked Kara questions like, "Who is the mysterious man you are meeting at night? Is he a teacher? Is he the teacher who is teaching your class in typing?"

Kara missed reading the forbidden books. But she didn't bring them home anymore. Not because Abram would have refused to give them to her, but because she didn't want Anka to ask any more questions about her other life. It wasn't that she didn't trust Anka—she did with all of her heart—but she felt certain that it was better for Anka if she didn't know about her and Abram. After all, she was becoming very serious with a man whose family openly hated Jews. So, if Kara had told her sister the truth, it would have posed a problem not only for her and Abram, but also for Anka.

Still, every time Kara returned after spending a time with Abram, she and Anka had a fight. "Mutti and Vater were looking

147

for you," she would say. "I had to lie again, and I don't think Vater believes me anymore. I wish you would stop seeing this man in secret. Why don't you just bring him home?"

"They think I am in class," Kara said. "Besides, Vater has his heart set on me marrying that Josef Beck fellow."

"Last night Mutti came into our room at two in the morning. She saw you weren't here, and she shook her head. If you would just bring your boyfriend home and stop staying out all night, I think you might be able to convince Vater to let you marry him instead of Josef. Besides, you're getting a bad reputation. I am sure of it."

"Oh please, don't be ridiculous, Anka. You know Vater better than that. He has his mind made up and he wants me to marry Josef. Even so, I wouldn't want to bring anyone here to our home, because I am ashamed of our parents. I am ashamed of how we live," Kara told her, and it was true. It was not the whole truth. It wasn't the real reason she didn't bring Abram around, but she was ashamed.

"So, you meet this fellow at night? What kind of a girl does this, Kara? Do you know that you are behaving like a common . . .?"

"Please, Anka. Don't say anything more."

Anka shook her head and walked out of the room.

We used to be so close, my sister and I, Kara thought. *Now she is marrying a Nazi, and I am in love with a Jew, and the beautiful friendship we have had since we were little, is being torn apart. I don't know what to do. I don't want to lose her, but every day we drift further away from each other.*

From the time Kara and Anka were little, they had vowed to each other that nothing in the world would ever come between them. They had even cut themselves once when they were children and blended their blood together, swearing that nothing would ever separate them. They would sit on the floor and play while they talked about their future. It was decided that some day when they grew up, they would marry men who were best friends, and then they would rent flats right next door to each other. They would raise their children together. And forever, they would be sisters and best friends.

Kara felt like she'd lost something she could never regain. It hurt her in a way she couldn't explain. But in order to hold on to the only good part of her past for just a little while longer, she decided not to go to see Abram for the rest of the week. She would spend this time with her sister. After all, soon Anka would be married, and things would change forever.

The week passed. Kara and Anka read stories at night. They talked until the wee hours of the morning. Mostly Anka talked, and Kara listened. But she was glad to hear her sister so excited about her coming marriage. But, before they knew it, it was Monday. That afternoon, Kara's father made a point of reminding her mother and Kara that Josef was expected for dinner that night.

"You'd better be here," he said to Kara, his eyes flashing warning signs at her.

"And as for you . . . don't you dare serve another dinner like the one you served last week. It was shameful. You made me ashamed of our home," Artur growled at his wife.

"But I don't have any money. I can't buy food without money, Artur. I only have some potatoes, parsnips, and bread."

"I can't buy food without money, Artur." He imitated her in an obnoxious singsong voice. "I don't want to hear your crap. All I know is, you'd better come up with something nicer than that lousy soup you served last week, or you'll pay dearly for it once Josef leaves."

Then Artur walked out the front door.

Kara's mother bit her lip. "What am I going to do?" she asked. "How does he expect me to get food without money?"

"I have some reichsmarks," Kara said. "I'll go and buy some food."

"What a good girl you are," her mother said in a pathetic tone of voice.

Kara couldn't look at her mother. She still couldn't understand why Heidi had not taken her daughters and left Artur years ago, but there was no point in asking now. So Kara just shook her head and slipped her jacket on.

Kara knew that the butcher always gave her a little extra because she was pretty. So she went into the butcher shop. As always, he gave her the extra chicken. She smiled and accepted it. When she got home, and her mother saw the chicken wrapped in white butcher paper, she started to cry. Then she hugged Kara, who tensed up at her touch. Heidi released her daughter and put the chicken into a pot to cook.

Josef didn't arrive at seven thirty as was planned. He didn't arrive at eight. And by nine, Artur was pacing the floor. "You scared him off by being the cold, heartless bitch that you are," he said to Kara. "Why would any man want to marry you?"

Then he pulled a leg off the chicken and ate it as he walked back and forth across the kitchen floor.

Kara didn't say a word. She tried to sneak off into her room, but her father caught her by the arm. "Where the hell do you think you're going?"

"I was just going . . ."

"You were just going to hell. That's where you were going. I had a good thing set up with Josef and you ruined it." He slapped her so hard across the face that her head whipped around. Then he pushed her into the wall and began punching her in the stomach.

"Stop it!" Anka had just come in, and she saw her father beating her sister. "Stop it right now!"

Anka started crying. She tried to pull Artur off her sister. But he shook her off and continued to beat his daughter with full fists.

"I am going to get the police," Anka threatened. "I swear I will if you don't stop."

Artur turned his attention to Anka. His face was twisted with rage. "All of you women defy me, all the time." He grabbed his coat. "I'm going to find Josef, and I'm going to beg him to come back. And when he does, you'd better treat him right, Kara. You'd better make sure he marries you, or I swear I'll kill you with my bare hands."

Kara was shaking as her father slammed the door. She ran to her room and got her coat. Anka stood looking at her. "Kara. You're hurt badly . . ." Anka said, trying to take Kara into her arms, but Kara pushed Anka away. Then she slipped out the bedroom window, and with tears running down her bruised and bleeding face, she ran all the way to the Mitte.

As she ran through the backstreets, a flash of lightning filled the darkness. The sky opened up and poured buckets of its own tears down on Kara, soaking her completely.

FINALLY, she found herself in front of Abram's window, protected by the darkness of the night, and with her hair and clothes drenched from the strong unexpected storm. Abram had been staring outside. He saw her, but her bruises were hidden by the darkness. Abram opened the window. Kara climbed inside. She was dripping rain-water all over the floor.

"Why haven't you come to see me? I have been worried sick about you. I was afraid something had happened to you." Then he saw her face and he stopped. "Oh, Kara, dear God, what has he done to you now?" Abram said, his voice filled with pain.

"Josef never showed up for dinner tonight. My father was furi-ous. He blamed me, and he punished me good. Then he went out to find him."

Abram took the blanket from his bed and wrapped it around her. "You're all wet. You must be freezing," he said, hugging her to him.

"I'm sorry," she whispered. "Look at the floor." Then she added, "Oh, Abram, I've made such a mess of your life."

"You have made my life. Before you, I had no life at all. I love you with all my heart. I was afraid that when I told you I loved you that it might have scared you off."

She shook her head. "It feels warm and good to know that you love me. When I am in your arms, I feel like I am at home. But not like the home where I grew up. With you, I feel like I am in a place where I feel safe and loved."

He cradled her in his arms as they sat silently together and watched the raindrops fall and trickle down the windowpane.

She began to weep softly.

"Don't cry. Please don't cry," he said.

"I know I'll be forced to marry Josef. I know it. Once my father makes up his mind . . ."

"Shhh . . . don't worry. You'll be safe," he whispered. "Please, put your trust in me."

He wanted to tell her about what he'd done to Josef, but he hesitated, afraid he might scare her. The fact that he'd committed murder scared him, so he could just imagine what her reaction might be. But still, he wanted her to know that she was safe. He wanted her to feel secure so badly that he waited until he was sure she had fallen asleep in his arms. Reaching up, he tenderly caressed her bruised cheek, and then he whispered, "You'll never have to marry Josef, my darling. You're safe. I promise you, you're safe. He's gone. Gone forever. I know. Because I killed him."

Then Abram wept.

CHAPTER THIRTY-SEVEN

KARA DIDN'T RETURN the following night. Nor did she return the night after that. A week went by, and then another. Abram was sick with worry. He was afraid that her father might have killed her. He knew where she lived. All he had to do was hide outside the building where Kara lived and wait to see if she came out. It might take days, but it didn't matter. Abram had to know. The next day, he made an excuse to his mother and told her he would be home late. Then, overcome with fear, he went to the apartment building.

He had thought it would take a long while before he could find out what happened. He hadn't expected to see her as quickly as he did. But an hour later, Kara came out of the building carrying a basket filled with clean, folded laundry. She didn't look sick or hurt. The bruises on her face had healed. Abram was relieved to see that she was all right. But at the same time, his heart was breaking. *Why hasn't she come to see me? What have I done? Oh . . . Oh no . . . is it possible that she heard me when I whispered that I killed Josef? I thought she was asleep. Did she hear me and decide that I was a monster?*

His heart ached as he watched Kara walk down the street and disappear around the corner. He wanted to run after her; he didn't care who saw him. He didn't care if he got arrested. All he wanted was to beg her to come back to him. But he knew if he did this, she would be angry. And more importantly, it might cause her problems. So all he could do was turn away and go back home.

CHAPTER THIRTY-EIGHT

ABRAM COULDN'T EAT or sleep. In the past, reading had always been his escape, but now when he tried to read, he couldn't concentrate. Two days later, Davina came to the store to see him. She wanted to tell him that she'd been accepted to Oxford, and that she was leaving for England.

"I am so happy for you," he said, but his face didn't look happy. There was a deep line between his eyebrows.

"And I am so worried about you, Abram. You look miserable." She shook her head. Then she offered, "Do you want me to ask my father if he can help you get into the university too?"

"No, but thank you for offering," he said warmly. *She's a good friend. A kind person.*

"I don't know if it would do any good anyway. But I would ask him if you wanted me to," she said as she studied him. "You are in love with someone. I can see it in your eyes."

He nodded. "Guilty, I must admit," he said.

"I wish it were me," she said wistfully. Then she shrugged.

He smiled at her wryly. "Best of luck to you at Oxford, Davina," he said.

She nodded and left.

After Davina left the store, he sat on the stool behind the counter and thought. *How easy my life would be if I had fallen in love with her. She is a pretty girl. She is kind, and she is smart. And . . . she is Jewish, like me. We would have had a good life together. But it's too late for that. Kara owns my heart. And even if I never see her again, she will always have my love.*

CHAPTER THIRTY-NINE

ALMOST TWO MONTHS LATER, on a frigid winter night when icicles formed on the trees, Abram felt lost as he walked home beside his mother. She'd convinced him to go to a Hanukkah party at her sister's house. His mother's sister had a daughter who was a few years older than Abram. Her name was Rebecca. And she and her husband, Ari, had a little girl who was the light of his mother's life these days.

Abram and Hoda had purchased several gifts for the child, and they'd brought the presents to the Hanukkah celebration. Abram had watched Rebecca and Ari together. He'd sat on the floor and played with the little one. And for the first time in his life, Abram felt that he might be missing something. Even as recently as a year ago, he would not have paid much attention to the child. He would have brought the gifts out of obligation, but he wouldn't have considered how empty his life might be if he never had a child of his own. In his younger years, he'd never wanted to marry. But that was before he'd met Kara. Now he could envision his life with her. He could see them eating their meals together. He thought about how they might raise their children. And how when their children grew older, all the fun they would have as a family ice skating in the winter, and swimming in the summer. But most of all, his heart yearned to smile at Kara in that special way that Ari smiled at his wife, Rebecca.

"It was a nice party," his mother said. She put her arm through Abram's so that she would not slip on the ice that covered the sidewalks.

Abram nodded. "It was nice, but the food rations make it so hard to have any kind of celebration."

"Yes, you're right, it's true. There's never enough to eat. But did you see the look on the baby's face when you gave her that dreidel you made for her? She liked it better than any of the store-bought toys we brought."

"Yes, I know. I saw the look on her face when I spun the dreidel on the floor. The way she watched me; you would have thought I was a wizard making some special magic. She's really adorable," Abram said, "and she is growing up so fast. How old is she now?"

"Four precious years old. She will be five in little over a month." Hoda sighed, then she added, "Do you ever think about getting married, Abram? Do you ever want to have children of your own?"

He shrugged, not wanting to talk about his feelings. He had no idea how he would explain that he wanted to marry, but only if his bride were Kara.

His mother went on, "You know that your father was a great deal older than me when we got married. He, like you, didn't want to marry. It took him a long time to settle down. Which was fine for him. But not so good for you and me. Because now he is gone, and we must go on without him. I know you wouldn't want your child to grow up without you. I know you would want to be a part of your wife and child's life as long as possible. Wouldn't you? You would want to see your child under the chuppah, under the marriage canopy. And maybe you could be blessed to live long enough to see your grandchildren. Nu, Abram? Wouldn't you want that?"

"I don't know, Mother," he said sharply. "I don't know what I want." *I am lying. Of course, I know what I want. I want Kara. But I can't tell her that. And besides, Kara is gone. She doesn't want me.*

"Well, I suggest you give all of this some very serious thought," Hoda said as they arrived at their apartment behind the bookstore.

Hoda turned the key in the lock and they went inside. "You want something hot to drink?" she asked Abram.

"No, thank you, Mother. I think I am going to get some sleep."

"All right. Good night, then," Hoda said.

"Good night, Mother. I'm sorry if I spoke harshly to you. I didn't mean to."

"It's all right, I understand. Sleep well. And . . . please, think about our talk. All right?"

"Yes, Mother," he answered. "I will."

Abram closed the door to his room and leaned against it. Then he shut his eyes. He was angry and frustrated. He wanted to break something. Preferably something glass. It would have felt good to hear the crash of the glass as it shattered against the wall. In his mind, he could make believe it was Adolf Hitler's head that was shattering. But, of course, he wouldn't do it because it would bring his mother racing into his room, and that was the last thing he wanted.

As Abram sat down on the bed to remove his shoes, he heard a soft tapping on the window. His heart leapt in his chest. Standing up quickly, he ran to move the drapes, but there was no one there. *Probably an icicle falling.* He felt suddenly very sad as his anger was now turning to grief. After rubbing his hands together to ward off the cold, which had seeped into his bones from the walk home, he got undressed and climbed into bed. Forcing his eyes closed, Abram tried to sleep. It was almost an hour before he drifted off. Then sometime after midnight, he was awakened by a soft tapping. *Was I dreaming?* He opened his eyes slowly, and then got out of bed and walked to the window. Moving the drapes, he looked out. There she was shivering, her face red from the cold. *Kara! Is it really you? Or am I dreaming?* he thought as he opened the window and helped her inside.

"Kara, forgive me. Please forgive me. I know I am a monster for killing Josef. I didn't want to kill anyone ever. But when I saw what he'd done to you, and when you told me that your father . . ." Abram was rambling. The window was still open. She turned to close it. Then she turned back to face him.

"I know. I know you killed Josef," she said. "I wasn't asleep. I heard you. And I was afraid that our relationship was hurting both of us." She hesitated. "Oh dear God, Abram, you killed for me."

"And I would do it again. I did it because I love you, Kara. I can't stand by and let someone hurt you."

She hugged him tightly. "I know. And I love you too. I couldn't stay away from you," she said. "I tried. I really tried."

"Thank God you came back," he said, taking her hands between his own and rubbing them to warm them. "You are so cold."

"Yes, I know," she said. "It's freezing outside. I borrowed a bicycle to get here because it was too late to take the bus."

He pulled her into his arms and held her tightly. "I thought I was never going to see you again. It was as if my life had ended. I love you so much."

"I feel the same way," she said. "I love you too."

He touched her face.

Then in a choked voice, she whispered, "Abram . . . I'm pregnant."

CHAPTER FORTY

March 1936
Berlin

Anka and Ludwig would have preferred to wait until summer to marry. They would have liked to have their wedding outside in a Biergarten filled with sunflowers. However, when Anka became pregnant, Ludwig's family decided it was best to rush the wedding. His father still had his doubts about the match. He didn't feel that Anka was a suitable match. He didn't think she came from a proper family background. But with a baby on the way, there was little else he could do.

The wedding was not the spectacular affair that Anka had hoped for. Ludwig's father didn't invite the men he admired and worked with in the Nazi Party. Which indicated to Anka that he was ashamed of his son's choice for a wife. Still, Anka and Ludwig invited several of the people they knew from school. And Ludwig's cousins came into town from Nuremburg for the wedding. His cousins were his father's brother's children. There were three girls, who were younger than Ludwig, and an older boy who Ludwig had always admired. His name was Wilhelm Babler, and he was a handsome man of twenty-three. At the wedding, Anka introduced Wilhelm to Kara.

"This is my sister, Kara," Anka said sweetly. "Kara, this is Ludwig's cousin Wilhelm. He came into town from Nuremberg for our wedding."

Wilhelm's face lit up when he saw Kara.

"A pleasure to meet you," Kara said respectfully.

"Would you care to dance?" Wilhelm asked.

"I'm sorry. I am not much of a dancer," Kara lied. But she didn't want to dance with anyone. She felt as if dancing with another man would be a form of betrayal to Abram.

"I am a very good dancer," Wilhelm said with a confidence that would have sounded as if he were bragging had he been anyone else. But coming from this tall, handsome stranger, the comment was almost charming. "I'll make sure you look like one too. All you have to do is follow my lead."

Kara managed a smile.

"One dance. That's all I ask." Wilhelm smiled. "I promise you that if you dance with me once I will not bother you anymore."

"Come on, Kara," Anka pleaded. "Just one dance?"

"All right," Kara said, and she stood up, taking Wilhelm's arm. He led her to the dance floor, and they began to waltz. *Well, he certainly wasn't lying. He is an excellent dancer*, she thought.

After the music ended, Wilhelm led Kara back to her table. "May I join you?" he asked.

She forced a smile. *What can I say? I can't say no.*

He sat across from her and gazed into her eyes. "I am going to tell you a little secret." He smiled. "I really didn't want to come to this wedding. I didn't want to make the trip. I am starting a new job, and I was afraid that coming here would interfere with my work. But now that I am here, I am going to consider finding a way to come to Berlin more often. Regardless of how it affects my professional life."

She smiled, her lips quivering.

"Do you have a boyfriend? Or a fiancé perhaps?"

How could I ever explain my situation? "No." She looked down at the table instead of meeting his eyes.

"Well then, I will be coming to Berlin more often," he said. "Can I get you another beer?"

"Yes, thank you," she said, glad he would be leaving her alone for at least a few minutes.

"I'll be right back." He smiled.

Anka was a beautiful bride. Her skin was glowing, and her eyes sparkled. It was too early in her pregnancy for her baby belly to show in her traditional German folk dress. Kara had braided her hair and put it into a bun with baby's breath. She looked light and happy as she danced with her new husband. But everyone whispered that as pretty as Anka was, there was something even more intriguing about her sister. Kara, with her hair that looked like spun white gold, and her eyes that sparkled like blue topaz, sat at her table. Several men came up asking her to dance, but she refused them all. It came as no surprise to the local boys. She'd already earned the reputation of being stuck-up among her neighbors and school chums.

But it wasn't that she was stuck-up. The truth was, she was in love, and it hurt her to know that she was unable to bring the man she loved anywhere. And most importantly, he could not be at her side at her sister's wedding. To make matters worse, Kara had missed her period again this month, and now she was certain that she was pregnant. If things had been different, she would have confided in her sister, but as they stood, the only person she could talk to was Abram. She knew he wished he could marry her, but the laws forbade it. It would have been so much fun if she and Anka were both getting married. And how delightful it would have been to have their babies born at almost the same time.

Her mind raced as she watched her sister laughing while she whirled across the dance floor. Kara considered having sex with one of the local men, and then telling him that she became pregnant. She was fairly sure that she could find one who would marry her. She wondered if that would be the best thing to do for the child. *But what about Abram?* She loved him. It was with Abram that she longed to raise this child, not with some stranger. He was the baby's father after all. *Why is this world we live in so crazy with hatred? Why has the government decided it is their right to keep Abram and I apart?*

After the wedding, Anka kissed Kara goodbye. She and Ludwig planned to leave for a short honeymoon the following day. And when they returned, they planned to live at Ludwig's parents' home. Kara knew it would be more difficult for her to escape at night now that Anka would not be there to cover for her when her parents came knocking on the bedroom door. And for the past few weeks she'd been so consumed with the wedding, that she and Abram had not had a chance to discuss what they planned to do about the pregnancy.

It had been a lovely wedding, but the bride and groom had just said their goodbyes, and now it was time for everyone to leave. The band played a final song. Wilhelm begged Kara to dance, but she refused.

Although Kara had refused to dance the last dance of the evening with him, Wilhelm insisted that he take Kara home. She could see in his eyes that he was smitten with her, and she didn't know how to discourage him without divulging the truth about her and Abram. So she walked silently beside him, all the while hoping that once he returned to Nuremberg, he would find he was too busy to return to Berlin. And with luck, he would forget all about her.

"So, what is this job you are starting?" Kara asked.

"I am going to be working in construction. It pays well, and it builds nice muscles, you know," he said. "Perhaps one day I can show them to you."

She didn't answer or even look at him, but she felt her stomach turn.

Once they arrived at her home, she turned to Wilhelm and said, "Thank you for escorting me home."

He smiled and pulled her to him. She felt her body tense up with resistance.

"You don't kiss on a first date?" he said, letting out a short laugh. "That's all right. I like a girl who gives me a little challenge."

She turned to open the door. "Well, good night," she said.

"Unfortunately, I am leaving Berlin tomorrow. I have to get back to start the new project. But since I walked you home, I have your address. So I hope it will be all right if I write to you."

"I don't think it's such a good idea. You live far away, and my life is here. My family is here." She tried to make an excuse.

"So? A letter or two can't hurt. I will write. You can tear up my letters if you'd like. But I will send them regardless."

She nodded.

"And maybe . . . who knows, perhaps you will answer."

"I don't know," she said. "I don't think it's a good idea."

"Give it some thought," he said.

Not wanting to continue the conversation, Kara just nodded. "Good night," she said more firmly than she'd said it the last time.

"Well, good night, then, lovely Kara," he answered teasingly.

She walked into the house and then ran to her room and shut the door behind her.

The last time Kara saw Abram, she told him that her sister was getting married. She explained that, because of the wedding, it might be a few days before she was able to get back to the Mitte to see him. He was disappointed, as he always was, when she was unable to see him. But he said he understood.

With Anka gone, Kara's workload at home doubled. Her mother made so many demands on her, that Kara was overwhelmed. She had never realized how much work Anka had done around the house. Now, because she'd been so busy, it had been almost a week since Kara's last visit with Abram, and she felt like she was going mad without him. That night after her parents went to bed, she stood in the hallway. Kara could hardly wait until she heard her mother's steady, even breathing, and her father's heavy snoring. It seemed to take forever. But once she was certain they were asleep, she slipped out of her bedroom window.

As she made her way to Abram's home, she thought about how much it worried him that she was outside alone at night. She'd promised him she would be all right. She caught the last bus of the night, and for some odd reason, as she was riding along trying not to make eye contact with any of the derelicts that were staring at her, she wished he could have accompanied her. And once again, she was angry at the unjust laws Hitler had put into place, for as she saw it, there was no reason at all.

Kara barely had to knock before Abram opened the window. He swept her into his arms and held her close to him. "I missed you so much," he whispered.

"I missed you too."

They made love. In the afterglow as she lay contented in his arms, he asked "How was the wedding?"

"Nice," she said. "I wished you could have been there."

She felt him nod in the dark. Then he said, "Every time you have somewhere you have to go, some kind of a celebration—like this wedding, or that Christmas party your girlfriend threw—I am always afraid you will meet someone else and you'll never come back to me."

She didn't answer for a few moments.

"I have something to ask you," she said. "What are we going to do about my being pregnant?"

"Kara, are you sure you are?"

"Yes, I've missed my period for the last two months."

He put his hand on her shoulder and said more to himself than to her, "What are we going to do? We haven't really discussed it."

She didn't answer.

"Marry me," he said.

"You know better. We can't."

"Leave your father's house and move in here with me. Marry me under Jewish law. I'll find a rabbi who will marry us."

"How? What rabbi would break the law like that? No one."

"I know someone who might. He's a rabbi in our neighborhood. We could try . . ."

"Did you attend his synagogue?"

"Not really. I mean . . . once in a while. But I have never been religious. My father wasn't, and I guess I followed in his footsteps. But my mother used to take me to the temple once in a while, when I would go with her. She knows this rabbi."

"What would your mother say about you asking him to marry us?"

He shook his head. "I don't know what she'll say. I don't think she would mind my talking to the rabbi. She always wished I would get closer to him and to the synagogue. But I never did. As far as you and I getting married . . . I figure she'll probably be worried about me. She'll be afraid that the Nazis will come and take me away for breaking their law. She'll cry and scream, but then she'll accept us. She will have to. I know her; she would rather accept you and I getting married, than risk losing me. She loves me. She's a good woman, Kara. She's just very nervous, and she was raised a certain way. She was raised to be afraid of non-Jews. So, it will be hard for her at first. But she'll come around. You'll see."

"I understand what it means to be raised to fear people who are different than you. I was raised to be afraid of Jews. And now . . ."

"And now?" he whispered, reaching up and affectionately tucking a strand of her hair behind her ear.

"And now, I love you."

"I love you too. We might have come from different backgrounds, but when I am with you, I feel like we are one person. Do you know what I mean?"

She nodded. "I do."

He kissed her softly. "Don't be so worried. This will all work out. You'll see. You'll move in here with me and my mother. No one will know you are here. Tomorrow, when you come to me, bring everything you want to keep. Then you will just never return."

"My parents may call the police when they find me gone," she said.

"But no one would suspect that you're here. Does anyone know you've been seeing me? Does anyone know you are coming to the store here in the Mitte?"

"No, no one knows about us. Not even my sister who, until you, was the closest person in the world to me."

"Hmm . . ." he said, "once you move in, you could pretend to be Jewish. We could tell my mother that you are Jewish, and you are from another part of Germany."

"And what about my papers? Where would we tell your mother I came from? Another city? How did we meet? She would know that it doesn't add up."

He shrugged. "You're right. She has seen you come into the shop in your adorable little German folk dress. She knows you're not Jewish. I am just grasping at straws," he said. "I suppose that was a childish idea."

"My friend Elke knows a Jewish doctor who can fix the pregnancy."

"How does she know him?"

"Her mother was his patient. Her mother got pregnant, and they couldn't afford another child, so her mother went to see this doctor in the Mitte. As a matter of fact, that's how I first met you. My friend—Elke is her name—was with her mother when she went to the doctor, and she saw your bookstore from the bus window."

"That's quite a coincidence."

"Yes, it is. I feel like it was fate," she said.

He squeezed her hand gently. "I'm glad you found me. But . . . Kara . . . I don't know a lot about these things. But from what I have heard, a woman can die from getting rid of a pregnancy. I love you, Kara. I can't put you at risk like this," he said, shaking his head. "And the idea of destroying our child hurts me. It's a gift from God. He gave us a baby as an expression of our love."

"I know what you're saying. I feel terrible about it. But what other choice do we have? I can't marry you and have your baby, which is what I would like to do."

"And that is what I want too. I never thought I would feel this way about marriage and children."

"But we can't forget that the law forbids it."

He nodded. "I should never have touched you. I should never have loved you. If I had known that my love would have ended up putting you in danger, I would never have made love to you."

"It wasn't all your fault. I wanted you to make love to me. I wanted you to because I love you too, Abram. And I believe that making love to someone who you really love with all your heart is being as close to God as a person can get."

He shook his head. "Yes, it should be that way. But now we have to fix this pregnancy, as if it were a mistake rather than a blessing. And, to make matters worse, you could face death. And . . . if anything happened to you . . ." He put his head in his hands, then in a tortured voice he said, "I don't know what to do."

"Look at me," she said, lifting his face so his eyes met hers. "I promise you I won't die."

"You can't make a promise like that," he said.

"Elke told me that the doctor is a good doctor. She said he was kind and understanding. And . . . her mother was fine. She said her mother told her that it didn't even hurt." Kara tried to smile, but her lower lip was trembling.

He put his head in his hands again and pulled the hair at his temples. "I wish I could go through it for you. I wish it were me who had to go through this and not you."

"You know better. There is no sense in making wishes that can't come true. I am the woman; the child grows within me."

"My child," he croaked out the words. "Our child. Our gift from God."

"Abram, stop, please. We have to be practical now. There is a child growing inside of me. A child I would love to give birth to. But it is not possible. So, we must take care of it."

Abram took a deep breath. "So, you've decided that this is what we must do?"

"It's our only choice. I don't know what it costs to have this procedure done, but . . ."

"Don't worry about the cost. I'll get the money. But more importantly, I will be with you every step of the way," he said.

"You are going to come to the doctor with me?"

"Of course, I wouldn't leave you to face this alone. This is not your problem, Kara. It's our problem."

"I suppose we should go to see the doctor tomorrow. I had a job interview tomorrow for a typing job," she said, smiling sadly. "I was going to surprise you. But this is more important. So, I could meet you at the doctor's office in the morning. I'll tell you how to get there."

"Do you have an address?"

"No, but the first time I came to your bookstore, my friend came with me, and she pointed out the building as we went by on the bus. It's a doctor's office. It's located right above Kasselman's Jewelry. Do you know where that is?"

"I know where it is," he said. "What time do you want to meet me?"

"I am thinking that if I leave here just before dawn, I can go home and take a quick bath. Then we can meet at the doctor's office at eleven in the morning."

He nodded. "All right. Whatever you want."

That night they didn't make love. Abram just held Kara tightly. After she fell asleep, he remained awake staring out the window. Tears of frustration ran down his cheeks. *My father always told me that a man should protect and cherish the woman he loves. He should shelter her from harm. But look at me. Hitler has reduced me to a simpering child. I am no man. I can't marry her. I can't provide for her and my child. And tomorrow she will talk to a doctor about sacrificing the greatest gift God can bestow upon a couple. Just look at me, I am worthless. I am nothing.*

CHAPTER FORTY-ONE

KARA AWAKENED to find Abram already awake as the sun began to rise.

"I've been so tired lately. I'd love to sleep until noon," she said more to herself than to Abram.

He didn't answer. There was a bitter taste in his mouth. And he felt like he didn't even deserve to hold her hand.

Neither Abram nor Kara spoke very much as she got dressed and ready to leave. He hung his head and stared at the ground. But when he did look up, he saw that she could hardly look at him. Then once she was ready to go, she turned and asked, "Are you sure you want to come with me? I could go alone, and then come back tomorrow night and tell you how much money we will need."

He shook his head. "No, I won't let you go alone. I will be there at your side. I can't do much for you. But I will do what I can."

"All right," she said. The sun had already begun to rise as she climbed out the window. He watched her as she walked toward the street and he chastised himself for how little he was able to provide for this woman he'd come to love. He couldn't marry her. He couldn't protect her or his unborn child. He couldn't even walk her home in the dark. Not only this, but if they were to have a child, his blood would be the blood that tainted their little one for the rest of its life. Abram began to hate himself. And although he'd never been religious before, and his Jewish background had never mattered to him one way or the other, as he watched the back of Kara's gray coat disappear around the corner, Abram began to hate being a Jew.

CHAPTER FORTY-TWO

THAT NIGHT when Kara returned home from visiting with Abram, Anka was waiting for her. Anka had returned from her honeymoon glowing like a ray of hope. Her eyes were luminous, and when she hugged Kara, she smelled of sunshine and fresh air.

"I have a secret to tell you," Anka whispered in Kara's ear.

"What is it?"

"Come into our room. I don't want anyone else to hear," Anka said, taking Kara's hand.

Kara followed Anka into the bedroom. She closed the door behind her and turned to look at her sister. Anka's face was illuminated by the sunshine that filtered through the window. "I'm pregnant," Anka said. "I was pregnant when Ludwig and I got married, but we didn't tell anyone. I wanted to tell you. I really did. But I couldn't; I promised Ludwig I wouldn't say a word."

"You're going to have a baby. How wonderful." Kara tried to sound happy, but her own unfortunate pregnancy haunted her, and for a moment she was jealous of her sister because she and Ludwig could have this child without anyone questioning them. Their love was accepted. Their child would be accepted. And their lives were planned like a perfect fairy tale.

"What's wrong? Are you angry that I didn't tell you?" Anka asked, seeing the strange look on Kara's face. "I really wanted to. I am sorry. I was wrong. I should have told you."

"No, it's all right, really. I'm just shocked, that's all it is. I didn't know. I didn't have any idea." Kara managed a big smile but her eyes were still sad. She was ashamed of being jealous of her sister. After all, she loved Anka. She wanted her to be happy. And she wished that she could see happiness in her own future. But her baby was not destined to be born into a loving home. It was destined to die on a doctor's surgical table.

Kara wanted to cry. She wished she could tell Anka everything and then weep on her sister's shoulder. Instead, she said, "I'm so happy for you, Anka. So happy." Then she embraced her sister so that Anka wouldn't see the tears forming in her eyes.

CHAPTER FORTY-THREE

As soon as she got off the bus the following morning, Kara could see Abram standing in front of the building that housed the doctor's office. He was pacing nervously. When she approached him, he tried to smile. *He's even more handsome when he's worried*, she thought. *Poor man. I feel sorry for him. Almost as sorry as I feel for myself.*

Abram took her hands in both of his. "You're trembling," he whispered. Then he put her hands up to his face and blew on them trying to warm them.

She nodded. Then she gently tugged at his hands and they walked inside the building. Dr. Klugmann's office was on the second floor. As soon as they opened the door, Kara was accosted by the scent of rubbing alcohol. She stole a glance at Abram. He was as white as the newly painted walls in the doctor's office. Kara walked up to the receptionist feeling like she was on death row and taking her last steps.

"May I help you?" A middle-aged woman with dark hair and a warm smile said.

"My name is Kara Scholz. I have an eleven o'clock appointment with the doctor."

"Yes, of course. Please have a seat. It will only be a minute"

Kara was glad there was no one else in the waiting room. She sat down on a hard wooden chair. Abram sat in the chair beside her.

"Mrs. Scholz, the doctor will see you now," the nurse said.

Kara and Abram followed the nurse back to an immaculate examining room.

"Wait here, please. The doctor will be right in."

"Thank you," Abram said.

A few minutes later, a tall, slender man entered the room. He wore a white coat with a stethoscope. His gray hair was very thin, so thin that his scalp showed through. He smiled warmly as he extended his hand to Kara. "I'm Dr. Klugmann," he said. She took his hand. Then he turned to Abram and extended his hand. "Dr. Klugmann."

"Abram Ehrlich." Abram shook his hand.

"So, Kara, what seems to be the problem?"

His wrinkled skin and soft-blue eyes made him look like a kindly old grandfather. "I-I missed my monthly period for the last two months," she blurted. "I think I may be pregnant."

The doctor nodded. "I see."

"And . . . for several reasons, for several very pressing reasons . . . we can't have a baby," Kara said.

"Let me guess. You are Christian. He is Jewish. And you are not married." '

"Yes."

"I would marry her. I would marry her in a minute, Doctor," Abram said, "but as you know, the laws forbid it."

"You are not the first couple to come to me with this problem. Nor will you be the last, I am afraid," the doctor said. Then he turned to Kara. "Well, the first thing to do is draw some blood. Then I will need some urine. After that, I'll examine you. We need to determine if you are actually pregnant before we can discuss our options."

"Yes," Kara said.

"I'll have the nurse come in to draw blood and help you to give us a urine specimen. Perhaps you should wait outside, Abram. As soon as we have finished the exam, I'll send the nurse to call for you."

Abram took Kara's hand. "Will you be all right?"

She nodded.

"I'll be right outside the door if you need me," Abram said.

"She'll be fine. And we won't do anything until we have all discussed the situation together," the doctor assured Abram in a gentle voice.

After Abram left, Kara said, "My boyfriend is nervous. He is very worried about me."

"You are fortunate. Some boys don't care at all. They take no responsibility. I can see in your Abram's eyes that he cares deeply for you."

Kara smiled. "I care for him too."

"I know. Believe me, I understand. These laws that were passed are a terrible thing that has happened to our country. I believe that it is against God's will to forbid two young people who are in love to marry." He shook his head. "The nurse will be right in to draw your blood and take your urine. Once she has finished, please take off your clothes and put on this gown. I will be right back to examine you."

Kara nodded. After the doctor left, she did as he had asked. The nurse was kind and gentle. She took blood and gave Kara a cup in which to urinate. Then she patted Kara's shoulder. "Don't worry, Dr. Klugmann is a very good doctor. He won't let anything happen to you," the nurse said reassuringly.

After the nurse left, Kara waited. Dr. Klugmann entered the room a few minutes later. Kara had never had a female exam before, and she felt embarrassed. But the doctor acted as if everything were perfectly normal. While he examined her, he asked her about school. She told him she graduated last summer. He asked her what she planned to do. She explained that Abram had taught her to type and take shorthand. And before she knew it, the exam was over.

"All right, my dear. I am going to leave for a few minutes while you get dressed. I will let Abram know that he can come back in, and then I'll return, and the three of us will all have a talk."

"Thank you, Doctor," Kara said.

The doctor gave Kara a reassuring smile. Then he patted her shoulder and left the room. Quickly she got dressed and then sat down on the examining table. She wished she had a blanket because she was shivering.

Abram and the doctor returned to the room at the same time. Abram stood at Kara's side, while the doctor sat down on a stool across from them.

"Kara, you are showing signs of being pregnant. Now, we can't be fully certain of anything until the tests are complete. That will take about two days. If you can make another appointment, we will know for certain then. However, in my professional opinion . . . you are pregnant. And you should both start considering what you plan to do."

Even though Kara had been fairly sure she was pregnant, hearing the doctor say the words aloud had left her speechless.

"All right, Doctor," Abram said, taking Kara's hand and helping her down off the table. "We'll make an appointment. Then we'll go home and discuss it further and be back at the end of the week."

Kara nodded. Her eyes were red, her face was pinched, and she was ready to cry.

"Don't be afraid. There is always adoption to consider as well. No one need know that the child is half-Jewish. You two would be the only ones privy to that information. Kara could go to a doctor in her own part of town and tell him that the father was a German. The doctor would help her find a suitable couple to adopt," the doctor said. "Whatever you decide, Abram and I will take good care of you. Isn't that right, Abram?"

Abram nodded. "I'll do whatever I need to do," he said.

Before they left, Kara and Abram made an appointment to return on Friday morning.

Once they were outside, Abram turned to Kara and said, "I love you."

She shook her head. Her eyes were glassy. Her body was trembling. He pulled her close to him, not caring that people on the street were looking on with curiosity.

"Please talk to me. I can't let you go home in this condition. Please just talk to me. Won't you?" he begged.

"Our love has caused nothing but grief for both of us. And now, even more grief for an unborn baby."

"I disagree with you. Loving you has been the greatest joy of my life," he said, putting his hands on her shoulders so that she could not turn away from him.

"Yes, and it has also been the greatest source of pain."

"If you want to leave me once this is all over, and we decide what we must do, I will understand," he said. "I want you to be happy, Kara. Your happiness is more important to me than my own. I would never do anything to hurt you. Never."

She pulled away from him and wiped the tears from her cheeks. "I am going to walk to the bus stop. Please don't follow me. I want to go home," she said as she turned away from him and began walking.

"I'll meet you here on Friday?" he said, standing there helplessly with his heart pounding and his hands at his sides as he watched her walk away.

"Yes," she answered without looking back at him.

CHAPTER FORTY-FOUR

ABRAM WASN'T SURPRISED that Kara did not come to see him at all that week. Even so, he waited, lying awake each night hoping to hear her knock on his window. He couldn't eat or rest at all. His mind was constantly filled with dread as he counted the days until Friday. *What if she hates me now? What if she does something terrible to herself. Oh, Kara, please, don't hurt yourself. I am begging you. Let me shoulder this with you. Why won't you marry me? Why won't you marry me even if the marriage isn't legal. It will be legal in the eyes of God. We could have this child, and we could raise it here in the Mitte. I would do whatever I had to do to provide for you both.*

But I know she would be giving up a great deal moving to the Mitte and marrying a Jew. She might not have money or prestige living with her parents, but she has the government's approval. She is a blonde-haired, blue-eyed, pure Aryan. Once she openly declares her love for me and tells the world that we are going to have a child together, she becomes as good as Jewish. And she is breaking their law. But I can't let her have this abortion. Anything could happen. She could die. Oh, dear God. What have I done to this woman? I love her so much, and there is nothing I can do to help her.

On Friday morning, Abram's stomach was in knots and his head ached. The days leading up to this fateful morning had taken their toll on him. His nerves were frazzled as he got dressed quietly before his mother awoke. He knew she would be worried when she found him gone. So he quickly scratched out a note.

"Mother, I went to meet with a man who wanted to buy one of my original signed copies of a Hemingway novel. I'll be careful. Please don't worry. I didn't bring the book with me, so there is no danger of being caught with it on my person. I'll be back by late afternoon. Love, Abram."

He put the note on the kitchen table under a coffee cup so it wouldn't blow away and then quietly left the apartment.

It was too early to go to the doctor's office. The office wasn't open yet, and besides, he wasn't scheduled to meet Kara for several hours. But he had to get out of the house while his mother was still asleep. If she'd awakened, she would have asked him a million questions. And he was so distraught that he was afraid he would just tell her the truth burdening yet another person who loved him.

Alone with his thoughts, his guilt, his love for Kara, and his fears, he walked the streets of the old familiar neighborhood where he'd grown up. *I am a Jew,* he thought. *I am not a Jewish man. I am just a Jew. The Nazis have taken away my manhood and made me into a weak and worthless piece of trash. I should never have started with Kara. It was selfish of me to bring her out of her safe, protected world and into my dangerous and uncertain one.*

It was mid-April, and the air was chilly. But Abram didn't care. He walked to the park and sat on the bench where he and Kara met that first day they'd made love. He studied the tree under which they'd lain together the first time. It was a thick, green tree with heavy branches and a sturdy trunk. *That tree prevails through the winter. It gets its strength from God. And although I've never been a religious man, and I've never really prayed, I've always known that there was something bigger than me. I guess I've always known that there is a God. And I have never needed him more than I do today. Hashem, come to me and help me, please. Give me strength. Give me answers. Let me know what to do. Forgive me for not coming to you sooner. I know I was an arrogant fool. I thought I could handle everything in my life on my own. But that was before I knew what it meant to love another person. I mean to truly love another person. To love them even more than you love your own life. Help me, please, Hashem. I need you. Please, I beg you; don't turn your face away from me.*

He waited for several moments listening to the beating of his own heart. Somehow hoping that God would come to him, and he would miraculously know what to do.

But there was no answer from the heavens. Only the songs of birds chirping and the whistle of the wind through the trees.

Abram sighed, then he looked at the watch on his wrist, which had once belonged to his father. If he walked slowly, he could head to the doctor's office and be there just as Kara arrived. He stood up and stretched his legs. Feeling old and heavy, he began to walk just as a light rain trickled down from the sky. Abram arrived on time, but Kara was not there yet. So he sat down on the steps outside the building and waited. The cold rain came down heavier and drenched his coat and hair, but he didn't mind. In a strange way, it felt good. Cleansing.

Abram glanced at his watch again. Kara was late. He wondered if she was going to come at all. If she didn't, he wondered if he would ever see her again. *Once again, I am helpless. There is nothing I can do but sit here and wait. If she doesn't come, I can go to her house and wait for her. But what will that do? If she doesn't want me, there is nothing I can do to change her mind.*

Finally, he saw Kara as she turned the corner and began walking toward him. "Sorry I am late. The bus was delayed."

"It's all right," he said, taking her arm. "How are you?"

She shrugged. "How should I be? I am scared."

"I know. Me too. But no matter what the doctor says today, I'll be at your side."

They walked up the stairs and into the building.

When they entered the doctor's office, Kara walked up to the desk and apologized to the receptionist for being late. Then she and Abram were escorted to an office rather than the examining room. "Please sit down. The doctor will be right with you."

Abram took Kara's hand and squeezed it gently. But it was limp. "You hate me, don't you?" he asked, feeling stupid for asking. But he had to know the answer.

"I could never hate you, Abram. But I wish we had never started this."

He felt tears burn the backs of his eyes. *She wishes she'd never met me.* He released his grip on her hand. And his heart broke when she took her hand away and laid it in her lap. *Don't cry. You can't cry. You have to be strong for her sake.*

There was a knock on the door, and then Dr. Klugmann entered the room. "Abram, Kara," he said, greeting them both. "I have the results of your test. I am afraid that due to the circumstances, the news is not good. You were right, Kara. You are pregnant."

Kara gasped. Abram reached over and took her hand, but she pulled it away. Abram cleared his throat, then he asked, "So, what do we do now?"

"That's up to you," the doctor said. "If you don't want to have the baby, I can help you. However, it won't be inexpensive. I am putting myself at great risk to perform this surgery for you. I will need my nurse to help me. All of this will cost money."

"I don't care about the money. I have a little bit saved. And what I don't have, I'll borrow. What I do care about is Kara. How safe is this procedure? Will she be all right?" Abram asked. The desperation he felt caused his voice to crack.

Dr Klugmann took a long breath. "There are no guarantees. I am afraid that I must tell you that there are never any guarantees with a medical procedure," he said, speaking slowly, choosing his words carefully.

"So I could die," Kara said coldly.

The doctor looked down at his desk for a moment. "It is possible," he said. "Of course, I will do everything I can to prevent it. I have done this procedure before."

"Have you ever lost anyone? Has anyone ever . . . died?" Abram asked.

The doctor bit his upper lip. "Yes, I am sorry to say, I have lost two patients. There were complications . . ."

"How many have you done?" Kara asked, her voice as cold and hard as a steel drum.

"Over twenty."

Abram glanced over at Kara. Her face was frozen, white like a stone statue.

"Do you want a few minutes to talk this over?" the doctor asked.

"No. There's nothing to talk about. I want to schedule the procedure," Kara said.

"All right. My receptionist can help you with that," Dr. Klugmann said. "Follow me. I'll lead you up to the front desk and you can schedule it with her."

They followed the doctor up to the front desk. There were several patients in the waiting room, so Dr. Klugmann leaned down and whispered in the receptionist's ear. She nodded. Then the doctor turned to Abram and Kara. "She will help you both from here," he said and walked away.

"The doctor wants me to schedule your appointment as soon as possible. However, we are very busy. Can you make a late-afternoon appointment next Tuesday, say about five p.m.? The doctor does these procedures at the end of the day, so I must schedule you for the last appointment."

"Kara?" Abram said, his voice cracking, "is that all right for you?"

"I can be here," Kara said, her voice a little above a whisper.

"Do you have someone to take care of you following the procedure? Because you will need to have someone," the receptionist asked.

"I'll find someone," Kara answered, but her voice held no conviction.

"All right. Your appointment is all set."

"Thank you," Abram said.

Abram opened the door for Kara, and they both walked outside. The rain had stopped but it had left puddles on the sidewalks. The sky was still gray. There was not a single trace of sunshine, and an umbrella of doom seemed to hang over the Mitte. Kara did not look at Abram as he walked by her side in silence. She kept her eyes glued to the sidewalk. She was headed back to the bus stop. He followed her without saying a word. There was no one at the bus stop, but the bench was wet from the earlier rain. Abram took off his coat and dried the bench. Then he turned to Kara. "Sit down . . . please."

She did. And as she did, their eyes met. It was then that the stone sculpture she had been portraying crumbled, and Kara began to weep into her hands. Abram sat beside her and wrapped her in his arms, holding her tightly. "Don't have this procedure. We can go to my mother. We can tell her our situation. She will be angry, but I know her. She's a good-hearted person. She'll help us. You'll move in with her and I and have the baby. Meanwhile, I'll try to find a rabbi willing to marry us. Please, Kara," His voice was filled with desperation.

"Abram . . ." she said.

"I love you, Kara. I love you more than you can ever know. I am begging you not to do this."

She sighed. "I am so afraid. I'm afraid of everything. I feel paralyzed with fear. If I have the procedure, I might die. If I don't, I have to leave everything and everyone I know behind. I don't care about anyone but my sister. And I couldn't tell her about you, because of her husband's family. So . . . if we did this, you would be all that I would have in the world."

"AND I WOULD MAKE sure that I would be all that you would ever need. Kara . . . I love you."

"But the Nazis. If they found out that we were married . . . that we broke the law . . ."

"The Nazis can't last. They are too crazy, too radical. Before we know it, Hitler will be gone, and we'll be able to live our lives in peace. For now, maybe you will have to leave everyone behind. But soon you'll be able to go back and see your sister. Please, Kara . . . I'm begging you. Don't do this. You mean everything to me. Please, Kara . . ."

She laid her head on his shoulder. Then in a soft voice, she said, "All right. Let's go and talk to your mother."

CHAPTER FORTY-FIVE

THEY WALKED hand in hand until they reached the bookstore.

Then Abram turned to face Kara. He took both of her hands in his and looked into her eyes. "Don't be afraid; my mother can be difficult at first, but underneath her tough exterior she's as soft as butter." He smiled, but his lips were quivering.

Kara forced a weak smile as they stood outside the bookstore.

"Wait right here. I am going to go in first and tell my mother you're here with me," Abram said.

"I don't know about this, Abram. I am nervous," Kara said as she looked at the bookstore window. She could see Hoda sitting inside the store, and because she could, she knew Hoda could see her. Kara walked a few steps until she was sure Hoda could no longer see her. Abram followed and stood beside her.

"It will be all right. Do you trust me?"

"Yes." She nodded her head.

"Then give me five minutes to talk to her. I'll be right back." Then he added, "Please, Kara . . . don't leave. Please wait right here for me."

"I won't," she said, looking down at her shoes. She could hear the bell ring as Abram opened the door to the bookstore. Then she saw him enter.

Hoda was sitting on a stool behind the counter. When the bell on the door chimed, she looked up at Abram. Her face was flushed with anger.

"Where have you been, Abram?" his mother asked. "I wake up to find you gone? You say you are meeting a man about a book? You leave me a note? What man, Abram? What book was it? Why didn't you mention it to me before? You are full of secrets these days, and I don't like it. I want to know what you are up to."

He walked over to her and said, "It's good that you asked, Mother. I am going to tell you."

"NU? So speak," she said abruptly, "what is it?"

"I have been seeing someone."

"A girl?" Hoda looked at him shocked.

"Yes, Mother. A girl." Abram took a deep breath and continued, "I love her."

"Well, this is news to me. But, I am glad to hear you are finally ready for marriage. Who is it? Davina?"

"No," he said, feeling the muscles in his back twitch. "She's not from around here."

"What is with all of the riddles. Who is she? Tell me about her."

"Mother . . ." Abram hesitated for a moment, then he said, "her name is Kara."

"Kara? What kind of a name is that? A shiksa name? Oy, Abram." Hoda shook her head. "She's a shiksa?"

"I hate that word. I hate the sound of it. You're right, she's not Jewish. But she's a good person, Mother. A very good person."

"Call it off. I will never approve—never. Do you hear me? Never."

He nodded.

"Besides that, it's against the law. You could get into real trouble for this. They could come and take you away," she was shouting at him.

"I can't call it off, Mother."

"You can and you will, if I say you will. You think you're all grown up, but I am still your mother."

"I can't, and I wouldn't even if I could. I told you, I love her," Abram said, then bravely added, "besides, she's pregnant."

Hoda threw her hands in the air. "What have you done?" She growled at him in Yiddish, "*Shemen zolstu zich in dein veiten haldz*! You should be ashamed of yourself."

Abram didn't answer. He knew she would respond like this. It was her way to scream and rant and go through hysterics until she exhausted herself. But then he knew she would settle down and accept the situation. For the next few minutes, Hoda screamed at her son, telling him that his dead grandparents would be ashamed. But she did not mention his father. Because they both knew that if Kaniel were alive, he would have accepted Abram's choice no matter what it was. They both knew that Kaniel would probably be congratulating his son right now and helping Abram find someone willing to marry the couple.

Hoda stared at Abram for a few moments, her eyes flashing like bolts of lightning. Abram was so much like his father. Finally, she threw her hands in the air. Her shoulders slumped and Hoda said, "All right. What's done is done." Then she sighed, and in a soft voice, she said, "I must meet her."

"Yes. You're right. She is waiting outside."

"Right now? I didn't mean now. I thought we would arrange a meeting."

"I am sure you realize that Kara and I are in trouble. Serious trouble. Kara cannot go home. She must move in here with us."

Hoda let out a long sigh of defeat. Then she nodded. "Go and get her. Bring her in here so I can meet her."

Abram went outside and found Kara leaning against the side of the building. Tears stained her cheeks. He put his arms around her and said, "It will be all right. She knows everything. She wants to meet you."

"I can just imagine what she must think of me," Kara said, wiping her face with her sleeve.

"It will be all right," Abram assured Kara as he led her inside.

"So, you must be Kara," Hoda said in a harsh tone of voice. She shook her head. "What were you thinking getting into trouble and with a Jewish boy, no less? Do you realize what you have done to him? To me? To yourself?" Hoda said, looking down at the desk in front of her and shaking her head.

Kara couldn't speak. She just shook her head. "I'm sorry. I never meant to hurt anyone. I just . . . ." Tears began to flow down Kara's face. She turned and headed for the door.

"Don't go." Hoda lifted her head and called out. Her voice was softer and kinder than before. "You are carrying my son's child. My grandchild. We will have to find a way to work all of this out. I cannot let you go and endanger yourself and the baby. I must do what is right. I must protect you both."

Kara let her eyes meet Hoda's. "Thank you," she said. "I really am so sorry for all of this."

"Well, I appreciate that, but sorry never did anyone any good. What's done is done. And there is nothing either of us can do to change it. So come, let me show you the apartment where you will be living."

Kara didn't let on that she'd already seen Abram's room many times. Instead, she followed Hoda silently as Hoda led her through the small apartment. Finally, they came to Abram's room.

"This is my son's room. You will be staying here with him. I would feel better about all of this if the two of you were married," she said, then she added, more to herself than to Kara, "but of course, with the laws being what they are, I realize that's not possible."

Abram trailed behind the two women, allowing his mother to take control of the situation for a few minutes. He knew her. He knew that if she were in control, her motherly instincts would take over, and she would come to be as protective of Kara as a mother cat with kittens.

"Are you going to go back home to get some of your things?" Hoda asked.

"Yes. I am going to go back this afternoon. I'll return tonight. If that's all right with you?"

Hoda nodded.

"This is very kind of you," Kara said. "I am very grateful to you."

Hoda sucked in a deep breath. "I'm not happy about it. My husband, his memory should be a blessing, was very indulgent with Abram. I suppose that was because Abram was our only child. But Kaniel never punished Abram, and so my son doesn't understand the meaning of consequences." Hoda shook her head, then she continued, "You seem to be a very nice girl. But as we both know, this government doesn't look kindly upon Jews. And they are even less kind to Jews who marry or have children with Gentiles. So this has put all of us in a dangerous predicament.

"Still, we cannot look backward. We must go forward. And the fact is that you are carrying my grandchild, and I must admit, I've always wanted a grandchild. You see, I was unable to have any more children after Abram was born. So I've been waiting for this day. The day when I would learn that I would soon have a grandbaby. However, I expected the mother to be Jewish and for her and Abram to be married." She sighed. "It seems Hashem has other plans. No matter. A child is always a blessing. So, welcome to our home, Kara."

Kara felt the tears well in her eyes. "You are so kind to me," she said.

Hoda nodded. Then she turned and walked away, leaving Kara and Abram alone in his room.

CHAPTER FORTY-SIX

KARA TOOK the bus home to collect what she could of her personal things. As she rode through the Mitte on her way to the part of town where her parents lived, she thought about Abram's mother. Hoda had made it clear that she preferred Abram would have become involved with a Jewish girl, but she was not cruel to Kara. *How strange this all is. I grew up believing that the Jews were mean and dangerous. My father hated them. My mother never cared much for them either. Everyone I knew at school hated and feared them, and yet now that I know Abram and his mother, and even Dr. Klugmann, I can see that all of the things I grew up believing were wrong. Jews are just people. They dress differently and speak a little differently. But in the end, they are the same as everyone else. I wonder why the world hates them so.*

Kara's father was asleep; she could hear him in his room snoring when she arrived at home. But her mother was sitting on the kitchen floor with the washboard in front of her and a large basket of dirty laundry at her side. On the other side of her was another basket filled with clean wet clothing.

"Where have you been?" she asked. "Look at the size of this load. I need your help. With Anka gone, you are going to have to do a little more around here. I am only one person. I can't do it all myself."

"I am sorry, Mutti. I went on a job interview," Kara lied. "Don't you remember I told you I was going?"

"I don't remember that," her mother said, wiping a strand of hair out of her eyes. Sweat dripped down her face.

"Yes. I told you," Kara said.

"Well, you're home now. I need you to help me get these clothes washed and hung outside to dry."

"Of course, Mutti."

"I'm so tired," her mother complained. "So tired."

"I know," Kara said. She knew that her mother was not only tired from the extensive physical work she did, but she was also tired of her husband's outbursts and his unwillingness to help in any way. Kara wished her mother had some way of standing up to her father. But she knew the years of abuse her mother had suffered had beaten her down.

Kara had seen pictures of her mother when she was young. She had been a pretty girl, who looked much like her daughter Anka, a blonde, blue-eyed, vivacious girl. But she could not see even a trace of that young woman in the woman who sat on the floor in front of her washing clothes. This woman was thin and developing a slight hump in her back. Her face was lined from years of pain. Her lips were thin, and on the rare occasions when she smiled, they almost disappeared. Kara knew her mother was too afraid to complain. She just endured whatever her husband said or did.

Kara quickly slipped off her coat. "Let me go and change my dress and I'll be right back to help you."

The two women scrubbed clothes for the remainder of the afternoon as a pot of thin potato soup for dinner simmered on the stove. Once they'd finished the wash, Kara took the heavy, wet bundle outside and began to hang all of the items on a line which was located right in front of the Scholzes' kitchen window. Heidi, her mother, had put the line there so she could keep an eye on the clothes to prevent anyone from stealing, because if any item of clothing were missing when she returned the clean clothes to her customer, she would be forced to pay for it.

"Kara," her mother called, "you had better hang those things inside. I am afraid it's too late in the afternoon to hang them out there. They won't be dry by nightfall, and I don't dare leave them out overnight."

Kara hated hanging the laundry inside. Her mother had set up a line in the living room, but it took up the entire room. Still, she did it rather than complain.

An hour later, one of Heidi's other customers arrived to pick up his clean and folded laundry. Heidi went to the kitchen where she had several baskets of clean clothes lined up and waiting for their owners to retrieve them. This customer appeared to be well over fifty. Everyone in town, including Kara, knew he had been widowed last year. She felt sorry for him, living alone after so many years of marriage and having to bring his laundry to her mother to have it washed. But when he smiled at Kara lecherously and let his eyes scan her body, she felt the skin crawl on the back of her neck.

"Looks like you are quite busy," the customer said to Heidi, smiling as he looked at the wet sheets dripping on the living room floor.

"Yes, I've been busy. I feel fortunate that so many people need my services. I have been able to keep a roof over our heads and food on the table."

"Well, good for you," the customer said as he took a few marks out of his pocket and handed them to Heidi. She put the cash the customer had given her into a money jar in the kitchen. The man thanked her, and then he took his basket of clean clothes and left, the door slamming behind him. Artur must have heard the door, because he came out of his bedroom just in time to grab some of the money that Heidi had earned out of the jar in the kitchen. Then without a word of explanation he walked out the door. Neither Kara nor her mother spoke. They both knew he was on his way to the tavern.

CHAPTER FORTY-SEVEN

THAT NIGHT, as Kara got dressed to leave, she looked around the room where she'd grown up. There were so many terrible memories, but there were wonderful ones too. For a few moments she thought about Anka and all the nights they'd lay in bed talking quietly. She remembered the books they'd read, and the laughter they'd shared. And for a few moments she felt sad that those days were gone forever. However, with Anka married, things had changed, and there was nothing left here for her. So Kara layered her clothing in order to take as much with her as she could. She dared not carry a suitcase, lest someone see her and ask her where she was going.

Stuffing undergarments into the pockets of her dress, she thought about how angry Anka would be that she'd disappeared without any explanation. Her mother would be too. And for that matter, so would her father. She didn't care what her parents thought. She hated her father. And even though she felt sorry for her mother, she was filled with conflicting feelings about her. She didn't hate her, but she found it hard to love a mother who would allow anyone to abuse her children.

Most importantly, she knew that no matter what she tried to do to help her mother, the woman would never change. *No!* she thought, *my mother, Heidi Scholz, will never change. She will spend the rest of her life serving Artur Scholz. She will always overlook any terrible things that Artur might do in the meantime. My mother knew that her precious husband had sexually abused me when I was too young to fight back, and she did nothing but look the other way.*

Once, when Kara was ten, she had mustered up her courage and tried to tell her mother what her father was doing, but Heidi refused to listen. That was because Heidi was afraid of her husband, so she lived her entire life avoiding the truth rather than facing it head-on and trying to stop it. *She wanted me to be that way too. She wanted me to forgive my vater. But I can't. I never will. And I will not be like her. I will leave my parents and my past behind. And never look back.*

However, she hated to leave Anka. Her beloved sister was all she'd had when growing up. The two girls had clung to each other in that raging and violent sea that was their home. As Kara tucked a small picture of her sister into her purse, she felt hot tears threatening to fall. Leaving without saying goodbye to Anka was the only part of running away that she found almost unbearable. If she could have, she might have turned back because of Anka. She might have endured the world she was born into. But the unborn child stirred in her womb and begged for protection.

She dared not bring this baby into the world in this house with Artur Scholz. *I will not subject my child to the horrors I endured.* As she climbed out the window, her thoughts were on Anka. *My sister will probably assume that I have run away with the man I told her I was seeing. The married man that doesn't exist. I hate lying to Anka. And I know she will be angry with me for not talking to her first. I can't do anything about that right now. I must wait until I have the baby. But I will go to see her once the baby is born. Although I can never tell her the truth, that the man I love is Jewish, at least I will be able let her know that I am all right.*

There were three ways to enter the Ehrlichs' apartment. One was through the bookstore which went directly through the kitchen, the other was through a side door which opened into the living room. And, of course, there was the third. Which was through the window in Abram's room. Until now, Kara had been coming through the window. But today, when Kara arrived, she knocked on the side door. Hoda opened it and let her inside.

"Have you eaten?" Hoda asked.

Kara shook her head.

"You must eat. It's important for the baby's health," Hoda said. "I made some soup earlier. Did you bring any clothes?"

"Yes, I have them all on under my dress," Kara said.

"Good. Now go, and put your extra things in Abram's room while I warm you a bowl of hot soup."

"Thank you again for all of this," Kara said.

"I wish that it had not happened this way. Don't ever mistake my kindness for my approval. I can't sanction what the two of you did. However, I was raised never to turn away a person in need. And I've tried to live to by that. So I certainly would not turn my back on a girl who is carrying my grandchild."

CHAPTER FORTY-EIGHT

THE FOLLOWING DAY, Hoda woke up early and left the apartment while Kara and Abram were still asleep. She walked down the main street of town to the butcher shop. The owner, and butcher, Yitzar Stein, had always been especially kind to her. Although he never made a single inappropriate comment, she knew by the look in his eyes that he liked her. He wasn't a bad-looking man, just not nearly as handsome or brilliant as her Kaniel had been. But a mother-to-be needed to eat meat in order to produce a healthy child. And that child meant the world to Hoda. So she was prepared to do whatever was required to ensure that the needs of her precious grandbaby were met properly. When she got to the butcher shop, she went inside. Yitzar stood behind the counter.

"What can I do for you Frau Ehrlich?" he said with a bright smile.

"I was wondering if you needed any help here."

"Oh." He looked at her surprised, then after pausing for a moment, he said, "You are looking for a job?"

"Yes, as you know, my son and I own a bookstore. But people are not buying so many books these days."

"Well, yes. I can imagine." He lowered his voice. "With the forbidden books and the burnings." He nodded his head.

"Yes, exactly. So I am here in search of work. I don't require a large salary. But I am hoping that perhaps you might be able to spare some extra scraps of meat for an employee?"

She could feel his eyes on her. He was quiet for a moment. Then he said, "Forgive me if I am too bold, but a lovely woman like you deserves far better than just scraps."

She felt herself blush, and so she turned away.

Then he added, "Of course, I will hire you. I will pay you what I can. And I will make sure you have meat."

Hoda smiled. "Thank you. When can I start?"

"Tomorrow, seven a.m."

"I'll be here," she said. Then she turned to leave, but she stopped before she got to the door and turned around. "Thank you for this."

He smiled and nodded.

CHAPTER FORTY-NINE

ABRAM WAS SIPPING a cup of tea when Hoda came into the kitchen dressed and ready to leave.

"Where are you going?" Abram asked his mother.

"I am going to work."

"You got a job? You're going to work?" Abram was stunned. His mother had never worked outside of the bookstore.

"Yes, there are two of you at home now to take care of the store. I expect the both of you to take care it."

"But a job?"

"Yes, Abram, a job," she said, a little frustrated with his disbelief. "We could use the extra money, and I will be working for the butcher, so we'll get some meat which is far too expensive to buy."

"You think he'll give you meat? I doubt that," Abram said, clearly anxious about his mother taking a job. It was so out of character for her. However, over the last couple of days, everything in their lives had changed. And Hoda's willingness to accept changes in their lives was surprising him.

"Like I said, you and Kara take care of the bookstore. I am going to work."

Abram watched his mother as she walked out the door and his

heart swelled with pride. He remembered his father once telling him that his mother was a stronger woman than they realized. "She's even stronger than she knows herself, Abram," Kaniel had said. At the time, Abram hadn't believed his father. His mother had always appeared to be such a delicate woman to him. But as he looked out the window at the slender figure walking toward the butcher shop, he knew that his father was right.

Kara woke a few minutes later and walked into the kitchen.

"Is your mother still asleep? I thought I heard voices out here. I must have been dreaming," Kara said.

"No, you weren't dreaming. She was awake and she's already left. You won't believe this, but she went to work. She got a job," Abram said.

"A job? Really?"

"Yes. She is working for the butcher. She says we could use the extra money, and she is hoping he might give her some meat."

When Kara found out that Hoda was working, she took it upon herself to offer to keep the apartment clean. "I will do the laundry and take care of dinner preparations as well," she told Abram.

He nodded. "I'll help you." Then he added, "I made a pot of tea, and we have some bread. You should eat."

"I can't, I'm a little nauseated," Kara admitted.

"Try. At least take a few sips of tea."

She sat down beside him as he poured her a cup of tea. Obediently, she tried to drink the tea, but she gagged. Abram didn't notice. He was busy cutting her a slice of bread. Kara felt her stomach turning but she didn't want to be a problem. So she tried to sip the tea and nibble on the bread.

They sat side by side at the table.

"I will do all of the food shopping," Abram said. "The people in this neighborhood can be very cruel. This is a very tightly knit community. Everyone knows everyone else. You are a stranger. A beautiful blonde stranger. They will stare at you and question who you are and why you are here."

"So what can we do about that? Nothing, I'm sure. People are like that everywhere. Don't you think they are like that where I come from?" she asked.

"Yes, I am sure they are. But until we are married, I think it's best that I go to the market. Why give the gossips fuel for their fires?" he said, and although he didn't tell her, he knew the cruel words they would say: "Abram Ehrlich is living with a shiksa. Hoda has gone mad. She's allowed her unruly son to bring a shiksa into their home. And, to make matters even worse, they are living together in sin, unmarried. Have you seen her belly? I think she might be with child. Abram's child out of wedlock." *No, I will not subject Kara to their cruelty.*

And even if he tried to lie to silence them, even if he told them that he and Kara were married, he knew how people loved to talk, and how they loved to believe the worst. Some people thrived on knowing about a shanda, an embarrassment. And there was nothing more shameful in their eyes than a girl who was pregnant out of wedlock. He could hear the old ladies speaking to each other in Yiddish, saying, "*Az es klingt, iz misstomeh chogeh.*" In other words, "Where there is smoke there is fire."

Abram loved the pretty traditional German folk dresses Kara always wore. But he decided that he must buy her some less conspicuous clothes. Not that he cared what the neighbors thought of her. But he didn't want her to feel uncomfortable, and he knew that the dresses would draw attention. He was afraid if they made her feel out of place, she might leave him and go back home. So he must do anything he could to avoid that end.

Because Abram's father, Kaniel, had been known as headstrong, highly intelligent, and unwilling to follow rules, people had always thought of the Ehrlichs as a rebellious family. There had been plenty of negative talk when Abram came of marriageable age and had chosen to travel rather than to find a good Jewish match and settle down like the rest of the young people of his age. And now he had brought home a shiksa; the old yentas had keen eyes. They would notice as soon as Kara's belly began to grow. And their tongues would wag. Abram longed to marry Kara. He hated the idea that his unborn child would face this hostility. So he planned to go and talk to a rabbi and beg him to marry them. Not that their being married would eliminate the criticism, but it might help a little. If they were wed, at least people could not call Kara a fallen woman.

"When my mother comes home from her new job, I am going to go out for a while," Abram said.

"Without me?" Kara asked.

"I want to speak to a rabbi about marrying us. I think it's best if I go alone."

"Let's wait for a while, Abram. With the laws being what they are, he is going to have to refuse you."

"I don't know about that. I am going to speak to a man who is known to be very progressive. Besides, we can't wait. The baby will not wait. And people can count the months. The sooner we are married, the sooner our child will be legitimized. I don't care what people say about me. I never have. But I care how they treat our child. And I care how they treat you. Do you understand?"

"Of course."

"So, you will stay at home and wait for me?"

"No, I will go with you, and I will tell the rabbi my side of the story too."

He let out a laugh. "All right. I fell in love with a headstrong girl. So, what did I expect?"

She laughed too. "I found your little hidden treasures this morning."

"What treasures?"

"Your forbidden books under the bed. I stubbed my toe on one when I got out of bed."

He laughed again. "Those are only the ones that I failed to put away. I'll show you where the real buried treasure lies."

"There are more?"

"Yep, they're hidden under the floorboards under the bed."

"So, when you're not teaching me typing and shorthand, we can read together."

"I'd love that." He smiled.

CHAPTER FIFTY

Hoda was surprised at how busy the butcher shop was and how difficult she found to keep pace. There were always lines of people waiting to be served.

"Yes, Frau Gladstone. We have chicken feet today."

"Nu, so what's the best price?"

Hoda had to go to the back and get Herr Stein so that he could settle on a price with Frau Gladstone.

"Next, who was next?" Hoda asked.

A shy girl, who Hoda knew had recently married, walked to the front. "I believe I was next," she said, but her voice was so soft that the other women spoke over her.

"I was next," one of the others said.

"No, I'm sorry. This young lady was next," Hoda said, indicating the shy girl. "All right." She smiled. "What can I get for you?"

"You have schmaltz?"

"Yes, of course we have chicken fat," Hoda answered.

"I would like some. But I don't know how much. I really don't know what I am doing. Can you help me? Please?"

One of the women in line said in a sarcastic tone, "A real *balabusta*. Didn't your mother teach you how to be a good wife?"

Several of the others laughed.

Hoda gave the sarcastic woman a frown. Then she turned to the young girl. "What are you trying to make?"

"Schmaltz with *gribenes*," the girl replied.

"Don't you worry. I'll tell you how. It's easy. You cut up the onions and fry them in the chicken fat with a bissel, just a bit of salt and pepper. Fry them until they get brown and crispy."

"That's it?"

"That's it." Hoda smiled.

"Thank you so much. You are so kind to help me."

"I'll get you some schmaltz."

After the girl left, Yitzar came out from the back wearing his bloody apron. "You did a mitzvah there, helping that girl," he whispered.

"Nu? I'm a mother too. I don't have a daughter, but if I did, I would want people to be kind to her."

Yitzar smiled.

"Enough with the talk. I need a kishke to stuff," Frau Greenberg said. "You have one?"

"Of course I have a cow's intestine." Yitzar smiled. "I'll go and wrap it up for you."

Hoda wasn't used to such a thriving business. She was surprised that Yitzar hadn't been forced to sell the butcher shop to an Aryan butcher for half its value, like so many of the other Jewish shop owners had been forced to do. There were waiting lines from the time she came in until they had sold out of everything. *After all, more people needed meat than they needed books,* she thought at the end of the day when Herr Stein handed her a few marks and a package wrapped in white paper.

"Some chicken," he said, smiling.

"Chicken! How generous of you, Herr Stein. I'll make soup," she said, taking the package.

"Chicken soup," he said with a sigh. "I haven't had a good chicken soup since my wife, Ruth, passed away five years ago. *Aleha hashalom,* may she rest in peace."

Hoda nodded. "Thank you," she said, looking down at the package. "Shall I come at the same time tomorrow?"

"Yes, you did a good job today. I know it was hectic, but you'll get used to it. I promise."

She smiled and turned to walk toward the door.

"I-I was wondering," he stammered.

She stopped walking and turned around.

"If I give you some extra chicken, would it be too much to ask for you to make a little extra soup and bring it to me? It would be a mitzvah."

Hoda looked at Yitzar. Until now, he'd always seemed like such a strong and confident man. But as she studied him, she realized that he was a lonely man who needed a friend. "Of course, I'll make some extra soup, and I'll bring it in when I come to work tomorrow."

"Wait here. I'll bring you the extra chicken," he said, smiling.

CHAPTER FIFTY-ONE

THE FOLLOWING DAY, Abram and Kara got ready to go and see a rabbi about marrying them.

"I hate to close the store," Abram said, "but I suppose if we put up a sign that we'll be back in an hour, it should be all right."

"I would stay behind and watch the shop, but I think it's important that I be with you when you talk to the rabbi."

"I would have to agree," Abram said as he put a sign outside the door to the bookshop.

The synagogue wasn't far. They walked without speaking. When they arrived, Kara was nervous as they entered the small synagogue. She had borrowed a simple dark dress from Hoda the night before, and she'd taken the braids out of her hair, which she now wore in a simple bun at the nape of her neck. Although she'd seen Jewish temples from the street, she'd never entered one before. But the stories she'd heard growing up, about frightening Jewish rituals, were now screaming in the back of her mind as she and Abram entered.

Her hands were cold, and she was trembling, but as she looked around the small auditorium, she realized that it didn't look very different from a church. *It's so clean. If these people were really performing human sacrifices, there would be traces of blood. This looks just like a church except there is no statue of Jesus. Otherwise, you couldn't tell them apart. So far everything I was told as a child about Jewish people has proven to be nothing but lies.*

"Cantor!" Abram said as an older, vibrant man walked up to them.

"Abram Ehrlich?"

"Yes, it's me."

"I haven't seen you since your bar mitzvah. You've grown into a man!"

"Yes, I have grown up. And about that bar mitzvah . . . it almost didn't happen," Abram laughed, "that's because I wasn't a very good student."

"You did all right," the cantor said. "I hoped you would attend shul more often after your bar mitzvah but . . ."

"I know. My family, especially my father, never set much store in religion."

"I was very sorry to hear that your father passed away. May his memory be a blessing."

"Thank you. My father was his own man; he refused to have a service at the shul. If he had chosen to have his service at a synagogue, of course my mother and I would have had it here."

The cantor nodded. "Of course. So, how can I help you today?"

"I need to speak with Rabbi Segal. Is he available, or shall I make an appointment?"

"Why don't the two of you have a seat, and I'll go and speak to him. I'll see if he has a little time this afternoon."

"Thank you, Cantor."

Kara and Abram sat side by side on the bench in the first pew right below the altar. Neither of them spoke. A few minutes later, a heavyset man with short gray hair covered by a yarmulke walked into the room. Kara was surprised that neither the rabbi nor the cantor had a beard or payot.

"Abram Ehrlich, it's good to see you!" Rabbi Segal said.

"I know it's been a long time since I came here. But I need to speak to you," Abram said sheepishly.

"Come into my office. We'll talk there."

Kara and Abram followed Rabbi Segal down a short corridor to a small office where the three of them sat down.

"Nu? So, what is it you would like to talk about today?" the rabbi asked.

"This is Kara," Abram blurted out.

"Hello, Kara," the rabbi said.

Kara smiled, but she thought she detected a look of disapproval on the rabbi's face. It was just a passing thing. There and then gone in an instant.

"Kara and I . . ." Abram started. Then he stopped to clear his throat. "Kara is not Jewish," he said.

The rabbi nodded.

"Kara and I are in love."

"I see."

"We want to be married."

Rabbi Segal rubbed his chin. "Married? You know that it's against the law for the two of you to marry."

"Yes, we know."

"And yet you want to marry anyway."

Abram nodded. He almost choked on the words, but he finally managed to say, "Kara is pregnant."

"Abram . . ." the rabbi said softly, "you are in trouble."

"Yes, we are."

"Oy," the rabbi said. He stood up and looked out the window for a few minutes. Then he turned and looked at Abram. In a firm but kind voice he said, "I am not as worried about God accepting your marriage as I am about the Nazis, and how they would react to the breaking of their laws. I believe that God would understand. But Hitler, he's another story. I am sorry, Abram. I wish you both the best. But I can't marry you. It would put my entire congregation in jeopardy. I really am sorry."

Kara glanced over at Abram. His hands were shaking. But he stood up and tapped Kara on the shoulder. "Come on, let's go home," he said without looking at the rabbi. He took Kara's hand, and they left the temple.

When they arrived at home, Abram and Kara sat down at the kitchen table. There they made up a story that they planned to tell anyone who asked. They decided they would say that they met and were married when Abram was traveling. They would tell the neighbors that Kara was from Munich and she had come to Berlin after she finished school. They planned to say that Kara was Jewish. Kara seemed satisfied with the story. But Abram knew there were people in that small community who wouldn't believe a word of it. They would continue to spread their gossip while they watched and counted the months until the baby would be born.

Hoda was afraid that when the butcher learned that she had taken Abram's pregnant girlfriend in to live with her, he would let her go. However, she discovered that Yitzar Stein was a stronger man than most. He was not afraid of gossip. Nor was he the kind of man to judge anyone. As time passed, Hoda would overhear someone telling Yitzar about Abram and Kara. But he never shared in the gossip. He would ask the customer to please refrain from spreading vicious rumors while in his store. And he never asked Hoda anything about Abram or Kara. However, Hoda noticed that once Yitzar found out that Kara was pregnant, he made sure to give Hoda extra meat. In turn, she brought him soup at least once a week. And so it was that they became friends.

CHAPTER FIFTY-TWO

November 1936

IT WAS in the dark of a cold autumn night that Kara felt her first labor pain. She glanced over at Abram who was sleeping soundly. She shivered with cold and fear as she pulled the blanket up over her shoulders. Another pain shot through her. *The baby is coming and I'm terrified.* Gently she nudged Abram. He woke slowly.

"I think it's time. I think the baby is coming," she whispered.

Abram had made arrangements with a local midwife who had promised to come to the apartment and help deliver the child as soon as Kara went into labor. He'd given her payment in advance, and now he had to go to her home to tell her that the time had come.

"I'll be right back with Sarah. Stay in bed," Abram said, jumping up and quickly pulling his pants on.

"All right," Kara said, shivering. Abram glanced over at her.

"Let me get you another blanket," he said. Abram took a blanket out of the closet and covered Kara with it. Then he went into his mother's room. "Mother, Kara is going into labor. She's very cold. I'm worried sick."

"I'll take care of her. Go and get the midwife."

"All right."

Hoda took her own blanket, and then she gathered her coat and Kara's and laid them all on top of Kara. After she'd finished, Hoda sat at the edge of the bed and took Kara's hand in her own. "Don't be afraid. You'll be all right," she said gently.

"I am so scared. I wish my sister were here with us," Kara said.

"I understand. But since she can't be here with you. I'll be here with you."

"You have been so good to me," Kara said. She'd begun sweating from the pain. Her face was red and scrunched. She looked at Hoda's kind and gentle eyes and she started to cry. "I have brought such terrible shame on you and your family."

"Shame? Who cares about shame when we are talking about a life? You are bringing my precious grandchild to me," Hoda said, squeezing Kara's hand. "Do you have any idea how I have longed for a grandchild?"

Kara didn't answer. She winced in pain as a contraction gripped her body. "I'm feeling very warm all of a sudden," Kara managed to say as the sweat ran down her face.

Hoda removed the coats and blankets and left only a sheet covering Kara. "Is that better?"

Kara nodded. "I've never felt so much pain," she said.

"I know. Childbirth is hard," Hoda said, "but I'll tell you what my mother told me when I was giving birth to Abram. She said that once my child was born, once I held him in my arms, I would not remember what the pain felt like. At the time I thought she was crazy. I mean who could forget such terrible pain, right?" Hoda smiled warmly at Kara, then she added, "But you know what? She was right. Once the midwife placed my baby in my arms, I couldn't remember the pain at all. I was filled with so much love. It was a love stronger than any I had ever felt before."

"Really?"

"Oh yes. I loved my family very much. And I loved Kaniel too. But there is no way to describe that feeling a woman feels when she holds her infant for the first time. It is a love like no other."

The pain gripped Kara again, and her whole body trembled. "Thank you," she said to Hoda, who took the sheet and reached up to wipe Kara's brow.

"You'll be all right," Hoda said.

And then they heard the front door open, and from the living room, they heard the loud, strong voice of Sarah, the midwife.

Abram went into the room and stood beside Kara while Sarah immediately went into the bathroom to wash her hands. When she returned, she smiled gently at Kara. "You are going to be fine," she said in a firm and steady voice that Kara found comforting. Then she turned to Abram, who stood beside Kara wringing his hands and looking helpless. Sarah touched Abram's arm and said, "Wait outside with your mother. I will take care of her now. I promise you."

Abram swallowed hard, and the Adam's apple in his throat rose and fell. "I don't want to leave you," he whispered to Kara, taking her small, delicate hand in his own and bringing it to his lips.

Kara nodded. She tried to smile, but instead she winced as a contraction shot through her body.

"I wish I could take the pain for you. I wish it were me suffering instead of you," he said.

"Please, go outside the room now and leave us," the midwife said.

"It's all right, please do as she asks." Kara mustered a smile. Tiny strands of her wheat-colored hair stuck to her face with sweat.

Abram shuddered as he gazed into Kara's eyes.

"I promise you, I'm fine," Kara said.

He nodded. Then he squeezed her hand, and she nodded at him trying to reassure him. He let go of her hand and left the room with Hoda trailing behind him.

CHAPTER FIFTY-THREE

November 1936

Kara labored through the night. By morning she was exhausted and spent. She could hardly bear another contraction. But Sarah was an experienced coach, and she helped Kara to find the strength to push the new life from her womb and into the world.

Karl Beynish Ehrlich came into the world at ten o'clock that morning. Kara and Abram had discussed names for the child, and the two had agreed to name the baby, Karl, for Kaniel, Abram's father. Abram had explained to Kara that the Jews always named for someone who they loved that had died. At first he had offered her the name to give.

"Is there someone you want to name the baby for?" he asked.

She knew he didn't want to be selfish when he had given her the option to name for someone in her family.

"No, I have no one. I would be honored to name the baby for your father."

"If it's a boy we'll call him Karl? Do you like that?"

Kara nodded. "If it's a girl?"

"How do you like the name Kivi?"

"I do," Kara had said.

They had decided upon the child's middle name together. Beynish meant blessed, and they had both agreed that their greatest wish for their offspring was that he or she be blessed.

Kara was exhausted but happy as she held the tiny infant in her arms. *Hoda was right. I can't remember the pain. How is that possible? All I can feel is overwhelming love and joy, and a strong sense that God is with us right now.* She counted Karl's toes and fingers and marveled at his tiny ears while the midwife went out to tell Abram and Hoda that the baby had arrived.

When Abram looked at his son, Kara melted. She could see the love in Abram's eyes.

"Do you want to hold him?" Kara asked.

Abram nodded. "He's a miracle," Abram said in awe as she handed him the bundle. Carefully, he took the baby into his arms.

"Yes, he is. Look at his hands and feet. Look at his ears . . . he is perfect," Kara said, tears in her eyes.

"A true miracle from God." Abram was crying now too.

Hoda came over and looked inside the blanket at the tiny form. Then she smiled at Kara. "He's beautiful, just perfect, such a blessing." Then Hoda turned to her son and said, "I know that your father is watching, and he is so proud, Abram."

Karl had been a good baby from the very beginning. He was not overly demanding. He slept through the night within a few weeks, and when he was awake, he was like a ray of sunshine. Kara had never been as happy. She had no desire to ever return home or see her parents again.

The only thing missing from her life was her sister, Anka. They had been so close, and now they had no contact. She would have loved for Anka to meet Karl. *I wonder how Anka is doing. Is she happy in her marriage to Ludwig? Does she miss me? When she returned from her honeymoon, she told me that she was pregnant when she got married. So I know that I have a little niece or nephew. And Karl has a cousin. I wonder if the babies look alike. Oh, how I would love to see her and hold her child. Wouldn't it be wonderful if we could live next door to each other the way we always dreamed we would when we were children? We used to talk about how, when we grew up, we would be neighbors. We would spend our afternoons walking our babies in carriages through the park together. And then this monster, Hitler, came into power, and because he decided that Abram was not a fit husband, all of my dreams for Anka and I became impossible. I was forced to choose between Abram and my sister.*

CHAPTER FIFTY-FOUR

May 1937

KARL FELL asleep in Kara's arms as she breastfed him. She knew he would sleep for at least two hours if she laid him in his crib. And even though her elbow ached, she so loved these quiet moments when she held him in her arms and watched the sun begin to rise from the living room window. Hoda would be awake soon, and Kara just wanted to cherish these precious morning hours alone with her son. She held him up to her and pressed her face against him, inhaling the sweet baby fragrance. Then she put him back down and offered him her breast. He suckled as she kissed the top of his head with its tiny white strands of hair.

There was no doubt that little Karl looked just like her. Everyone said so. But she pondered what he would be like when he grew up. Would he have Abram's love of traveling? Like his father, would he want to see the world and discover everything around him with a childlike wonder? "Oh Karl," she whispered, "my little bitty man, you don't know it yet, but you have brought such joy to the lives of your father, your grandmother, and me. Even when business in the bookshop is slow, and we are struggling to make ends meet, you have the power to take us away from our troubles. All you have to do is do something funny and all of us will laugh. Even with the Nazis causing more and more trouble with their lies about Jews, your little smile still has the power to give us hope for the world." Then she began to sing an old German folk song to him.

Hoda walked out of her bedroom and smiled at Kara. She was dressed and ready to leave for work. She walked over quietly and looked down at Karl whose eyes were closed contentedly. Then she smiled. "Because you sing to him and talk to him in German, he'll be fluent in both German and Yiddish," she said.

"They're so close that it's almost the same language," Kara mused.

Hoda nodded. Then she asked, "Are you hungry? I can take the baby and put him in his crib so we can have a nice breakfast together," Hoda offered.

"Sounds perfect. I'll start the coffee," Kara said. Hoda gently scooped Karl into her arms. He woke up and cooed for a second but then fell back to sleep.

Kara went into the kitchen and began to prepare breakfast for herself and Hoda. This was their regular routine on the days when Hoda went to work. She and Kara would have a quick breakfast before she left. Abram would sleep for another hour, until it was time to open the bookstore. Then he would drag himself out of bed, dress quicky, and go into the store. Kara would bring him some bread and coffee for breakfast. They would talk for a few moments, then Kara would return to the apartment with Karl where she would straighten up the apartment and do the wash, while Hoda and Abram spent the rest of the day at their jobs.

Hoda walked into the kitchen. She reached into the pantry for a jar of jam and placed it on the table. Then she sat down across from Kara and sliced two pieces of bread. She took one for herself and handed the other to Kara. "I brought this jam home from work yesterday. It's homemade," she said. "I got it from a customer at the butcher shop as a gift. I gave her some extra chicken livers one day when she was short on money, and she was so grateful that she brought it for me." Hoda popped the jar open and put the jam on the table between herself and Kara.

"That was nice of you. To give her the extra chicken livers, I mean," Kara said.

"It's Yitzar. I couldn't do it if he didn't approve. But he's so generous. He'd never let anyone go hungry. Especially, a woman like her who has a family with little children. Everyone in the neighborhood loves him. He isn't rich; he doesn't have much, but what he has he is always willing to share."

"You like him," Kara said boldly. "I can tell."

Hoda laughed. "I suppose I do. But I am too old to be thinking about those kinds of things."

"What do you mean, 'those kinds of things'?" Kara said. The two women had become good friends. They'd bonded over the birth of Karl. Then Kara continued, "You're not old at all. You're very beautiful. And you might want to get married again someday."

"Me?" Hoda smiled and shook her head. "No, the days of being with a man have passed for me. They ended when I lost Kaniel." Then she took a bite of the bread with jam and closed her eyes. "I can't believe how long it's been since I tasted jam."

Kara took a bite. "I know, me too. It's delicious."

"Kara . . ." Hoda said in a serious tone, "there is something I want to talk to you about."

"What is it?"

"You seem to be sad lately. Are you all right? Is there something wrong between you and Abram?"

"No . . . Abram is wonderful. He's a loving man and a very good father. I do wish we could marry though. I wish our union was legal."

"Is that it? Is that what is making you so sad?" Hoda asked softly.

"No, it's not that. I know better. I know it's not possible. So I force myself to accept the fact that we are married in our hearts, and that must be enough for us . . . at least for now."

"Then what is it? What is making you sad? You have everything any woman could want. You have a man who adores you, a beautiful, healthy child . . ."

"It's my sister, Anka; I miss her terribly."

"I didn't know you had a sister."

"Yes, when we were growing up, my sister and I were always close. But she married a man whose family is high up in the Nazi Party. I fell in love with Abram, and I felt uncomfortable around her husband's family because of the way they feel about Jews. So, I stayed away. The last time I saw Anka was at her wedding."

"I always wondered why you never went back home to see anyone in your family. But I didn't dare ask because I didn't want to pry."

"My parents were horrible. I don't miss them. But my sister . . . I miss her so much."

"Does she know about you and Abram?"

"No, I couldn't tell her the truth. So I lied to her. I am ashamed of lying. I am ashamed because I should be proud of Abram, and I am . . . but"—she looked down—"anyway, I told her that I was involved with a married man. A Gentile man. She has no idea about me and Abram."

"Why don't you go and see her? You don't need to tell her the truth. In fact, you shouldn't tell her the truth. It's too dangerous. Just tell her you are still with the Gentile man and because he is married you can't give her his name. I am sure she will be glad to see you."

"I would love that. I would really love that," Kara said, "but . . . I don't want to bring Karl with me because I am not sure what will happen when I go there. After all, her husband is a Brunner. They are strong members of the Nazi Party. That's why I haven't gone back home since I moved in here with you."

"If you do decide to go, you must not tell your sister about you and Abram. I understand that the two of you have always been very close. But she is married now, and chances are good that she will tell her husband whatever you share with her. He may think he is doing you a favor by arresting Abram."

"Oh dear." Kara sighed. "So I can't even tell her about Karl?"

"Well, that's not exactly true. You could tell her that Karl is the child of your married boyfriend, and you can't disclose his identity because you have promised him that you wouldn't, in exchange for his supporting you and the child."

"I hated lying to her before. I will hate it even more now. But if it keeps Abram and Karl safe, then I will do it," Kara said.

Hoda nodded. "I wish things were different in the world. You have no idea how much I wish this. But we must be careful. If we are careless it could cost us dearly."

Kara chewed on her lower lip. "I agree," she said.

"Why don't you leave Karl at home with me the first time you go back to visit? I'll take the day off work," Hoda said.

"Are you sure?"

"I am," Hoda said.

CHAPTER FIFTY-FIVE

THE LAST KARA HAD HEARD, Anka and Ludwig were living with Anka's in-laws. They owned a large home, and there was no reason for the young couple to rent an apartment before Ludwig finished school. When Kara got off the bus, she knew exactly where to go because Anka had shown her the house where the Brunners lived before she and Ludwig were married. Having spent so long living in the Mitte, she'd forgotten how beautiful some of the homes of the rich people who lived in Berlin were. She slowly walked up the walkway, then climbed the three stairs to the door. The brass door knocker was cold in her hand. It made a loud sound as she rapped it against the wooden door. She felt a chill shoot through her, and she almost turned and left, but Herr Brunner, Ludwig's father, was leaving the house at that moment, and he saw her standing there at the door.

"Kara?" he said, "is that you?"

He must remember me from the wedding. That was the only time we ever met, Kara thought.

"Herr Brunner! How good to see you." Kara tried to sound cheerful, but she couldn't take her eyes off the perfectly fitted black

Nazi uniform he wore. "I was in town, so I decided to drop by your home, to see my sister."

"Well, isn't that nice." He smiled warmly. "I'm sure she will be happy to see you."

The door opened, and a young girl in a maid's uniform stood looking at Kara. "Can I help you?" she asked.

"It's all right, Helga. This is Kara; she's Anka's sister. Show her in, and let Anka know she's here," Herr Brunner called out as he climbed into the back of his automobile. A driver in full uniform sat in the front seat. The driver started the car. As they began to pull out of the driveway, Herr Brunner opened the window and said, "Enjoy your visit."

"Thank you," Kara said as she followed Helga into the house.

"Wait here, please," Helga said.

In a few minutes, Anka came running down the stairs. When she saw Kara, she let out a small cry. Then she ran into her sister's arms. "I've missed you so much. What took you so long to come and see me? Where have you been? I went back to our parents' home to look for you, but Mutti and Vater said they haven't heard a word from you."

Kara hugged her sister tightly but didn't answer any of her questions for several moments. Then she said, "I have been living with my boyfriend. You remember I told you about him?"

Anka nodded. "Yes."

"We have a son together."

Anka gasped. "I have a nephew?"

"Yes. His name is Karl."

"Karl," she said softly. "Oh, Kara, are you all right?"

"Yes, I'm fine. I just couldn't come back here until I was settled."

"I've been so worried. I didn't know if you were all right or not."

"I'm fine, Anka. I think I must be an aunt too? You were pregnant when I left."

Anka turned away. She quickly wiped her eyes, which had begun to cloud up and then looked back at her sister. "I lost the baby. When I was going through the miscarriage, the only person I wanted to see was you. And . . ." She began to cry. Then she stopped herself. "I'm sorry. I don't want you to feel bad and go away again. I'm glad you're here now."

"I'm here," Kara said.

"How long can you stay?"

"Just the afternoon. I'm living in Frankfurt," she lied. "I have to catch a train home." Then she looked into Anka's eyes and her voice cracked as she said, "I'm so sorry about the baby."

Anka looked away. Then she forced a sad smile, "Oh, I was hoping you could stay for a while," Anka said. Kara thought Anka looked so much older and sadder than Kara remembered her. "Where are my manners," Anka said, still trying to smile. "Let's have something to eat. You must be famished."

Kara took her sister's hand and held it in her own for a few moments. "I missed you more than I can ever express, but I couldn't come back until now. Please forgive me."

"I could never stay angry at you, Kara. You're my sister. You know me better than anyone else in the whole world." Anka squeezed Kara a little tighter, then she added, "I'm so glad to see you."

They spent the day drinking tea and reminiscing about funny moments they'd shared as children. Both of them were careful to avoid discussing the painful memories that their parents had stamped on their young, impressionable souls.

The afternoon passed quickly. It was getting late, and Kara knew she must return home. "It will be dark soon," she said.

"Oh, please don't leave, Kara. Ludwig will be home shortly. He'd love to see you. Can you stay for dinner?"

"It's a long ride back. A very long ride. I'd love to stay, but I can't. I must go."

Anka nodded. "Will you come back, please, Kara. Promise me you'll come back . . . soon."

"I will. And I'll bring Karl with me. I know you would love to meet your nephew."

"I would. I really would," Anka said with tears in her eyes. "Oh, Kara, I missed you so much." Kara and Anka embraced. They held each other tightly for several moments. Then Anka added, "I hope it won't be too long before you come back."

"I'll try to come as soon as I can. It's a long distance to travel." Kara hated herself for lying. But in a way, it was a long distance—not a physical distance—but Anka's home and the Mitte were like two different worlds. And it was so hard to come here in Anka's world and remember to keep all of her secrets. When she was with Anka, it was like they were two young sisters again. Two young girls who had never kept a secret from each other. Kara looked into Anka's blue eyes, and she longed to share all that had happened in her life since they were apart. She wanted to tell Anka all about Abram and Hoda, and how kind they were to her. She wanted her sister to know how wrong the Nazi government was about Jews. But as she looked around Anka's beautiful home, her eyes fell upon the huge painting of Adolf Hitler hanging right over the expensive plush sofa in the perfectly furnished living room, and she knew she couldn't share her feelings. It was too dangerous to take such a risk.

On her way back to the bus stop, Kara felt sick to her stomach as she walked past the windows of several shops which displayed signs that read, "No Jews Allowed."

She had been hopeful when Berlin had hosted the Olympics last year. It seemed that the sentiment toward the Jews had been less harsh. During that time, many of the signs restricting Jews had been removed. And somehow in her naïveté she'd convinced herself that maybe things were going to get better. They hadn't. It was only for a short time, and now that the Olympics were gone, there were signs forbidding Jews more than before. For a long time, Kara tried not to acknowledge all of the privileges that were being taken away from the Jewish people. But it was very hard. Jews were losing their jobs; they were unable to hire workers who were of Aryan decent; they were being ostracized—thrown out of schools and universities.

And then, of course, she couldn't ignore the fact that all relations between a Jew and an Aryan were strictly forbidden. But she'd been so happy with Abram that she had been almost childlike, trying to make believe that somehow, something would happen, and these things would change. Perhaps, she hoped, Hitler would be overthrown, and a new and less harsh government would take over. But as she stood at the bus stop, she shivered. It was getting harder and harder to make believe this would just go away. It was more and more difficult to ignore the growing hatred toward the Jewish people.

CHAPTER FIFTY-SIX

1937

IT WAS late autumn before Kara returned to see Anka. She carried Karl in her arms. When she knocked on the door. It was Ludwig who answered.

"To what do we owe this wonderful pleasure?" he asked, smiling. "Come in, come in. It's cold outside."

Kara walked in, her cheeks slightly pink from the cold.

"How are you, Ludwig?" Kara said, smiling at him. "How is my sister?"

"Fine, we are both fine. What a beautiful child. So blond and blue eyed. He resembles you."

"Oh, thank you." She blushed. "I have been meaning to come by and bring my son to meet you both."

"So, you have gotten married? Who's the lucky fellow?" Ludwig said. "I know my poor cousin, Wilhelm, would have done anything to be in his place. He was very attracted to you."

Kara didn't answer.

Anka walked into the room. She let out a shriek of joy when she saw Kara and the baby. She immediately went over to Kara and scooped Karl into her arms. As she held her nephew with one arm, Anka hugged her sister. "It took you so long to come back. I never want to let you go back home again."

"Kara, have you gotten married?" Ludwig asked again.

"No," Kara said, a little embarrassed. She wished Ludwig had not persisted with the question, but she realized he'd always been awkward. "Karl's father and I aren't married," she admitted.

"Oh," Ludwig stammered, "I-I didn't mean to embarrass you. I just . . ."

"Hush. You are always saying the wrong thing," Anka said in frustration.

"I am truly sorry, Kara," Ludwig said sheepishly.

"It's all right," she said, trying to smile.

"I'm sorry," Ludwig said, hanging his head.

Kara nodded. "Really, it's all right." Then trying to change the subject, she looked down into the bundle in Anka's arms and said, "Karl, this is your Auntie Anka and your Uncle Ludwig."

Ludwig looked at the baby. "He really is a beautiful Aryan boy, isn't he?"

Until she came to Anka's home with Karl in tow, Kara had never thought about how Karl would be seen by a Nazi. But as she looked at her son, she realized he was the ideal Nazi child: his white-blond hair, his sapphire-blue eyes, the strong bone structure in his face. These were all characteristics that were coveted by the Nazis and considered perfectly Aryan. She had to smile. It was a secret smile because she knew that although her son resembled her, he was half-Jewish.

"I'll go and tell the maid to have the cook prepare something special for lunch today. Our dear Kara is here!" Ludwig said.

"That would be perfect," Anka said.

Over lunch they talked about Ludwig's studies and how he planned to be an architect. And, in a half-joking manner, Ludwig mentioned once again how his cousin Wilhelm had been taken with Kara at their wedding.

"He told me he thought you were the prettiest girl he'd ever seen," Ludwig said.

"Oh." Kara laughed a little.

"No, really. He really liked you. And . . . he is still single, you know," Ludwig offered.

"Ludwig!" Anka said.

"I'm sorry. It seems I've said the wrong thing again. Well, I didn't mean to offend you. I just meant that . . ."

"Ludwig?" Anka said again.

"So, how is the chicken?" Ludwig asked, changing the subject.

"Delicious," Kara said.

Once they finished eating, Kara took Karl into the bedroom and fed and changed him. Then she returned, and the three adults played cards while Karl slept on a blanket on the floor. But a little over an hour later, Karl awoke. He was getting fussy. "I should get home," Kara said.

"It has been such a pleasure having you here," Ludwig said.

"I wish you could stay forever," Anka said.

Kara smiled. "I'll come again in the spring."

"Why so long?" Anka said.

"It's hard for me to travel during the winter with the baby."

"I could come and visit you."

"It's better if you don't. The baby's father doesn't want anyone to know about us. He's very secretive because he's married. He would be unnerved. I'm sorry."

"I understand. But please come. Will you? Do you promise?"

"I do," Kara said.

CHAPTER FIFTY-SEVEN

Spring 1938

KARA WOULD HAVE RETURNED to visit her sister as soon as the winter ended, but in April the Jews received notice that they were now required to register and report all their assets. So many of the Jewish business owners in the Mitte had been forced into giving their business away to non-Jews. This program was instated by the Nazis. They called it Aryanization. Even the Jewish doctors could no longer treat Aryan patients. Abram had watched in terror as so many of the local stores had changed hands from Jews to Gentiles. Thus far, he and Yitzar, the butcher, had been lucky. No one had come to take them over. At least not yet. Abram was worried, and he made it clear to Hoda and Kara he thought it best that they try not to draw any attention to them. So it was best that Kara not return to Anka's home to visit. At least for a while.

"We don't want to do anything to make them notice us," Abram said. "It's bad enough that the other Jews in this neighborhood know that you and I are together, and you are not Jewish. If the Nazis find out, who knows what they'll do."

"Don't you think they already know?" Kara asked. "Don't you think they see me on the street?"

"I don't think they know. I think if they knew, they would have already arrested me. But more importantly, I am concerned about what they might do to you and Karl. He is a half-Jewish child. They don't like that."

"I won't go," Kara said.

"Are you sure your sister doesn't know where you are living?"

"I'm sure. She thinks I am living in Frankfurt and that I am a mistress to a married man."

"For now, let's do what we can not to draw any attention to ourselves."

"I would have to agree with him," Hoda said. "I think it's best for now."

"This will all blow over. It has to. The German people are too intelligent to let a government like this go on forever," Abram said. "We just have to be careful just for a while. Just until something happens to get the Nazis thrown out of power."

"I hope you're right," Kara said.

CHAPTER FIFTY-EIGHT

November 1938

EVERYONE in the family wanted to do whatever they possibly could to make Karl's second birthday special. Yitzar gave Hoda extra chicken and as much sugar as he was able to come by so she could bake a birthday cake. Hoda considered inviting Yitzar to the celebration, but she decided it was best not to get involved with her boss even though she knew he really liked her, and as time had passed, she had come to like him too.

Abram had spent months before Karl's birthday illustrating and writing a small book for him in which Karl was the subject of the story. Kara agreed that Karl would love the book. He was immediately fascinated by any story that Abram told him in which he was the main character. Kara loved to watch Abram and their son in the evenings after dinner. Abram would hold the boy in his lap and invent a wild fantasy about Karl. He named his stories *The Adventures of Karl Ehrlich, the Boy Who Could Fly.*

. . .

KARL'S EYES would grow big as Abram spun the tales. And sometimes Kara and Hoda would have to laugh at how engaged Karl became. He would flap his little arms and pretend he was flying as Abram told him the tales. So, being that money was tight, Abram had come up with this idea of writing and illustrating a book for Karl, knowing that his son would cherish the book even after he grew up.

For two weeks prior to Karl's birthday, Hoda, Kara, and Abram had each contributed to building the excitement of the coming day and the party they would have. They would tell Karl that his birthday was coming, and it was going to be a very special day. Karl would squeal with delight, and they would laugh. Kara loved to see the look on Karl's face each morning when he asked, "Is it today?"

"No, not yet," she would tell him, "but almost! Your birthday is only two weeks away."

"Is it today?" he would ask again.

And she would laugh. "Not yet."

Finally, on the morning of November 8, Karl asked, "Is it today?"

"Yes, it is! Today is your birthday!"

Karl let out a cry of joy. He was so excited that he clapped his hands and giggled.

"When is party?"

"Tonight, after dinner."

"No, Mama, now—"

"We have to wait for Papa to finish work, and for Bubbie to come home from the butcher shop."

Just like a two-year-old, Karl asked Kara every few minutes that day, "How much longer?"

"Not until tonight," she said patiently. "Meanwhile, I have to cut up the vegetables for the soup."

"Chicken soup?"

"Yes, your favorite."

Karl laughed. "Matzo balls?"

"Yes! Bubbie is making matzo balls," Kara said as she kissed the top of his head. Then she added, "And . . . I am going to bake your birthday cake."

"Cake!" Karl said. It was a rare treat for the family to have cake. But Karl had tasted cake once before and he remembered it. It was when a wealthy patron of the bookstore brought a piece for Hoda as a gift for giving him a special price on a first edition.

"Yes, cake too."

It had been a golden autumn day, when the sun gleamed brightly through a crystal-blue sky, and the autumn air was brisk and fresh. Blankets of vividly colored leaves covered the ground. Soon there would be snow, but for today, the earth was an oil painting of magnificent proportions. Kara watched her son playing on the floor, and her heart swelled with love. *My life is so good*, she thought. *It would be perfect if Anka could be here with us to celebrate Karl's birthday.* She let out a long sigh because she knew it was impossible.

Hoda had insisted on preparing the soup to boil before she left for work. Everyone loved her chicken soup, and she wanted it to be perfect. The pot of vegetables and chicken simmered all day, filling the house with a wonderful aroma that made Kara feel safe and warm. When Hoda returned from work, she prepared the matzo balls and dropped them into the hot soup. Then she changed out of her work clothes. Abram closed the bookstore and came into the kitchen. He kissed Kara and then bent down to pick up his son. He held Karl high above him and Karl laughed with delight. "It's my birthday," Karl said.

"Is it?" Abram teased the little boy. "I didn't know."

"Yes, you did," Karl said. "Did you forget?"

"Never! Of course I know it's your birthday," Abram said, "and I have a present for you."

"Can I have it?"

"Yes, but not until after dinner."

"Oh . . ." Karl said, disappointed. But then Hoda walked over to Karl and took him from his father. She gave him a hug. "Don't you want to eat Bubbie's matzo balls? I made you my special matzo balls!"

"I love Bubbie's matzo balls," Karl said.

"And you know what comes with Bubbie's matzo balls?" Hoda said as she kissed both of Karl's cheeks.

"Bubbie's soup!" Karl said.

"Yes! You're right. It's your favorite. Isn't it?"

"Yes," Karl laughed and nodded his head.

Dinner was delicious. Thanks to Hoda's boss, there had been enough chicken to go around. When everyone finished, Kara placed the cake she'd baked on the table. Karl giggled. "Cake!" he said and clapped his hands. Karl was so happy and excited that it made Kara's heart ache with love for him.

Then as the family began to sing "Happy Birthday," and Karl clapped along, the room began to shudder, the ground shook, and there was a loud, thunderous explosion followed by the crash of glass shattering somewhere outside the small apartment. A bowl fell off the stove and smashed, sending half of a matzo ball rolling across the floor. Karl's eyes were wide. His laughter turned to shrieks of fear. And in an instant, the lives of the Jewish people in Germany were changed. They were suddenly covered by a dark and ominous shadow. It was a night that would be remembered by the Jewish people forever. They would call it Kristallnacht: The Night of Broken Glass.

CHAPTER FIFTY-NINE

KARA SHIVERED as she remembered the events of the day. It was only two days ago that her life had seemed almost idyllic. But now, she was sitting under a stairwell with her mother-in-law and terrified two-year-old son. And worse, Abram had not yet returned from his venture out onto the street. *Abram has been gone for over an hour. What if something happened to him.*

Hoda stirred awake. "Kara," she said, looking around frantically, "where is Abram?"

"He went out to find food."

"Dear God, no."

"I didn't want him to go, but he insisted. I wish I hadn't stopped breastfeeding two months ago. If I hadn't, I could have fed Karl. And then maybe Abram would have waited at least another day."

"He wouldn't have," Hoda said, shaking her head. "He's stubborn, and when he makes up his mind, he can be impossible to reason with. Right now, he feels like it's his responsibility to take care of us. He knows that we can live without food for a while, but we must have water." Hoda hesitated, then added, "How long has he been gone?"

"I'm not sure exactly, but it's been at least an hour."

"That's a long time." Hoda bit her nail.

"Yes."

"Who do you think did all of this? When we were still in the apartment, I looked outside, and from what I could see, it seemed like it was a gang of boys. They weren't wearing any type of uniform, so I don't think they had anything to do with the government," Hoda said.

"I can't say. The Nazis are so tricky and full of propaganda and lies. I don't know who is responsible. All I know is that this is terrifying."

"Bubbie, I'm hungry. I want more soup." Karl was awake. "And I'm wet too."

"Yes, I know," Hoda said. "I will do my best to change you as soon as I can."

"I want Little Bear," Karl said.

Hoda looked over at Kara. "We forgot his stuffed bear," she said.

Kara nodded.

"Get Little Bear," Karl said again. "I need Little Bear."

Just then they heard footsteps on the stairs. Kara felt her heart rise into her throat. She held her breath.

"I couldn't get anything to eat or drink." It was Abram. "I tried, but our apartment and the bookstore are gone, burned to the ground. So is the synagogue and lots of the other businesses in town. All of the windows along the street are broken. There is glass everywhere. And"—he took a long, hard breath—"there are people lying on the street. They look as if they've been beaten to death."

"Oh, dear God," Kara said. She stood up and went to Abram. She put her arms around him. "What are we going to do?"

"I don't know yet," Abram said. "I don't know."

"Did you go by the butcher shop?" Hoda asked.

"Yes, I walked up and down Liepziger Street. Most of the stores were destroyed. But as for the butcher shop, the front window was gone, shattered. There was glass everywhere, but the store wasn't burned."

"I'll go to the butcher shop and see if Yitzar is all right. I pray he is. And I know if he can, he will give us food and water," Hoda said.

"Let me go. I am the man of the house. I will tell him that you sent me," Abram said.

"I can't wait down here for you. I can't let you go alone," Kara said. "I want to go with you."

"Please, Kara. Do as I ask. Stay here. I'll be careful. It's easier for me to navigate the streets unseen if I am alone. If you are with me, I have to watch out for you. It's better this way," Abram insisted.

"What if someone comes and finds us here? We have no weapon?" Hoda said.

Karl started crying. "I want Little Bear," he pleaded. "I want Little Bear. Get Little Bear—"

"Shut up," Abram yelled.

Karl was shocked. His father had never yelled at him. He'd never spoken to him in anything but a soft voice before. Karl stared at his father and his eyes flew open. Hoda and Kara exchanged glances with each other.

Abram took a deep breath. Kara could see he was trembling. But he forced himself to smile at Karl. Then he reached down and gathered Karl into his arms. "I'm so sorry. I didn't mean to yell at you. Forgive me"—Abram held the child close to him and kissed his forehead—"I don't know what got into me."

Several moments passed. Tears fell down Abram's cheeks, but he still continued to embrace his son. And Karl was quiet in his arms.

"I have to go," Abram said, handing Karl to Kara. "You be a good boy for your mama. I will be back as soon as I can."

Abram nodded to Kara and Hoda, then he climbed the stairs and was gone again.

CHAPTER SIXTY

IT WAS late afternoon when Abram returned. He carried a glass jug filled with water, and a loaf of bread. In his other hand, he held a blackened and soiled, but otherwise intact, stuffed bear.

"Papa!" Karl screamed, "you brought Little Bear."

Abram nodded. "Of course. I wouldn't think of leaving Little Bear behind," he said, handing the bear to Karl who held it tightly to his chest.

Kara began to cry. "I love you so much," she whispered. "It was dangerous for you to go into the building after a fire to get his bear."

Abram smiled. "I'm all right," he said as he placed the food and water down on the cement. "Eat," he said, tearing a piece of bread off the loaf and giving it to Karl, who climbed onto his lap still holding the stuffed animal in his arm.

As everyone was eating and drinking, Abram began to speak, "I saw Yitzar. He is all right."

"Thank God," Hoda said and let out a sigh.

"I told him that the store and our apartment were destroyed. He says he wants us to come and stay with him."

"Stay with him?" Hoda asked.

"Yes, at his home."

Hoda contemplated the idea for a moment. Then she said, "This is very kind and generous of him. I think we should accept his offer."

"We have no other choice," Abram answered.

"It has been quiet out there today. I haven't heard any screaming or yelling. Do you think it's safe for us to take Karl and go to Yitzar's house now?" Hoda asked Abram.

"Yes, as soon as we have all finished eating, we should go," Abram answered.

CHAPTER SIXTY-ONE

Yɪᴛᴢᴀʀ ᴅɪᴅ ɴᴏᴛ ʜᴀᴠᴇ a big home. But it was clean and comfortable, and he made room for everyone. He gave Abram and Kara his bedroom. Hoda and Karl slept on thick blankets in the study, while Yitzar made a bed for himself on the sofa in the living room. Once they'd settled in, Yitzar and Abram went to the butcher shop and brought all the meat home.

Yitzar gave a small smile, then he winked at Hoda. "I know that Hitler banned kosher meat, but I never listened. All of this meat is kosher."

Hoda smiled. "Nu? So, it is your own small protest?"

"Yes. We Jews don't have much power left. So, we do what we can to resist, right?"

"Are you religious?" Abram asked. He was wondering because he knew that if Yitzar was religious, it would be only fitting that they all make sure to respect his house rules.

"Not really. But my papa was a kosher butcher, and my parents were religious. So I grew up that way. Then as the years passed, I got lazy."

"I am only asking because I cannot lie to you. Kara is not

Jewish. And although we are unable to marry legally, we are married in our hearts. This is our son, Karl."

"I know all of this. Hoda told me. And it's fine. I welcome all of you with open arms," Yitzar said. Then he smiled at Hoda. She returned his smile.

It was late in the evening. Abram had fallen into a deep sleep, but Kara lay beside him unable to rest. She watched him sleep. She loved him dearly. No one had ever been as kind to her, and her heart sank when she thought of the danger he faced being Jewish. And what about Hoda? Or Yitzar? They were good people too. What fate awaited them? But most of all, she was worried about Karl. Her innocent little boy with his big toothless smile. Would the Nazis be so heartless as to hurt a child?

Her mind was whirling when she heard Hoda and Yitzar speaking quietly in the living room. It was difficult to make out what they were saying. But from the way they looked at each other, Kara was certain that they were falling in love. She knew how hard this must be for Hoda, who had always told her that she knew she would never give her heart to another man after Kaniel died. Once Karl was born, Hoda had devoted her life to her grandson. *She is a good bubbie,* Kara thought, smiling as the Yiddish word surfaced in her mind. *And I must admit, I am glad for her and Yitzar. She is still a young woman, and she should not be alone. He is a good person. I can see that already.*

Kara was right. It was almost a week later when Hoda and Yitzar announced that they planned to marry. Kara congratulated them and hugged them both. When Karl felt the joy in the room, he giggled with pleasure. At first, Abram seemed a little upset. He left the room and went to the bedroom where he stayed for about fifteen minutes. Kara wondered if he was thinking about his father. But when he returned, Abram smiled warmly at his mother and then turned to smile at Yitzar. "Mazel tov to both of you," he said with sincerity.

"Thank you, Abram," Hoda said.

"I know Papa would want you to be happy. You should have someone in your life. And Yitzar is a wonderful person. I approve," Abram said.

CHAPTER SIXTY-TWO

HODA AND YITZAR were married in a quiet ceremony in the study in a rabbi's home. Hoda stood beside Yitzar as the rabbi pronounced them man and wife. They looked at each other with eyes filled with deep affection. Kara smiled when Abram's eyes met hers. "I'm glad she will have a second chance at happiness," he whispered in Kara's ear.

That night Abram and Kara insisted that Hoda and Yitzar sleep in the bedroom. Until now, Karl had slept with Hoda. But to make the change easier for Karl, who was very attached to his grandmother, Abram put Karl on his lap and said, "You are a big boy now. You are too old to sleep with your grandmother. It's time for you to have your own bed. So, I am going to make you one. And you can help me."

Karl looked at his father skeptically. But when Abram took an empty drawer out of the dresser and lined it with sheets and blankets and then put Little Bear inside, Karl nodded with delight. They put the makeshift bed at the end of the small bed that Kara and Abram now shared, which was in the study.

That night, Hoda and Yitzar retired early. They said good night to everyone and went into the bedroom. Immediately, Karl forgot about his bed and cried out for his bubbie.

"Remember? You're a big boy now. You're going to sleep with Little Bear in your own bed."

Karl nodded. But he stood staring at the closed door. "Bubbie," he said.

Hoda came out and kissed Karl. "Good night, my love. I'll see you tomorrow, and I promise you we'll do something very special."

"I want to sleep with you," he said.

"I know. But your father told me that you are a big boy now. You and Little Bear have your very own bed."

Karl nodded.

"I am very proud that my bubbala is all grown up."

"I am grown up, Bubbie."

"I know," she said. "Would you like me to tell you a story or sing you a song before you go to sleep?"

"Yes, Bubbie."

"All right, then, come with me. Hoda took Karl's hand, and they went into Kara and Abram's room in the study. She tucked Karl into his bed and told him a story. Then she sang to him. And by the time she'd finished, he was asleep.

Hoda slipped back into the bedroom where Yitzar waited. She was nervous. "I have something I must tell you," she said. "It was wrong of me not to tell you before. But I couldn't find the courage. Once I've told you, if you want to annul the marriage, I will understand."

"Hoda? What is it?"

Hoda took a deep breath. Then she began in a slow and steady voice, "When I was just five years old, I was helping my mother to make soup. I was standing on a chair because I was too short to reach the stove. The pot boiling soup was sputtering. A drop of water flew up and hit my cheek. I reacted by jumping back and grabbing the handle of the pot. As I fell off the chair, the boiling soup splattered all over my chest and my arm. It was a very bad burn." She swallowed hard. "What I am trying to say is that I am scarred."

Yitzar rose and took Hoda into his arms. Then he slowly unbuttoned her blouse. Her entire chest was covered in scarred flesh that reached across the top of her right arm. "Hoda," he whispered and gently touched her marred skin. Then he bent down and kissed her chest and arm gently. "I love you. I am so happy to have you as my wife."

Tears fell down her cheeks. She couldn't speak. She drew him to her, and they made love.

CHAPTER SIXTY-THREE

The Mitte had been ravaged on those fateful nights, and people were still cleaning up the mess that had been left behind. They were trying desperately to salvage whatever they could from their homes and businesses. There wasn't much to recover from the Ehrlichs' bookstore or their apartment. The books and the wooden shelves on which they stood had been the perfect fuel for the flames. Abram's family had lost everything, including all of Abram's forbidden books and his treasured photographs of Kaniel. But there was no time to mourn the losses. Abram, like all of the Jews who lived in the Mitte, had to forge on and find new ways to survive.

Hoda and Kara combed the neighborhood to see what they might recover. They found half-burned sheets and brought them home. They scrubbed them until their hands bled and then cut them into pieces to make diapers for Karl. Times were tough. There was hardly enough meat to keep one butcher busy, so Yitzar was not able to hire Abram. This forced Abram to go out in search of a job. He went to his old friend Davina Cooperman's house to see her father, who was a scientist doing freelance work in several different laboratories. Abram was hoping that perhaps Herr Cooperman might know of some janitorial work that was available at one of the laboratories where he worked. But when he arrived, Herr Cooperman told Abram that he, too, was out of a job.

"I was fired for being a Jew," the old man spit the words at Abram. "I'm glad at least that my daughter got out of Berlin before all of this began," Davina's father said, sucking his teeth. "Too bad you two didn't marry. Isn't it? If you had married her, you would have been with her at Oxford now. Instead, you're here stuck in Berlin like the rest of us poor souls. Us poor Jews, huh? And I hear that you have stooped very low. I hear you are living with a shiksa."

Abram glared at the old man. Abram knew that Davina had been crazy about him. But he wasn't able to return the feelings. He liked her well enough as a friend, but he couldn't see himself spending his life with her. It wasn't that Saul Cooperman had ever really liked Abram or wanted him as a son-in-law, but Cooperman resented Abram for rejecting his daughter, who was the light of her father's life. Abram would have liked to punch the old man in the face for what he said about Kara. But with the world falling apart around them, the last thing Abram needed was to get into a fight. And besides, he knew his father would be ashamed of him for punching a man who was so much older than himself. "Respect your elders," Kaniel had always said. Without another word, Abram left Saul Cooperman's home.

Finding a job wasn't easy, but Abram was willing to do whatever he could to help the family. He'd changed in so many ways. Before he met Kara, he'd been a selfish boy always in search of new adventures. Travel and women had been his passion. Now, he couldn't even remember what it felt like to be such a free spirit, because now his wife and child were first in his heart. So when he landed a job as a cleaning man at the Charite Berlin, a teaching hospital in the Mitte, he was glad to have the work. In his early years he would never have accepted such a lowly position. But not only had he accepted it, he was eager to start contributing to the family.

Hoda and Kara took turns helping in the butcher shop and caring for Karl. When they were in the store, they worked the counter while Yitzar cut the meat and kept the store clean. They shared the chores of keeping the small house clean and washing the clothes. The extra money that Abram brought in helped to buy things like flour and vegetables, and on rare occasions, sugar.

One evening as Abram was coming home from work, he turned down Neue Friedrichstrass. He wanted to stop at the leather maker to try and purchase some used shoes for Karl. The shoemaker's shop had been ransacked during the horrible attack on the Mitte. The large picture window was broken, and most of the shelves lay shattered on the floor. But at least it had not been burned. Abram walked inside the cobbler's shop and made his purchase. When Abram left the store, he saw Saul Cooperman coming out of the clothing store a few doors down. There was no one else on the street. The two men were face-to-face. When Herr Cooperman saw Abram he walked quickly toward him and stood in front of him, glaring at him.

Abram, not wanting to start an argument, said, "Good evening, Herr Cooperman." Then he tried to walk away. But Saul Cooperman's face had turned red with rage and he blocked Abram's path. The old cobbler was looking out from his store.

"You are a very rude young man," Saul said. "You walked into my home last week asking me for help. Then you walked out without even saying goodbye."

"Move out of my way," Abram said, trying to stay calm.

"That's how you talk to an elder? Your father would be ashamed. Well, I always said that Kaniel indulged you too much. He was a real nar, a fool. If he could have seen the future, he would be shaking his head. If he could see you living with a shiksa in sin. A blonde *kurveh*, a whore."

"Don't you dare call my wife a whore."

He laughed. "She's not your wife. No rabbi in his right mind would marry you. The *goyum*, your girlfriend's people, wouldn't marry you. They don't want you. In fact, they made laws to keep you away from their women, Jew boy."

It had been a particularly hard day at work for Abram. He'd cleaned vomit and feces, almost throwing up himself. The smell still lingered in his nostrils. He was exhausted. All he wanted was to go home and clean himself up.

"Please move out of the way," Abram said to Herr Cooperman, who was blocking the street.

"Why should I?"

Abram was losing patience. With his elbow, he pushed Saul Cooperman out of his way. But he didn't realize how hard he'd shoved him. Saul Cooperman lost his footing and fell through the already broken window of the leather goods store. He was cut severely in several places. When Abram saw the blood on Saul's face, all of the anger flooded out of him. He was still weary from his day, but he felt bad. *He's just an old man. And a friend of my father's,* Abram thought as he knelt down beside Herr Cooperman.

"I'm so sorry. Are you all right?"

Herr Cooperman turned his head away from Abram just as a black police car came around the corner. The cobbler ran out the back door of his shop. Abram got up to run, but it was too late. Two large Gestapo agents jumped out of the automobile. The Gestapo men grabbed Abram and Saul Cooperman and threw them both into the back seat, and then they drove away.

CHAPTER SIXTY-FOUR

BINAH ROSENBLATT WAS USED to hearing the word *rachmones*, pity, when people looked at her. She knew that everyone pitied her. That was because she had no parents, no family at all, in fact, and she lived on the street. Her hair was a mass of tangles; her clothing was dirty and too small for her. Everyone thought she was mentally slow because she didn't speak to anyone. Most of the time she walked through the streets unnoticed. In the winter, she shivered as she sat on the sidewalk. People walked by her and seemed not to see her. Sometimes she wondered if she were invisible.

But Hoda Ehrlich had always been kind to her. Once on a very cold night, Hoda had brought her blankets. And sometimes Hoda had even brought her a bowl of hot soup or a thick piece of challah that she baked. Hoda never waited for Binah to say thank you. She just gave her the gifts and then left.

This had gone on for as long as Binah could remember. There had been a sweater one winter that Hoda gave her which had been one of her most treasured possessions. When it became much too small for her to wear, she'd unraveled the yarn and used two sticks as knitting needles to make it into a hat.

There had never been a single word spoken between them. Hoda did not expect anything of her, so when Binah saw the Gestapo take Abram, Hoda's son, away, she knew she must go and tell Hoda what happened.

She knew where Hoda lived. In fact, she made it a point to know where everyone lived in the Mitte. Where they lived and what they did for work. She knew their sins and their mitzvahs. She had learned that as long as everyone thought she was mentally challenged, they would speak freely in her presence. And nothing went on in the Mitte that Binah was not aware of.

Binah walked quicky, and unseen, to the butcher shop. The bell that hung over the door clanged as she entered. Hoda had been in the back, so Yitzar saw her first.

"Can I help you?" Yitzar asked.

Binah just stared at him.

Yitzar walked into the back of the store and whispered in Hoda's ear. "The little beggar girl is here. She's in the store. I tried to ask her what she wants, but she doesn't answer. She's just standing there looking."

"You mean Binah?"

"Yes"

"That's strange. She never comes into the stores. She has no money. Poor thing must be hungry. Let me go out to the front and see what we can do to help her."

Hoda walked out and smiled at Binah. "Food?" she said, expecting Binah to nod but not speak.

"I must talk to you," Binah said.

Hoda was shocked. No one she knew had ever heard this poor child speak. "Yes, what is it?" Hoda asked gently.

"Can I please come in the back where we can speak alone?" Binah said, glancing at Yitzar.

"Of course."

Hoda led Binah into the back of the store. "I have a pot of ersatz coffee on the stove. Would you like a cup? It's not much, but it is hot." Hoda smiled.

Binah ignored the question. "I was hiding in the alleyway behind the leather store on Neue Friedrichstrass when I saw your son, Abram. He got into a fistfight with Herr Cooperman, and Herr Cooperman fell. Herr Cooperman got hurt. And then the Gestapo came. They took Abram and Herr Cooperman away. I think they have been arrested. I wanted to come and tell you because you have always been so kind to me."

Hoda's hand flew up and covered her mouth. "Oh, dear God, no."

"Since that night when the mob of German boys came and broke all the windows, the Gestapo have been coming around and arresting a lot of Jews. Every day, more and more. I see it happening. They don't see me because I hide in alleys and behind buildings. But I know what the Nazis are doing," Binah said. "Most of the time they don't even need a reason to arrest someone. They just stop the car and go into a store and pull out the owner and take him away. Now, please know that I don't mean any disrespect, but with your daughter-in-law being a shiksa, they have probably been watching your son. And when he got into this fight, it brought their attention to him."

Hoda was too shocked and worried about Abram to take notice of how smart and aware Binah was.

"I don't know what to do," Hoda said more to herself than to Binah. She was rubbing her eyes and pacing.

"I know I am nothing but a poor beggar. I might even be a little slow, but I think it would be wise for you to get your daughter-in-law and your grandchild out of the Mitte. These Nazis are heartless. I've seen them beat old women and children to death. They would think nothing of taking an innocent child away from its family. They killed plenty of innocent people on the streets that night when they attacked the Mitte."

"Do you think it was the Nazis," Hoda asked, "or do you think it was just a gang of thugs?"

"I know it was the Nazis. Remember, I am invisible. No one pays any attention to me. So I was able to hear the gangs as they ran

through the streets. They were under the direction of this government. You can be sure of it."

"Dear God," Hoda said. She felt beads of sweat forming on her
forehead and the beginnings of a dizzying headache. She looked at
Binah and put her hand on the young girl's cheek. Then she added,
"Thank you for coming to tell me about my son. I have to speak to
my husband so we can decide what to do."

Then her eyes fell upon Binah's ragged dress and hair and upon
her painfully thin body, and even though Hoda was overcome with
her own problems, her heart ached for the young orphan. "Come,"
she said, "follow me." Hoda walked over to the money box where
she and Yitzar kept their cash. Taking out a few reichsmarks, she
handed them to Binah. "Here. Take this. Go and buy yourself
something to eat."

Binah nodded. She took the money and then left the store.

"Yitzar!" Hoda cried out. "Yitzar, come here."

He had been working in the back of the butcher shop, but when
he heard the desperation in Hoda's voice, he rushed over to her.
"What is it?" he said.

She was shaking. Her face was covered in sweat, and he was
shocked by what he saw.

"It's Abram. He's been arrested for fighting in the street. That's
why Binah, the little beggar girl was here. She came here to
tell me."

"Do you believe her? I thought she didn't speak," he said,
confused.

"I do believe her. She has never spoken to me before, but she
spoke today. She said the Gestapo took Abram away."

"But why?"

"He got into a fight in the street. I don't know why. All I know is
that they have him."

"Abram? That doesn't sound like Abram. Maybe the poor girl
made the whole thing up so that you would give her some money."

"I don't think so. I am sick with worry."

"I'll go to the police station and find out what I can. Perhaps
they will take a little money to let him go. I'll give them whatever

we have," Yitzar said. But Hoda grabbed his arm and held it tightly.

"No. Please don't go there. I am afraid," Hoda said, "they might take you too."

"That's absurd. I've done nothing wrong. I follow all of their rules. At least they think I do. They don't know the meat here is kosher." He tried to smile. "Let me go and talk to them. I'll give them whatever I can."

"No, I am afraid for you. And besides, we haven't followed their rules. We've allowed Kara and Abram to live together."

Yitzar looked at her. "You're right. I never thought about it." Yitzar stared down at the countertop, lost in thought. Then he added, "And they probably would love to get their hands on our little Karl. Oy vey. *Gott im himmel.*"

"I think we must get Kara and Karl out of here once they are gone. We can go together to the police station and see what we can to do help Abram."

"Let's close early and go and talk to Kara. We must hurry."

They cleaned up quickly and then walked to the house. "You two are home early. Did you sell out of meat?" Kara said as she stirred the pot of noodles on the stove.

"No," Hoda said, "we came home because we must speak with you."

"What is it?" Kara said, drying her hands on her apron.

"Abram has been arrested," Hoda said.

Kara sank down into a kitchen chair. "What? Why? Is it because of me? Dear God . . ."

"No, it's not you. He got into a fight in town."

"I'll go to the police station. I'll talk to them. I'll get them to release my husband," she said, her face flushed.

"Kara," Yitzar said gently, "you can't go to the police. You are a German living with Jews. You have a half-Jewish son. Hoda and I are worried about you and Karl. If the police find out that your son is half-Jewish and that you and Abram broke the law, who knows what they'll do to Karl."

"My son," she gasped, and her eyes flew open wide.

"Yes. We must stay calm and be logical so we can protect Karl," Hoda said. "Now, I have been thinking. You told me that you have a sister. You said she doesn't know that Karl is half-Jewish. In fact, she knows nothing of you and Abram. Is that correct?"

"Yes."

"Then you must take Karl and go and stay with her. I will contact you when everything has settled down here. But you must get Karl out of here. Do you understand me?"

"But Abram? I must help Abram."

"Abram would want you to take Karl away before . . ."

"But—"

"You must do this. Do you think I want to part with my grandson? Do you think I want this?"

Kara was crying softly. The pot of noodles had boiled over onto the stove, but no one paid any attention.

"I don't want this any more than you do," Hoda continued, "but I would rather know that Karl was safe than have him here and know that at any time they could come and take him away. He is little and he is helpless. It's up to us to protect him."

"Abram"—she wrapped her arms around herself and began to rock—"my sweet Abram. What about Abram?"

"Don't you think I am sick with worry about him also? But let's face facts. There is a greater chance that they will let him go if they don't find out that he is living with a Gentile woman. If they find out about the two of you, they will punish him for sure."

Kara bit her lip. "Do you promise that you will contact me as soon as you hear from Abram?"

"Of course. Before you go, you will leave me your sister's address. I will send you a letter as soon as I know anything. It may be a while, a month, perhaps two, before you can return. But I promise not to keep you in the dark. I promise I will write, and I will always tell you everything I know," Hoda said. "Now, get ready. I want you to go tonight."

"That soon?"

"Yes, that soon. Yitzar and I want to go to the police station as soon as we can, and we can't do that until you and Karl have gone.

Besides, I've heard that they are arresting people in the Mitte for no reason at all. You must go before they come looking for you and Karl."

"I'll start packing," Kara said.

"Use Abram's small suitcase; it's under the bed," Hoda said.

CHAPTER SIXTY-FIVE

WHEN KARA WAS PACKED and ready to leave, she called for Hoda to come into her bedroom. Karl was sitting on the bed playing with Kara's handbag. "Bubbie!" he said when he saw Hoda reaching his arms up for her to lift him.

Hoda picked him up and held him in her arms. She breathed in the essence of him. Tears fell down her cheeks as she nuzzled his small cheek and ear. "Bubbala, you have to go away for a while. But you must promise me that you'll be a good boy. Your mama needs you to be very good and do everything she tells you to do," she said.

"Why are you crying, Bubbie?"

"I'm not," Hoda said, wiping her tears away with the back of her hand.

"You are crying."

"No, sweetheart. I'm fine. I was just cutting onions. You know how onions make my eyes tear." Hoda smiled, then she held Karl tightly and kissed his forehead. Taking a deep breath, she whispered, "Always remember that you are loved."

"I am loved," he repeated.

Hoda nodded. "You are deeply loved," she said. Then she handed Karl to Kara.

"Kara, I never thought in a million years that I would feel this way about you. I always thought that people should stick to their own religion. But I have come to love you; you have been like a daughter to me," Hoda said, pulling Kara and Karl into an embrace. "Be careful and be safe."

"Here, this is my sister's address." Kara took a small sheet of paper out of her handbag and gave it to Hoda.

"I'll be in touch as soon as I can," Hoda said.

Yitzar walked in, announcing, "Kara, I want you to take this." He handed her an envelope, "It's not much, but you should have it in case you need it."

"Money?"

"Yes, it's our savings. Take it."

"I couldn't." Kara looked at Hoda.

Hoda nodded. "Yitzar and I discussed it. We want you to take it. That way, if something happens and you need money, you'll have it. We kept some aside; we hope to use it to bribe the police to release Abram."

Kara hugged Hoda, then she hugged Yitzar. "I love you both. Please . . . as soon as you hear anything about my beloved Abram, let me know."

"I will. I promise you. And as soon as it's safe, you'll come back to us. God willing."

"God willing," Kara said, her face covered with tears.

CHAPTER SIXTY-SIX

KARA HELD Karl on her lap and looked out the window of the bus as they rode through the Mitte. *I can't believe that I was once afraid of this place, of these people. Now I feel as if I am leaving my real family behind. I will be glad to see Anka again. But as for my parents, they are nothing but a distant, and hurtful memory.* Her heartbeat fast with fear as she thought about Abram. *All I can do is pray that the Gestapo did not hurt you. And that soon they will let you go.* She didn't want to leave Hoda and Yitzar. She would rather have stayed and waited for Abram's return. *But I know Hoda is right. If the Nazis find out that I was living with Abram and that Karl is half-Jewish, they will make me pay for breaking their ridiculous laws. And they might very well extract that payment through Karl.* So even though she knew the laws were absurd, she still did not dare put Karl at risk.

The motion of the ride had put Karl to sleep. He was groggy and cranky when she stood up at their stop. They would have to catch another bus in order to be close to her sister's home. "Where is Little Bear?" Karl asked as they waited at the bus stop.

"I packed him in my handbag," Kara said.

"I want him, now."

"You can have him when we get to Anka's house."

"No! Now!" Karl demanded "I want Little Bear now."

271

"Be quiet. If I give the bear to you, you'll lose it," she said sharply. Karl moaned. Then their bus rounded the corner. "I don't want to go on another ride," Karl said.

"I'm sorry, but we have to take this bus to get to Anka's house."

"I don't want to."

"I understand, but please be good."

"No!" he said. She picked him up and he let out a cry. But she carried him on board. At first, he was fussy, but the motion of the bus put him to sleep. When they came to their stop, he woke up crabby. They got off the bus. Kara took Karl's hand and they began to walk toward Anka's house. Then Karl started to cry. He sat down on the sidewalk and wailed.

"I'm sorry," Kara said, and she took the stuffed bear out of her purse and gave it to him. He was dragging along, gripping the stuffed bear. She was tired and cold, and she wanted to get to Anka's as soon as possible, so she picked him up and held him in her arms. It was easier to carry him than to try and make him walk. Carrying Karl in one arm and the suitcase in the other, she made her way through the wealthy area of Berlin.

When she arrived at Anka's house, she knocked on the door. The maid answered and let her in.

"Kara!" Anka came running down the stairs. She threw her arms around Kara who was still holding Karl. "Look at how big he has grown. He is so beautiful, Kara. He looks just like you."

Karl woke and looked at Anka.

"What lovely dark-blue eyes you have," she said.

Karl started to cry.

"I'm so sorry. He must have forgotten who you are," Kara said. Then she turned to Karl. "This is my sister. She is your Aunt Anka."

"I want Bubbie."

"What did he say?" Anka asked.

"I don't know," said Kara, pretending not to understand Karl. The last thing she needed was for Anka to hear him use the word bubbie. "He's tired and he's rambling. Is it all right if we stay?"

"All right? Of course it's all right. It's not only all right, it is wonderful!" Anka said, eyeing the small suitcase that Kara carried.

"I would love to change his clothes and put him to bed. Then I need to speak to you," Kara said.

"Follow me. I have a spare room where the two of you will be very comfortable."

Once Karl was asleep, Kara came downstairs. She found Anka in the living room, knitting.

"I broke up with my boyfriend. He went home to his wife," Kara lied. "Karl and I have been abandoned. We have no place to go."

"Oh my. Are you all right?"

"Yes," Kara said, wanting to cry. Her heart was heavy with worry for Abram. "I'll be all right. But I was wondering if we can stay here with you for a while."

"Of course, I am happy to have you. And I know Ludwig will feel the same." Anka put her hand on her sister's shoulder. "You can stay as long as you like."

"I don't think it will last with my boyfriend and his wife. They have had troubles in their marriage long before he and I met. He left me as a last attempt to work things out with her. I am hoping that this last attempt to make things right will finally be the end of their marriage. He and I have a child together. Besides, they are very different people, and they don't belong together," Kara said. *I can't believe I am spinning this lie. I wish I could just tell her the truth. But it would be dangerous for her to know that I am in love with a Jewish man and that her nephew is half-Jewish. This is the best way to keep both Anka and Karl safe. When I hear from Hoda and I know that things have settled down in the Mitte and Abram is home, I will tell Anka that my boyfriend has left his wife for good. And then I will return.*

.

CHAPTER SIXTY-SEVEN

February 1939

IN THE BEGINNING, Karl asked for his father and bubbie often. But because he was so young, only Kara could fully understand him. And she was relieved, because the term bubbie would have given away her secret.

A month passed, and then two. Each day when the mail arrived, Kara ran out of the house to get it. She didn't want to risk anyone seeing an envelope addressed to her, but nothing arrived. When Anka approached her about why she was so interested in the mail, she said sheepishly, "I am always hoping that Bruno will come to his senses, divorce his wife, and ask us to come back to him. And if not, then perhaps he could at least send money for his child."

"Bruno is his name?" Anka asked.

"Yes."

"Do you want to tell me his last name? I can see if one of Ludwig's friends can check up on him and see what he is doing."

"No, please, don't pressure me." Kara began to cry fake tears. "I can't have everyone know what happened. You know how people talk. I was a mistress to a married man. I am so ashamed of how he threw me over."

"Of course. I understand," Anka said, hugging her sister. "No need for anyone to know any more than they already know."

The winter was bitter cold. Most days were spent with Kara and Anka playing with Karl on the rug by the fireplace.

Anka was in a much better mood since Kara had moved in. She was always happy, and Ludwig was pleased that Kara had come. He was so pleased, that when Wilhelm wrote to him to say hello, he invited Wilhelm to come and stay for a weekend. Ludwig wanted it to be a surprise, so he did not tell Anka or Kara that Wilhelm was coming.

Wilhelm arrived on a frigid winter day when the sky looked like blue ice that could crack at any moment. He wore a smart black uniform with a black hat bearing a death head symbol.

"Kara!" he said when he saw her, "you are still as beautiful as I remember."

She mustered a smile.

"When Ludwig told me you were here, I had to come and see you."

"It's good to see you, Wilhelm," she said, looking at the swastika on his sleeve.

"I brought a little something for your son."

"How did you know I had a child?"

"Ludwig told me," he said. Then taking a small wooden bus out of his pocket, he handed it to Karl.

"Thank you. That was very thoughtful."

"If you give me a chance to prove myself, you'll see that I am a very thoughtful fellow," he said.

Kara didn't answer.

The following day, Karl wanted to go outside and play in the snow. Kara tried to discourage him, but Wilhelm said, "I used to love to play in the snow when I was a child. Why don't we go out together, the three of us? It will be fun."

Kara shrugged her shoulders, but she agreed. They spent a full hour making snow angels and attempting to build a snowman. "It's so cold out here. I think I should take Karl back inside," Kara said.

"No," Karl said.

"Yes." Kara picked him up.

"Don't be upset, little man. Perhaps we can convince your mutti to let us do this again tomorrow," Wilhelm said.

"What a beautiful little boy he is," Wilhelm said when Karl was napping that afternoon. "He's so blond and Aryan. You must be so proud."

"I am proud of my son," Kara said. *Not because he looks Aryan, but because he is a kind and sweet little boy.*

"I'm the sort of man who wouldn't mind marrying a woman who already has a child."

Kara smiled.

"Do you know what I am saying?" he said.

"I am not ready to start anything new with anyone. My breakup with Karl's father is too fresh in my mind. I'm sorry, but I don't want to lead you on."

"I have plenty of time," he said.

That night at dinner, Wilhelm was seated beside Kara. His table manners were impeccable, but then the conversation between Ludwig and Wilhelm turned to affairs of the state. They talked about how good Hitler was for Germany.

"He's done a wonderful job restoring our economy," Wilhelm said, "and he's getting the filthy Jews in line too."

"It's about time someone did," Ludwig said.

Kara glanced over at Karl, and she felt a chill run down her spine.

Two days later, when Wilhelm left, Kara breathed a sigh of relief.

CHAPTER SIXTY-EIGHT

May 1939

AFTER SIX MONTHS without a word from Abram or Hoda, Kara was beside herself with worry that something had happened to all of them. She was sure of it, because even if Hoda and Abram could not write, if Yitzar were able, he would have written. The fact that no one had contacted her sent chills through her. Kara knew that regardless of the risk, she had to go to the Mitte and find out why she hadn't heard from anyone.

"Will you keep an eye on Karl for me?" Kara asked Anka.

"Where are you going?"

"I have some business to attend to."

"You're going to see Bruno, aren't you?"

"No!" Kara said afraid that Anka would insist on going with her, "I am going on a job interview."

"But you don't need a job. We have plenty of money. Besides, who would watch Karl if you went to work?"

"I was hoping you would help me out. I was hoping that perhaps the maid might watch him for a few hours a day. I need to have some money of my own. I feel awkward having Ludwig support my son and me. I'm sure you understand."

"I do. But I can promise you that neither Ludwig nor I mind at all if you stay at home with your son. It is better for the boy, you know."

"Yes, but I feel like I should do this. I feel like I need to have some money of my own. I can't ask your husband for everything Karl and I need."

"I understand." Anka sighed, then added, "If you'd like, I can ask Ludwig if he knows of anyone who needs a secretary, although I still do have to admit that I would prefer you didn't work."

"I know, and I love you. But please don't ask Ludwig. I want to see if I can get a job on my own. Won't you please do this for me? Won't you just stay with Karl for a few hours for me? I won't be long."

"If you want to go on this interview, of course I will watch my nephew. I adore Karl."

"And he adores you," Kara said. She hated herself for all the lies she was getting herself wrapped up in. "I'm going to get ready. I'll be back here late this afternoon. Will that be all right?"

"Yes. Of course."

CHAPTER SIXTY-NINE

KARA KEPT LOOKING AROUND to see if anyone was following her as she rode the bus to the Mitte. If anyone saw her or told her sister that she was on a bus headed to the Mitte, she would have to come up with another elaborate lie in order to cover the truth. Lying to Anka felt wrong. It felt like a betrayal of all she and her sister had once shared. She would have liked to tell Anka everything. But then she reminded herself, *That would be selfish of me. If she knew about Abram and me, she would be conflicted as to whether to tell her husband or to carry my secret like a stone in her heart. Right now, she's carefree and happy. I love her, and it's safer for her if she doesn't know the truth.*

The bus stopped and Kara climbed down the stairs to the street. She was a block away from Yitzar's store. She looked around her for a moment. Much of what had been destroyed on the Night of Broken Glass was now cleaned up. All of the windows had not yet been replaced, but the broken glass was gone and the windows were boarded up. She'd read in the paper that laws had been passed requiring all Jews to wear badges, so that they would be recognized as Jews immediately. And as she walked through the Mitte, she saw these badges. She'd also read that the Jewish shop owners were required, at their own expense, to fix any damage that had been done on those fateful November nights. It wasn't fair; what had been done to them was no fault of their own, yet the German government required it.

It was early on a Wednesday afternoon, and she knew that Yitzar and Hoda would be at work, so she walked to the butcher shop. But when she arrived, she felt a pang of fear shoot through her heart. The Star of David on the window had been removed, and the name Yitzar Stein's Kosher Meat was gone. In its place was a large sign that read, Meier's Butcher Shop, and underneath it in the display window that had been replaced, was a large, butchered pig. This was a definite indication that this was no longer a Jewish meat store.

Leaning against the side of the building, Kara tried to catch her breath. *Where was Abram? Where was the rest of the family? Who was Meier?* She had to know the truth. So she walked inside. A heavyset man with thick auburn hair and a matching mustache stood behind the counter.

"How can I help you today?" he asked in a cheery voice.

She mustered up her courage to ask, "Are you Herr Meier?"

"Yes, actually I am." He smiled. "And who are you?"

Kara didn't want to give him her real name. "Ingrid Albrecht," she said.

"A pleasure to meet you. Now . . . what can I get for you today?"

"I'll take two bones for soup, please."

"I'll get that for you right away."

While Herr Meier was packing the soup bones, he smiled at her. "These bones have plenty of marrow. They'll make a rich soup."

Kara nodded. She was quiet for a moment, then she spoke to him, trying to sound casual as she asked, "Wasn't this formerly a Jewish butcher shop?"

"Yes, it's undergone a possession transfer."

"What does that mean?" Kara asked, trying to sound as if she were making light conversation, but she could hear her voice cracking.

"It means that I am the new owner."

"What happened to the people who were here before?"

"No one knows. They've disappeared. They were Jews, you know. It happens all the time. Jews are leaving the country."

"Oh," she said, her hand shaking as she took the package he handed her wrapped in butcher paper. Then she fished into her handbag and took out a reichsmark, which she laid down on the counter. "Well, thank you," she managed to say.

Kara walked outside. She gulped the air. Then she walked as fast as she could, having to force herself to keep from running, to Yitzar's house. Her mind raced. She was terrified of what she would find, but she had to know, so she knocked on the door. A pretty young woman with braided hair answered. "Guten Tag," she said, looking at Kara skeptically. "What do you want?"

"Who are you?"

"I suppose a better question is, who are you?"

Kara ignored the question. "What happened to the family who lived here before?"

"How should I know? My husband was awarded this home. It's our home. We live here now," she said. "I don't know anything else. I am sorry." Then she slammed the door.

Kara stood in front of the door for a few moments. Her feet and legs felt so heavy. It was hard to move. But there was nothing else to learn here. And if she stayed, there was a good chance that the young girl who was living in Yitzar's house might call the police. That was the last thing she needed. So she forced herself to go back to the main street. Trembling, she walked to the doctor's office, the one who had offered to help her when she wanted to rid herself of her pregnancy. Kara shivered at the thought that she'd almost given up her child. At the time she had no idea how much she was going to love her son and how precious he would be to her. And now, as the heels of her shoes clicked on the pavement as she made her way to the doctor's office, she said a prayer thanking God that she'd not gone through with it.

Dr. Klugmann's name was still on the window of the office building. *At least he's still here.* Relieved, Kara climbed the stairs.

"I must see the doctor," she told the receptionist.

"Is it an emergency?"

"Yes," Kara said. Then she glanced around the waiting room. It was filled with people. Some were coughing; one was hunched over holding her stomach. "Well, yes and no," she said, "I just need to see him. I only have a quick question. I promise you; I won't take up much of his time."

The receptionist nodded. "What is your name?"

"Kara Ehrlich," she answered, using Abram's last name.

"Wait here."

When the receptionist returned, Kara was escorted back to a small office area. The doctor entered. "I remember your face," he said, smiling. "How are you?"

Dr. Klugmann looked as if he'd aged twenty years. He could hardly stand up straight, and he walked very slowly and unsteadily.

"I'm all right, but I have an important question to ask you."

"Go on."

"Do you remember Abram Ehrlich? He and his mother owned the bookstore?"

"Of course, I remember them. Abram was your boyfriend."

"Have you any idea where they are?"

"I don't know where they are, but I know that they were arrested. Along with the butcher, Yitzar Stein."

"Arrested for what?"

"No one knows. You don't have to commit a crime anymore to be arrested. Being Jewish is a crime enough for the Nazis. People are here one day and gone the next. No one knows what happens to them. The Gestapo takes them away, and they are never heard from again."

"What? Never heard from again?" Kara asked. The room was turning dark, and she was afraid she might faint. She forced herself to breathe deeply.

"Yes, my dear child. It's been happening for several months. It's not safe to be a Jew in Germany. I would leave here and go to live with my brother in France if not for my patients. They need me. If I go, who will they turn to? They have no one else."

Kara's mind was reeling. "I am going to go to the police station and see what I can find out."

"I wouldn't do that. They might take you away too. There is no reasoning with them. I know you are an Aryan, but if they find out that you are in association with Jews, you need not commit a crime to be arrested and disappear. Be careful, child," he said. "I must go now. I have a roomful of patients waiting for me."

Kara stood up. She felt weak, but she left. It was hard for her to breathe as she climbed down the stairs. When she stepped outside, she gulped the air. Tears rushed to her eyes as she began to walk to the bus stop. While she waited for the bus, she considered her next move. *If I go to the police, they might very well take me away. Then Anka and Ludwig would find out that Karl is half-Jewish. I don't know how he would react. But I am afraid his feelings toward Karl would change and that would put my son in danger. And I wouldn't be there to help Karl. I can't ask Ludwig to see if he can get me any information about Abram and his family. He would want to know why I was interested in what happened to a Jewish family in the Mitte. As far as Anka and Ludwig are concerned, I don't have any contact with Jews at all. But I have this constant nagging fear that Abram is dead. My Abram, my friend, my lover, my husband. I can't even imagine a world without him. And what about Hoda and Yitzar. Are the Nazis really this cruel? Dear God help us.*

Kara wiped the tears from her face with trembling hands before she boarded the bus. She sat down and lay her head against the dirty window. *Now I know why I haven't heard from anyone.*

That night, Anka came into Kara's bedroom. Karl was already asleep, so she sat down on the bed across from her sister.

"How was your interview?"

"My shorthand is too slow. My typing too."

"Don't worry yourself about any of it. Like I said, you don't need a job."

Kara felt so broken that she longed to weep in Anka's arms. She wished she could just tell her sister everything. *If I were able to share my grief and worry with Anka, I might find some relief. But I won't do it. I won't. Anka is married into a family that believes in the Nazi doctrine more strongly than they believed in the Bible. And although I don't think Anka has any personal reason to hate the Jews, she has to be influenced by her husband's family.*

"Thank you," Kara said.

"You're my sister. My flesh and blood, and my best friend. I am glad that we have the means to care for you and my precious nephew. Don't even think about getting a job. Stay at home with me and raise Karl. Perhaps you will meet a nice man at one of the parties we attend, someone you might consider marrying."

"Perhaps," Kara forced herself to answer.

"Get some sleep, and don't worry about the job." Anka smiled. "I promise you, Ludwig is glad to have you and Karl here with us. He doesn't want you to worry about money."

"Thank you, Anka."

"Good night. Sleep well," Anka said, and she closed the door behind her.

After Anka left, Kara got into bed. She lay there staring at the ceiling and thinking about Abram. *He was so tender and kind, and he'd given me everything he had without question.* She glanced over at Karl who was sleeping in the crib that Ludwig had purchased for him. The child's angelic face was illuminated by the rays of moonlight that came through the window. *My son. You are the living manifestation of the love between your father and me. You embody all the joy and wonder of God's love.* Then she wept until she had no more tears.

Over the next six months, Anka and Ludwig attended parties that were given by Nazi officials, friends of Ludwig's father. Kara didn't want to go, but Anka insisted, so Kara accompanied them. It made her sick to her stomach to see how these people were living in comparison to the Jews in the Mitte. They had plenty of everything, while the Jews had made do with so little.

Often the conversations at the table would touch on what the Nazis referred to as the Jewish Question. Kara longed to tell them what she thought about their views on Jewish people. She had so much to say, but she forced herself to remain silent, lest she cause trouble for Karl.

Every few months Wilhelm returned to visit. He continued to try and woo Kara. But she made it clear that she had no interest in him, and finally he stopped coming.

Meanwhile, Ludwig had finished his schooling and had begun looking for work as an architect.

Then on the first of September in 1939, Ludwig was late coming home from a visit with several of his friends. He had not telephoned Anka to tell her that he would be late, and she was worried.

"Shall I hold dinner?" the maid asked, "or would you like me to feed you and Fraulein Scholz now?"

Karl had been fussy all day. Anka looked at Kara. "Let's hold dinner until Ludwig comes home. I'll feed Karl and put him to bed now."

Anka nodded.

It was a little after nine that night when Ludwig arrived.

"Where were you?" Anka asked. "I was worried. Why didn't you call me?"

"I'm sorry. I should have called. But I have news. Important news: Germany is at war with Poland.

Anka's face was pale. "Do you think we will be invaded?" she asked.

Ludwig laughed. "Germany is the strongest country in the world. It's a good thing we didn't follow that ridiculous law in the Treaty of Versailles, about not having our own army. They were trying to keep us down. But it's a good thing that our führer had the foresight to see that we needed an army to make Germany strong and to help our beloved fatherland rise to its rightful place in the world. We are bombing the Poles into the ground. And between defeating Poland and getting our Jewish problem under control, we have grown into a force to reckon with. Now Germany can conquer anyone."

"Jewish problem?" Kara asked carefully.

"Yes. You know that if it hadn't been for the Jews, we would never have lost the Great War. Our führer will never let the Jews have so much control in our country again."

"So, what is he doing about it," she pressed further, hoping to discover something about Abram. "I mean what is he doing with the Jews?"

"Arresting them, confiscating their homes, their businesses. That sort of thing."

"Where is he sending them?"

Anka broke in, "This is terribly morbid. As long as we are not in danger, I don't want to hear anything more." She paused, then continued, "Shall we have dinner?"

"Yes, of course. I'm sorry that you both waited for me. I was thoughtless; forgive me?" he said.

"I am just glad you are home safe. Now, let's not talk about Jews. That is a depressing subject."

"You are absolutely right, my dear. I am sorry," Ludwig said. "I should never have brought it up."

Anka told the maid to serve dinner.

Kara was silenced. She could not ask any more questions about the Jews without creating suspicion. So she sat at the table pushing her food around her plate and wishing she could speak. Instead, she just listened while Anka told Ludwig about a new dress she saw in the window of a shop and how she wanted to purchase it to wear for a dinner they had been invited to.

Two weeks later, Germany conquered Poland.

CHAPTER SEVENTY

November 1940

On November 8, Anka had the cook prepare a special dinner in honor of Karl's birthday. She ordered a cake from a bakery with pretty roses made of candy on top. There were gifts that had been wrapped with newspaper and tied with string, piled on the coffee table in the living room. Kara forced herself to smile as everyone sang happy birthday to Karl. He giggled. *He's forgotten his father and his grandmother,* she thought. *He's young. Of course, he's forgotten. But I will never forget.*

She could not share her memories. But in her silence, she remembered how this date had been a date of such significance in her life. First, it had brought great joy when Karl was born. And then on Karl's second birthday it was the beginning of terrible hardship and the persecution of her husband and their family. She wanted to cry, to scream, to release the festering anger, but she could not. She must keep her pain buried, hidden, and smile as Karl blew out the candles on his cake. When her slice was served, she found she could not swallow the cake. It stuck in her throat. She drank some water to wash it down. But the water had a bitter taste to her, and she could not eat the cake.

"Do you feel all right?" Anka asked, looking at Kara's plate.

"Yes, I'm fine. I'm just trying not to eat sweets. I've been gaining weight."

"You're imagining it," Anka. "You have a lovely shape."

"I can't eat sweets and keep a lovely shape," Kara said, then she smiled.

"My sister has always been stubborn. If she thinks she's fat, no one will be able to convince her otherwise," Anka said to Ludwig.

After dinner, Karl ran to the pile of presents and began to open them. Kara gave him a small shovel and pail as well as some new shirts and socks. Ludwig and Anka were extremely generous with their gifts for Karl. They gave him a handmade, wooden rocking horse and a pair of new, finely crafted leather shoes. And Ludwig bought him an illustrated book. The cover was green with a picture of a mushroom with a human face. The mushroom was surrounded by other mushrooms and it wore a Star of David on its chest.

"Read it to me, Mutti?" Karl said, giving Kara the book.

"Very well," Kara said.

"What's the book called?" Karl asked with curiosity.

"*Der Giftpilz*, the poisonous mushroom."

"It's written by a very famous German author. His name is Ernst Hiemer," Ludwig said proudly to Karl. Then he turned to Kara and said, "This book is meant to help children learn valuable lessons."

"A poison mushroom, Mutti? What does that mean?" Karl looked up into Kara's face.

"I don't know exactly. Let's read it and see," Kara said to Karl, taking him into her arms. She opened the book and read the first sentence aloud. "Just as it is often hard to tell a toadstool from an edible mushroom, so, too, it is often very hard to recognize the Jew as a swindler and criminal." Kara's voice cracked. She was outraged. There were hideous pictures of old Jewish men trying to lure blond-haired, blue-eyed children by giving them candy.

Kara stopped reading. Quickly, she thumbed through the rest of the book. The words were frightening. "Money is the god of the Jews. The Jews are devils in human form." She came upon a picture of a Jewish doctor attacking a blonde Aryan girl who was wearing a League of German Girls' uniform. The book stressed that pure Aryan children must be careful of Jews, because Jews have dark and terrifying agendas. They have plans to take the children and kill them in ritual sacrifices. When Kara saw a picture of a Jewish man with a black hat holding a knife over the body of an animal, torturing the animal, while children stared through the window, she closed the book. Her hands were shaking. Ludwig must have seen the look on her face.

"This is too scary for a child," Kara declared. *And not only is it scary, but it's wrong and it's horrific.*

Ludwig smiled comfortingly. "I know you hate to scare your child. But it's far better to warn them in advance. You would rather have them be careful than to be kidnapped and murdered by Jews."

Kara forced herself to half smile. There was nothing she could do right now. But she decided that Karl would never see that book again after tonight.

Karl rocked on his rocking horse until he was exhausted. Then he began to get fussy, and Kara took him upstairs to clean him up and put him to bed. When she returned, a bottle of schnapps and three glasses had been placed on the table.

"I have news," Ludwig said proudly. "I saved it until Karl went to bed because I wanted this evening to be his special night."

"Go on, tell us. What's the news?" Anka said eagerly.

"I've been given a position. It's a very good position. An honor, in fact. I will be working on the Wolf's Lair. This is a retreat for our führer and his high officials. The design seems brilliant. It's a group of bunkers housed deep in the forest, affording our führer and the high-ranking officers safety and privacy. It will be a place where the high officials and some of the guards can come to relax and be entertained. There will even be a casino on the grounds." He smiled broadly, then added, "Well . . . all I can tell you is that the Wolf's Lair will be filled with all of the comforts a man could dream of."

"Oh! That's wonderful!" Anka said, her face lighting up with excitement.

"Yes, congratulations," Kara said, trying to sound enthusiastic.

"There is only one small catch. In order for me to take the job, we must move to Rastembork in Poland."

"Poland?" Kara said.

"Yes," Ludwig said.

"Is it safe there?" Anka asked.

"Yes, Poland now belongs to Germany," Ludwig said, smiling. "We will have a nice comfortable home where we will live."

Anka sat back in her chair. "Poland?" she repeated. Then she shrugged and said, "Will there still be parties to attend?"

"Of course."

"Then why not!" Anka smiled. "You know how much I love parties."

"I do," Ludwig said, putting his arm around her shoulder.

"It's so exciting," Anka said, turning to Kara, "and, of course, you'll be going with us. Won't she, Ludwig?"

"Of course, you and our little Karl," he said and smiled. "We will have a nice life. I promise you."

Anka smiled at Kara. "It will be fun. An adventure! I've never been out of Germany."

Kara managed to smile at her sister, but her mind was whirling. *Poland. So far away from here. I will have no chance of ever finding Abram again if I leave this address. This is the only known address Hoda has for me. But I can't stay here without Anka. I either go or find a way to stay in Berlin with Karl. I don't have a job. And if got one, who would watch Karl while I work? Besides, it would make no difference if I were in Berlin or in Poland. If I am not at this address, there will be no possible way for Hoda to find me. If I go, I will have Anka. If I stay here, I will be alone.*

"What is it, Kara? You look like you're so lost in your thoughts," Anka asked.

"It's just that this is such a big move. And what will I do once Karl starts school?"

"You needn't worry about Karl getting a strong German education. We'll be living in a community with other Germans. There will be Aryan teachers there who will see to it that he gets a good and proper German education. I'll see to it," Ludwig said. "And . . ." He hesitated. "You can be sure that Wilhelm will come to visit us in Poland. It's not that far away."

As if I was at all concerned about Wilhelm, Kara thought. But she said nothing. Instead, she just nodded and smiled.

CHAPTER SEVENTY-ONE

1940

IT TOOK over two weeks for Kara and Anka to pack up everything in the house. But once they'd finished, they were on their way to Poland. Kara's heart was heavy, and she was uncertain whether she'd made the right choice. She begged Anka's father-in-law to forward any mail that was addressed to her. He promised he would.

They arrived in Poland on a cold, gray afternoon at the end of November. Evidence of the bombs that the Germans had rained upon the country were everywhere. People, mostly women, in drab garb with sad faces stood outside with buckets clearing away the rubble.

Kara was shocked at the magnificence of the house that had been awarded to Ludwig. It was even nicer than the house where they'd lived with his parents in Berlin. This two-story brick home had beautiful crown molding and exquisite white marble floors. It was exquisitely furnished.

Kara knew she must never ask how this house had come to be so beautifully decorated, with its authentic works of art hanging on the walls. But she was afraid that it might have been confiscated from a Jewish family who had been arrested and sent to the place that no one talked about. Perhaps they were in the same place as Abram, Hoda, and Yitzar. She decided that it would do her no good to know anything about it, because if she did find out that it had been stolen from Jews, then what was she going to do? She was powerless. She couldn't complain or state her feelings. She had nowhere else to go, and besides, it would be unsafe for her to show any warm sentiment toward the Jewish people. Ludwig was always kind and generous toward her and Karl. But she decided that since she was going to stay, she needed to earn some money of her own. So she went to Ludwig to tell him that she planned to look for work. She admitted to him that she was feeling guilty that he and Anka were supporting her and Karl. Ludwig listened without speaking. Then in a kind voice, he offered to tell the others who worked with him at the lair, that Kara was available to tutor their children in reading. "You do love to read, don't you?"

"I do."

"Then if any of their children are having trouble with reading, they could come to you. And you would earn a bit of spending money. Would that make you feel better?"

"Oh yes," Kara said.

"I'll take care of it tomorrow." Ludwig smiled at her. And he did. Within weeks, Kara had three young students who came to see her twice a week for an hour each time.

Every Sunday, Ludwig's family had dinner with the family of one of the men who worked with Ludwig. It was a different family each Sunday. Anka easily made friends with the wives. They talked about recipes and fashion. Many of the wives were young, and they admired Anka because she was so pretty. They even told Anka as much. And Anka admitted to Kara that she loved being a part of this community. Little Karl enjoyed the company of the other children. Everyone they met raved about Karl's coloring. They said he was the most beautiful Aryan boy they'd ever seen, leaving Kara feeling lost and alone in her silence.

She knew that because of what she'd been through in her life, she could never be a part of their world. Nor would she ever want to. And when she thought of how appalled they would all be if they ever learned the truth about Karl, she vowed to do whatever was necessary to make sure they didn't find out. They loved Karl now, but Kara was certain that if they discovered Karl was half-Jewish, they would turn on him instantly and their wrath would be merciless. The thought made her shiver.

Each afternoon, Kara took Karl to a nearby park to play. Sometimes Anka accompanied them. Other times Anka was tired, and Kara and Karl went alone. On those occasions, Kara found that her thoughts always drifted to Abram. Although she hated to believe it, she was fairly sure he was dead. If he had been alive, she was convinced he would have found a way to get word to her before she left Berlin. *All I have left are memories.* Tears would run down her cheeks as she watched Karl play in the sandbox with his pail and shovel.

Ludwig often expressed that he loved the town of Rastembork, and he enjoyed working on the Wolf's Lair. Anka always agreed with him. And since they'd come to Poland, their relationship seemed to be better.

One evening, Ludwig came home from work. Anka and Kara were in the living room playing cards. Karl was on the floor playing with a toy train that Ludwig had bought for him. Ludwig walked in and kissed Anka. Then he smiled at Kara. "I have some good news," he said. "An old friend of mine is in town. He's an architect as well, and he's come to see how we're doing with our project."

"Oh?" Anka said. "Do I know him?"

"No, unfortunately. He left Berlin before we started dating. I don't think you ever met him. But he is very nice, and I've invited him to dinner this Sunday. I hope it's all right with you."

"Of course," Anka said. "What's his name?"

"Oskar Lerch. Hell of a nice fellow. And"—he glanced at Kara—"handsome and single too."

Kara forced a smile, but she had no interest in meeting another man. She'd given her heart and soul to Abram. And now that he was gone, she planned to devote the rest of her life to her son. Many nights since she had moved in with Anka, she would stay awake praying, "Dear Jesus, please, please, please, let my Abram be alive. And I beg you please to help us find each other again." However, as time was passing, she was losing hope.

CHAPTER SEVENTY-TWO

Ludwig had been accurate when he told them that Oskar was a handsome man. When Oskar arrived on Sunday, Kara saw a flash of appreciation cross Anka's face. Oskar was tall and regal in his well-fitting black SS uniform. His blond hair was perfectly combed, and his eyes were the bright cornflower blue of a robin's egg. He had perfectly straight white teeth, and the soft refined voice of a rich boy who had been well educated. In his hands he carried a colorful bouquet of flowers and box of chocolates from Switzerland.

"This is my wife, Anka," Ludwig said with pride, "and this is her sister, Kara. Ladies, this is my dear friend, Oskar."

"It's a pleasure to meet you both," Oskar said, handing the flowers and candy to Anka, but all the while his eyes glued to Kara's face.

"Yes, it is a pleasure," Kara managed to say.

For a moment, Anka seemed awestruck when Oskar turned his gaze upon her and smiled. However, she quickly recovered her composure and said, "Welcome to our home; it's so nice that you could come to dinner."

"I am so honored that you would have me," Oskar said.

During dinner, they spoke mostly about the Wolf's Lair and how wonderful the design was. Then when Ludwig changed the subject by mentioning something concerning the confiscation of Jewish property, Oskar gave him a warning look. Then he said, "Let's not bore these lovely ladies with talk of Jews and other political subjects."

And Kara was grateful that he'd changed the subject. At least she wouldn't have to endure any vicious words about her loved ones.

After dinner, Oskar sat down on the floor and called Karl over to him. "What a beautiful Aryan boy you have here," Oskar said to Kara, "however, I hope you don't mind my saying so, but you really should cut his hair. He looks like a girl."

"I love his hair. I love to run my fingers through it. And he'll only be a baby for so long. Then he'll grow up, and it will always be short," Kara answered.

"Yes, I suppose you're right. Enjoy his long hair now while he is still young," Oskar said, smiling at Kara.

Karl giggled as Oskar lifted him high in the air. Then they sat down on the floor and began to play together. Kara glanced up at the oil painting of Adolf Hitler, and then she looked around the room at her sister, her brother-in-law, and Oskar, and she thought, *I am so thankful they don't know my son is Jewish.*

The two, Oskar and Karl, played for almost an hour. Kara watched as her son enjoyed the much-needed attention of a man. Although Ludwig liked Karl, he never seemed to have the time to play with him. Ludwig was kind, he gave Karl gifts and treated him very well, but as Kara watched Karl and Oskar, she realized that her son needed more. Karl's laughter rang through the house, and Kara felt a warm glow as if a tiny candle had been lit within the dark hole that was inside her heart.

After Oskar left, Kara went to her room to put Karl to bed. She was tucking the covers around him when Anka knocked on the door.

"Come in," Kara said softly.

"Is Karl asleep?"

"Almost. I gave him a hot bath. He was very excited to have someone to play with. He needed the warm bath to calm down."

"He looks like an angel. Don't you think so?" Anka said as she looked at Karl who had already fallen asleep.

"You can't ask me. I'm partial, he's my son."

"I wish I could have a child," Anka said wistfully.

Kara looked at her son. He did look angelic with his head on the pillow and his eyes softly closed. Kara ran her fingers through his hair and marveled as his blond curls fell onto the pillow. She sat down on the bed and then patted the bed beside her. Anka sat. "You've never told me what happened when you lost the baby."

"I know. It's too painful."

"You don't have to talk about it."

"There's nothing to tell. I lost the baby. The doctors say I can't carry a child full term. So, Ludwig and I have to be careful that I don't get pregnant again. If I do, there is a good chance that I might die in childbirth," Anka said as she forced a trembling smile. "So, I have to live with it, I guess." Kara could see Anka's eyes were welling up with tears. "But I want you to know," Anka added, "that having you and Karl here living with us has been a joy to me. You are my sister and my best friend. And I feel like little Karl is my own son."

"He adores you too," Kara said.

"I'm glad. I really am so glad that you and Karl are here." She took Kara's hand and squeezed it. Then she went on to say, "By the way, I think Oskar was quite taken with you."

Kara shook her head. "I'm not interested."

"You can't wait forever for Karl's father to return to you. He has a wife. And it's been a long time since you last heard from him, hasn't it?"

"Yes, it has. And I know you're right." Kara longed to tell Anka the truth. She had to force herself to remember the danger. "But I am happy to just be here with you, and Karl. I can't see myself becoming involved with anyone again. And by the way, Ludwig turned out to be a pretty good husband, yes?"

"He loves me. That's for certain. But our love has never been magical. For him it has, perhaps. But not for me."

"I can see that you care for him, don't you?"

"I do. It's just that sometimes I want more. I suppose that's just human nature. I should be happy to have a man who is so good to me," Anka said. Then she stood up. "Well, it's late, and I'm very tired, so I'm going to get some sleep. I'll see you in the morning."

CHAPTER SEVENTY-THREE

May 1941

ON A SUNNY SPRING MORNING, Kara and Anka had taken Karl to visit one of the other families who had come from Germany to work on the lair. They had a child Karl's age, and Kara felt that it was good for her son to have a chance to play with other children. After they returned home, they had lunch, then put Karl down for a nap. They spent the rest of the afternoon talking. Anka told Kara she was hoping that once the lair was finished, Ludwig would be awarded a holiday in Munich. They lay on Kara's bed and talked about Munich and how much they both wanted to go until they fell asleep. They slept until they heard the front door close.

"Anka, Kara? Are you girls at home? I have some news." It was Ludwig.

Kara opened her eyes and looked at Anka who was still sleepy. Ludwig knocked on the open door.

"I hope I didn't wake you both," he said, "but I'll bet you two can't guess who has come to town?"

"Who?" Anka asked in a sleepy voice.

"Oskar Lerch. He's in Warsaw. And . . . that's where we are going too. Do you know why?"

"Warsaw? Why?" Anka asked.

"Well, because we have been putting all the finishing touches on the lair and . . . Himmler is so pleased, he is throwing a huge gala to celebrate. So we are all invited."

"A party?" Anka asked, waking up.

"Yes, a big party! And, to make things even more wonderful, we don't have to leave Poland once the project is finished. I've been offered a job as a pit boss in the casino at the lair," Ludwig said with a broad smile.

"That's wonderful news," Anka said. "Is our führer coming to the party? I would think he would want to stay at the lair?"

"The führer won't be attending this gala. That's because we wouldn't ask our führer to come and see the lair until it's absolutely perfect. Therefore, we are planning to take a little extra time before we invite our führer to make sure that everything is in order. Then the plan is that next month our führer will arrive, and he will honor us by spending a week at the Wolf's Lair."

"Oh, how exciting! Perhaps I will get to meet him." Anka clapped her hands together.

"Perhaps. That is as long as he is pleased with our work. Well, anyway . . ." Ludwig smiled. "How do you feel about staying here in Poland? It's important to me that you are happy."

"I am. But we must return to Germany from time to time. I do miss it. And I was hoping that we can take a holiday in Munich soon."

"Of course we will, darling. In fact, you must have read my mind, because it was just yesterday that I put in a request for a holiday in Munich. If we are granted the request, we will spend a week there . . . all expenses paid by the party."

"Oh, dear! That sounds like fun!" Anka squealed. "And the gala sounds wonderful too. When is it?"

"Next weekend. But Oskar will be here for dinner tomorrow night. I hope it's all right with you. He's staying in Warsaw, but he's taking a drive out to the lair in the morning. He says he can't wait to see it."

"Of course it's all right. In fact, it's wonderful! I'll have the cook prepare something special," Anka said. Then she turned to Kara. "You remember Oskar?"

"Yes, of course I do."

CHAPTER SEVENTY-FOUR

Oskar arrived with Ludwig after work the following day. He handed Anka a bottle of schnapps. Then he looked around. When he saw Kara, his eyes fixed upon hers. "How have you been?" he asked.

"I'm doing quite well," she answered quietly.

"You're as lovely as I remember."

She smiled.

"I brought Karl a present from Warsaw," he blurted.

"You didn't have to do that."

"I know I didn't have to, but I wanted to. He'll love it. I'm going to go out to the car and get it. I'll be right back."

When Oskar returned with a train set, Karl screamed with delight. Oskar gathered the child in his arms and lifted him high in the air. "After we finish dinner, you and I will assemble this thing together. What do you say?"

"Can't we do it now?" Karl asked.

"Now, you don't want your mutti and your aunt to be angry with me, do you? They've put together this wonderful meal. We must eat first. But then we'll have fun."

"All right," Karl said as Oskar ruffled his hair.

Oskar turned to Kara. "He's such a handsome young boy. Any man would be proud to adopt him and claim him as his son."

Kara didn't answer. She couldn't look at Oskar. And she was glad when the maid interrupted, announcing that dinner was served.

The meal was delicious: roasted chicken, potatoes, green salad, and a rich red wine.

Oskar was the perfect gentleman, pulling Kara's chair out for her before he sat down beside her.

I must admit he is charming, and handsome. And he's wonderful with Karl. He makes a lovely impression on everyone. And he even looks debonair in that uniform. But I know what that uniform stands for, and I know what he is. He may look good, but he's a Nazi.

"The casino opened today!" Ludwig announced with pride. "We started the games. And you'll never guess who our biggest winner was." He smiled broadly, then he said, "It was Oskar!"

Oskar laughed, looking embarrassed.

"Congratulations!" Anka said excitedly. "How much did you win?"

"Oh . . . a gentleman never discusses money in mixed company." Oskar smiled.

"He won enough, that's for sure," Ludwig let out a laugh.

"Congratulations," Kara said.

"Perhaps you will allow me to take you to dinner to celebrate. I could stay here in Rastembork for another day or two before returning to Warsaw."

Kara felt her face flush. "I'm sorry. I can't."

"Perhaps, then, we might take Karl on a picnic or a hike?"

"I don't think so. But thank you so much for the kind offer."

"Well, you will be attending the gala next week, won't you?"

"Of course she will," Anka chimed in.

"That's good. Then I would be honored if you would allow me to be your escort," Oskar said to Kara.

"Come on, Kara," Anka said.

Kara's shoulders slumped. She didn't look at him, but she said, "All right."

CHAPTER SEVENTY-FIVE

ANKA LAY beside Ludwig after they finished making love. She'd resigned herself to his lackluster lovemaking, and it no longer bothered her. It was just a part of their marriage, a job that must be fulfilled.

"I wish you could see how wonderful the lair turned out," Ludwig said. "I am so proud of it, and I am so excited about the upcoming gala. I have never met Herr Himmler, but I am looking forward to it."

Anka giggled. "Everything is going so well for us," she said. She could hardly contain her excitement about the upcoming gala. She had a request, and she knew how to get whatever she wanted from her husband. She leaned over and kissed Ludwig, brushing her naked breasts against his arm. Then she begged him to allow her and Kara to go into Warsaw a few days early. "I need to find a new dress to wear to the party. Kara needs something special to wear too. After all, dear, the way we look is a reflection on you."

"I find it hard to believe that you don't have anything to wear," Ludwig said.

"I have dresses, but everyone has seen them before. If I am

going to make a good impression, I'll need something new. Something stunning and appropriate for a woman whose husband has been recognized for completing such an important job for the führer the way that you have. Besides, Kara and I want to see if we can find a nice Polish lady to watch Karl while we are at the gala."

"You could leave him here at the house with the maid."

"The maid goes home at night. So does the cook," Anka said.

"You could pay her extra to stay overnight."

"Or we could take Karl with us into Warsaw and take him to the zoo the day after the party. He would love that."

"You do adore that little boy, don't you?" Ludwig said, his eyes filled with love as he looked at his wife.

"I do. Don't you?"

"Of course I do. I love him because you do," he said, touching her cheek.

"Do you ever miss not having children? I've always been afraid that our not having them was holding you back in your career. The Nazi Party is so clear on their feelings about family."

"Anka, come here," he said, turning on his side and pulling her close to him. "I have always felt like the luckiest man in the world, because I have you for a wife. Never in my wildest dreams would I have thought that a girl as beautiful as you would look in my direction, let alone marry me. You have made me the happiest of men. I don't miss anything. I am fulfilled beyond my wildest dreams," he said, taking her hand and kissing it. "So, if you would like to take little Karl to the zoo in Warsaw, then let's plan to do it! You and Kara can go to the city tomorrow and buy some outrageously expensive gowns. Which, of course, I will gladly pay for." He smiled in the darkness and added, "Then you two can find a babysitter to watch Karl the night of the gala. The following day, we'll all go to the zoo."

Anka giggled with delight. "Thank you," she said, then kissed him warmly, deeply.

"I love you," he said, and his voice cracked with emotion.

"I love you too." Anka put Ludwig's hand on her breast, and they made love again.

After Ludwig fell asleep, Anka got out of bed and went to Kara's room. She knocked softly on the door.

"Come in," Kara said.

"Karl is still awake?" Anka asked in surprise.

"He couldn't sleep. I was reading to him."

"Hello, little man," Anka said, bending down to kiss Karl's head. The she turned to Kara and said excitedly, "I have great news."

"Oh?" Kara said as she gently and rhythmically stroked Karl's hair. "Tell me."

"You and I have permission to go to Warsaw a few days early and get a hotel room with Karl."

"Why would we do that?"

"That's the exciting part! You and I are going shopping. Ludwig gave us permission to purchase the most beautiful gowns we can find. Regardless of the cost! We'll have plenty of time. Ludwig will meet us in Warsaw at the end of the week, so we'll have several days to shop. And while we are there, we'll ask around at the hotel and see if we can find a suitable babysitter for Karl for the night of the gala."

"I'd really rather stay here with him. You and Ludwig can go to Warsaw."

"Kara! Please don't be that way. I know you are still mooning over your old boyfriend. But please, let's have fun. Besides, Ludwig and I have something wonderful planned for Karl the day after the gala. How would you like to take him to the zoo for the day? We could even have one of the local restaurants pack us a picnic lunch. I know Karl would love to go to the zoo. Wouldn't you, Karl?"

"Yes, Aunt Anka. Mutti, please can we go to the zoo? I've never seen bears or lions. Please?"

Kara shook her head, then sighed. "All right."

"We're going to the zoo! We're going to the zoo! Can we see the monkeys? Will we see tigers?" Karl asked excitedly.

"Yes, yes, and yes," Kara laughed.

Karl stood up and took Anka's hands. She stood up, and he began to dance around her. She giggled and joined him in the dance. Kara watched them and decided that even though she would rather have stayed home, a boring night at a Nazi gala was worth the waste of her time if it meant that the next day would be devoted to Karl's happiness.

CHAPTER SEVENTY-SIX

THE EVIDENCE of Germany's two-week violent takeover of Poland was even more apparent in Warsaw than it had been in Rastembork. Although a cleanup effort had begun, there were still plenty of bombed-out buildings that had not been repaired. The streets were filled with rubble. And Nazi flags could be seen everywhere. They seemed to taunt the defeated Polish people. Kara found the whole business very sad. As they walked through the city, down Grzybowska Street, toward their hotel, they saw a large red-brick wall surrounded by barbed wire. Kara couldn't see over the wall and couldn't imagine what this could be.

"I wonder what that place is?" Kara asked Anka.

"I don't know."

"Do you think we can go inside?"

"You could ask someone, but why bother. It doesn't look very appealing. I'd rather have lunch and go shopping," Anka said.

Kara nodded. They walked a little farther and stopped for lunch at a German owned restaurant. Anka became friendly with their waiter. She was like that. She could talk to anyone, from a waiter to a high government official. And Kara had no doubt that if Anka were introduced to the führer, she would be able to engage in a conversation within minutes. Anka and the waiter talked for a while before Kara found the nerve to ask the waiter what the red brick wall with the barbed wire surrounding it was.

The waiter looked at Kara and nodded. "Oh, so you passed the ghetto?"

"The ghetto?" she asked.

"An unpleasant place, I'm afraid," the waiter said. "It's a small area where the Jews are imprisoned."

"Criminals or Jews?" Anka asked curiously.

"Jews are criminals," the waiter explained. Then he went on, "All the Jews have been rounded up and sent to the ghetto. They can be carefully watched there. That way they can't cause any trouble."

"You mean to tell me that all of the Jews have been imprisoned?" Kara said boldly. "*All* the Jews?"

"I think there are some that are trying to hide, but the Germans are working hard to find them and get them off the streets," the waiter said with a smile. "I have no doubt they will succeed, and Poland will be the better for it. Now, what can I get for you ladies?"

Kara looked at the waiter. She had lost her appetite. "I'm not very hungry," she said.

"Are you ill?" Anka asked, concerned.

"No, just not hungry."

"How about a beer?"

"Yes, that sounds good," Kara said in a soft voice. But she was furious inside. *I wonder if there is a place like this in Germany now, a place where Abram, Yitzar, and Hoda are imprisoned. How can I find out?*

After lunch, they checked into their hotel. Anka had secured rooms in the same hotel where the gala was to be held on Saturday night.

"Three days of freedom!!" Anka announced with glee as she threw her hat on the bed. "Ludwig won't be here until Saturday morning! We can shop all day. We don't have any time restraints. We aren't required to be home for dinner. We can do as we like." She picked Karl up into her arms and held him high above her head. "We're going to have fun, aren't we?" she asked.

"Yes, Auntie Anka," he laughed.

"It will be so much fun, Kara. Aren't you excited?"

"Yes, of course I am. But I'm very tired," Kara said, feeling the heaviness in her heart. "Would it be all right if I took a long, hot bath? Would you mind keeping an eye on Karl?"

"Suit yourself. And, of course, I will be happy to watch my nephew. Tell you what: Karl and I are going out to explore. We'll be back in a few hours so we can all have dinner together."

"Very well," Kara said.

After Anka and Karl left the room, Kara drew a hot bath. As she lay in the warm water, she thought about the ghetto and Abram, Hoda, and Yitzar. *How can I help them?* But even as the thoughts crossed her mind, she knew she was powerless. All she could do was pray and hope God would hear her prayers. Kara stayed in the bath until the water grew cold. Then she got out and dried off. Tossing on her nightgown, she pulled down the covers and climbed into bed. It was a thick, comfortable mattress, and she fell quickly into a deep sleep. She might have slept through until morning if Karl and Anka had not returned. But when they entered the hotel room, her eyes opened immediately. It was already growing dark outside.

"Did you have a good rest?" Anka said, sitting down on the corner of the bed.

"I did. I slept so soundly."

"You must have needed the rest." Anka smiled as Karl took off his shoes and curled into his mother. "I have some good news," Anka added.

"Oh, did you find a dress?"

"No, silly. We are going shopping together tomorrow. You need a dress too. So, I wouldn't shop without you."

"I have dresses. Or if you don't think they are dressy enough, I would be happy to wear one of your old ones. I'm not comfortable spending Ludwig's money, and I hardly have enough from tutoring to buy a fancy dress."

"Don't even think about it. I want you to have a lovely new gown. Not one of mine, but one that is all your own, that is fitted to your lovely shape. Ludwig has plenty of money. I insist."

Kara shook her head. "You're so good to me, to us," she said, indicating Karl.

"Of course, you're my sister, he's my nephew. You're my blood." She sat down on the bed and reached over to hug Kara. "Anyway, about that good news. You'll never believe it, but I found a babysitter for Karl for Saturday night. We met her at the bakery."

"You went to a bakery?"

"Of course, my nephew needed a treat after all of the walking we did."

"Who is this lady you met?"

"She's an older lady. She's a *grossmutter*, a grandmother with five grandchildren. Her name is Sonia Smolak, and you should have seen her with Karl. She was wonderful."

"Yes, I understand that. But, Anka, we don't even know her," Kara said. "I would prefer to find someone who is working for the hotel."

"I asked. They don't have anyone available."

"Then, please, just let me stay at the hotel with Karl. I really don't mind. You and Ludwig go to the party and have fun."

"Absolutely not. I want you to come. Just meet this woman. I know you'll love her. She's a real grandmother type. If you don't like her after you meet her, we'll think of something else. But you must come to the party. You simply must."

Kara loved her sister. But there were times when Anka tried her nerves. "Anka . . . she's a stranger. I just don't know." Kara frowned.

"Just meet her. That's all I ask."

Kara didn't want to argue. "All right. I'll meet her. But if I don't feel comfortable . . . ."

"Yes, yes, I know. If you don't feel comfortable, then we'll think of something else. But for now, won't you please try to be happy. You aren't the same girl since you met Karl's father. You are always so sad, and you never want to have fun," Anka complained. "Just smile, Kara. Everything will be all right. Why don't we go to Sonia's apartment first thing tomorrow? You'll have a chance to meet her and then decide for yourself."

"Very well," Kara said.

"Now, you haven't eaten all day. So why don't you get dressed, and the three of us can go out to some quiet restaurant and have a nice dinner."

Kara nodded.

CHAPTER SEVENTY-SEVEN

THE FOLLOWING DAY, after breakfast, they headed to the address that Sonia had given Anka the day before. As they walked through the streets, Anka hummed to herself.

"I'm just curious; did you even discuss babysitting with this woman?" Kara asked.

"Of course. I wouldn't just drag you over to her apartment to meet her if she hadn't already agreed. Please, stop worrying. Everything is taken care of."

"I haven't said yes to all of this yet," Kara reminded her sister in a stern voice. "We are just going over to this woman's house so I can meet her. That's all."

"I know, I know," Anka said, "but I am confident that you are going to like her."

Sonia's apartment was on the third floor of a well-maintained brick building. Anka carried Karl as they walked up the three flights of stairs. Once they arrived, she knocked on the door.

"Who is it?"

"It's Anka from the bakery yesterday. Do you remember, I am the woman who asked you to babysit?"

"Yes, of course."

"Well, I brought my sister, Karl's mother, to meet you."

Sonia opened the door and immediately smiled at Karl.

"I wasn't expecting you until Saturday afternoon. I thought we'd agreed that you would drop Karl off early on Saturday so that you could have time to get ready for the party," she said.

"Yes, we did actually agree on that, but my sister wanted to meet you before we agreed to leave Karl with you."

"Well, that's perfectly understandable. Come in. I'll make us all some tea."

Kara liked the old woman immediately. Her tone when she spoke was calm, gentle, and sincere. Her home was clean and organized. She served the tea in delicate china cups. "These belonged to my grandmother," she said when she saw Kara looking at the cups. "I received them when my mother passed, God rest her soul."

"They're beautiful," Kara said, admiring the lovely pattern.

"Thank you," Sonia said, then turned her attention to Karl. "Would you like a cookie?" she asked him.

"Yes!"

"Yes, what?" Sonia asked patiently.

"Yes, please?" Karl said.

Sonia handed Karl a cookie. "What do you say?"

"Thank you."

She smiled.

They talked for over an hour about Sonia's grandchildren, who were living in Krakow. Then Anka said, "This has been a lovely visit, but we must be leaving."

"Will I see you on Saturday, then?" Sonia asked.

Anka looked at Kara. Kara shrugged. "All right," Kara said.

"Perfect. We'll see you on Saturday, then," Anka said to Sonia.

"I am looking forward to spending time with Karl, my new friend," Sonia said, and she smiled at Karl.

Karl smiled back.

CHAPTER SEVENTY-EIGHT

THE FOLLOWING days in Warsaw were filled with visits to women's formal-wear shops. At first Karl was cooperative because his aunt gave him candy. But after sitting for several hours in several different dressing rooms while his mother and aunt tried on an endless array of gowns, he began to grow fidgety and restless. He tried to run out of the dressing room and hide under the clothing racks. He was hoping that either his mother or his aunt would chase him.

But instead of laughing and searching for him through the store, Kara was annoyed. She reprimanded him in stern voice for being unruly, while the shop owner, who looked like an old spinster with wiry, gray hair in a bun and a frown on her wrinkled face, stood looking on. Karl began to cry. Kara told him to sit quietly, and for a few minutes he did. He watched his mother with wide eyes as she tried on one dress after another.

She'd hardly ever chastised him. Most of the time his antics made her laugh. He stopped crying, but his bottom lip was jutted out in a pout, his eyes were red, and he looked so sad. Seeing him that way made Kara lose interest in the dresses. Wearing only her slip, she went over to Karl and picked him up. She held him tightly in her arms. "I'm so sorry," she whispered in his ear. He nuzzled into her neck. "Just let me and Auntie Anka finish here, and I promise you I won't go to any more stores. All right?"

Karl lay his head on Kara's breast. She held him for a few minutes. The whole event had exhausted him. He lay down on the bench in the dressing room with his head on Kara's handbag. Then he put his thumb in his mouth. *It's not his fault. This is no place for a child.* And she felt badly about having been cross with him. His eyelashes were still wet with tears when his eyes closed, and he fell asleep.

Kara decided to hurry and find something to wear so that she would not have to put Karl through this again. She tried on a few more dresses, all the while keeping her eye on Karl who slept. And finally, Anka found a dress she loved. Kara was so relieved that her sister had decided on something. To ensure that the shopping would end, Kara chose the next dress that the saleswoman brought into the dressing room for her.

Anka decided upon a blue satin dress. It was lovely on her. "That shade of blue really brings out your eyes," Kara told Anka, who smiled broadly.

Kara chose a stunning black gown that hugged her body in just the right way. She carried Karl in her arms not wanting to wake him, but Karl woke up as they were leaving the store. "I'm hungry, Mutti," he said.

"We'll stop and get something on the way back to the hotel," Kara told him.

They stopped at a café. Karl was singing loudly, and Kara asked him to please be quiet. When his food arrived, he gobbled half of it, and then he began playing with the rest. Kara knew he was full and bored, but he was talking loudly and disturbing the other diners. "Stop that, please," Kara said softly.

Karl frowned. He was used to being the center of attention at home. Everyone, even Ludwig, was taken with him. However, on this trip, his mother and aunt were distracted. And when he tried to amuse them, instead of laughing, they seemed annoyed. After they finished lunch, they went back to the hotel room. Kara sat on the bed with Karl drawing pictures while Anka took a nap.

That evening, Karl was still fussy and trying hard to attract attention when they went to dinner. As they waited for their meal to arrive, Kara tried to entertain her son. But he was out of control, hitting the table with a spoon. "Please, stop that right now," she said, taking the spoon away from him. He let out a shriek. "Karl, stop it. I mean it," Kara said. But he wasn't quietening down. Kara turned to Anka. "He's upsetting everyone who is dining here. I'm going to take him back to the room. You finish eating."

"No, it's all right. I'm done," Anka said.

They left and walked back to the hotel. It was then that Kara realized that Anka was right to have hired the babysitter. She still would rather have not gone to the party, but she couldn't disappoint Anka. And if she was going to be forced to attend, it was better that they were dropping Karl off early so she and Anka could get ready in peace.

After they got back to the room, Anka read Karl a story. That seemed to calm him down and he fell asleep. The following day was Saturday, the day of the gala. Anka whispered, "Shall we make arrangements to have our hair done tomorrow morning, as soon as we drop Karl off?"

"I don't need to go to a beauty shop. I can do my own hair," Kara said.

"Have you ever had your hair done at a beauty parlor?"

"No, actually I haven't. Don't you remember, you used to cut my hair and I cut yours?"

"Of course I remember. Who has been cutting your hair recently?"

"Me," Kara said, "with a mirror."

"That settles it. I'll go downstairs while you and Karl get ready for breakfast, and I'll make an appointment at the beauty parlor across the street. Then we'll go to Sonia's apartment and drop Karl off. Once he's settled in at Sonia's, we'll go right to the hairdresser," Anka said. Then she reached over to turn off the lamp.

"Anka . . ." Kara whispered.

"Yes?"

"I'm nervous about leaving Karl. Do you really think it's all right?"

"Yes, I do. I think it will be fine. I wouldn't do it if I thought there was any chance of a problem. Sonia is a nice old lady who needs the extra money. She has grandchildren of her own. She'll be good to him."

"But he's so young and vulnerable. What if she resents us because we're Germans? The Poles aren't exactly fond of us Germans. What if she takes her anger at Germany out on Karl?"

"Did she seem like that type of person?"

"No, not at all. But even so, I'm a little nervous."

"That's only because you've never left him before. But he'll be fine."

"I would still rather stay in the hotel with him," Kara said.

"Don't be silly. You have a beautiful new dress which looks gorgeous on you. Come on, Kara, you need some time with adults. It's only a few hours, and I think it will be good for both of you."

"You're probably right," Kara said. But she couldn't sleep.

CHAPTER SEVENTY-NINE

As they were having breakfast the following morning, Kara decided that if Karl cried or seemed to be uncomfortable with Sonia, she would insist on missing the party and staying with him in the hotel room. But when they arrived at Sonia's apartment, the old woman seemed excited and ready to entertain her young guest. She'd arranged several toys on the rug in the living room, and Karl was immediately drawn to them. He was playing with a dog that had been carved out of wood when Kara asked him if he was going to be all right staying with Sonia.

"I'll stay with her," Karl said. "She reminds me of Bubbie."

The mention of Hoda shook Kara to her very core. Karl had not used that word in years. *How did he remember? He was so young the last time he saw Hoda.* Kara turned white. Anka stared at Karl for several moments. Sonia had heard him too.

"I don't know where you would have heard a word like that. But I think it's a Jewish word. So, don't ever say that again. You don't have a bubbie. You're not some dirty Jew," Anka said in a stern voice. Kara cringed to hear her sister use the term "dirty Jew," but she said nothing.

Karl looked crushed. Then Anka took him into her arms. "I'm

sorry," she said, "you probably heard that word from one of the other children at the park."

"Oh, you know how children can be. They hear a word, and they think it sounds interesting, so they use it," Sonia said. Then she ruffled Karl's hair. "You go on to your party. He'll be just fine here with me."

Kara was trembling as she kissed Karl. "We'll be back in the morning to pick you up. Remember the special day we have planned for tomorrow?"

"The zoo!"

"Yes—that's right!" Kara said, kissing him.

"How early do you plan to arrive to pick him up?" Sonia asked.

"Not too early," Anka answered, "the party will go on until late tonight. I am assuming we'll be ready to pick him up at about eleven."

"All right. I'll make sure he's eaten his breakfast, and he's ready to go by eleven," Sonia said.

Kara was afraid that Anka suspected something when she heard Karl use the word "bubbie." *What if she asks me questions once we leave here? What lies am I going to tell her now? She is so good to me and Karl, and I just keep getting buried deeper and deeper in lies.*

Once they left, Anka turned to Kara and said, "We have to hurry. We don't want to miss our hair appointment."

Kara breathed a sigh of relief now that Anka was more worried about her hair than she was about Karl using a Yiddish word.

CHAPTER EIGHTY

Oskar and Ludwig arrived in Warsaw together in Ludwig's black automobile. It was late afternoon when they checked into the hotel where the girls had been staying. The plan was that once Ludwig arrived, Anka would leave the room she shared with Kara and move into her husband's room. Oskar had secured his own room. He'd paid extra to make sure that it was located right across the hall from the room where Kara would be staying. That way, should she want to come to his room during the night, she could discreetly slip across the hall. And he hoped that by the end of the evening, she would do just that.

Ludwig knocked softly on the door to Anka and Kara's room. Anka opened it just a crack. "We're here. I've missed you," he said, grinning like a schoolboy.

"Hello, Ludwig. You'd better hurry and get dressed. It's getting late," said Anka, then added, "I'll finish getting ready here in this room with Kara, then I'll move to our room after the party," Anka said.

"Let me in. I feel like a fool standing in the hall like this," Ludwig said.

"Absolutely not!" She giggled. "You must not see me until the party. I bought the most beautiful dress, and I want to make a grand entrance."

Kara overheard her sister and Ludwig talking, and she had to smile. *Anka is still like a young girl. She is still so naïve and innocent.*

"You always make a grand entrance, my love," Ludwig said, "but very well, I suppose I shall be forced to go and get dressed in my room all alone . . . and I, who have endured all of these long, miserable days that you have been away," he said dramatically, in mock distress.

"Oh, please," she said, "you've been busy with your work. You don't fool me. I know you've been perfecting that place you're building. Haven't you?"

"I must admit that you're right. I have. But I certainly am glad to see you. I'm so proud to be your escort tonight, beautiful wife."

"You talk so silly, but I like it," she laughed, "still, you'd better go and get ready. We have less than an hour before the party begins," Anka said, closing the door.

"I am miserable without you!" he said through the door in that same mocking tone.

She shook her head and laughed.

CHAPTER EIGHTY-ONE

WHEN IT WAS time for the gala, Ludwig and Oskar came together to the door of the women's hotel room. Anka opened it. She let them both in and poured them each a glass of schnapps.

"You look like an angel," Ludwig said. "That blue brings out your eyes." Then he came up behind Anka and whispered into her ear. "I can't wait until the party is over and we are alone. I've been without you for far too long."

"You are so silly," she giggled.

Then he kissed her neck, and she gently pushed him away.

Kara walked out of the bathroom in her black gown. Anka handed her a glass. She drank the schnapps quickly without looking around the room. She felt nervous, self-conscious, and very out of place. These people who would be at this gala were the same people who had kept her and Abram apart. They'd taken him away from her, and they might have hurt or killed him. She wanted to scream. If only she could just stay in the room and not have to face them all and pretend that everything was fine.

"You look beautiful," Oskar said in a husky voice. Kara's head whipped around. His words had broken into her thoughts. He smiled at her admiringly, then he added carefully, "You both look beautiful. I can easily see that these two sisters will be the most stunning women at the party tonight."

"Of course they will," Ludwig chimed in.

With trembling hands, Kara placed the glass down on the table. She tried to smile but her lips were quivering. She longed to hold her son, and suddenly she was worried about him.

"I don't know how to say this," she said in a broken voice, "but I don't want to go to this party. You three go on, and I am going to take a taxi and pick up Karl."

"Kara, please. Karl is fine. I promise you," Anka said. "You're all dressed. Just come to the party. Do it for me?"

Kara looked at her sister.

"Please?" Anka said.

Kara nodded.

Both men looked elegant in their perfectly fitted, newly pressed black uniforms. But Kara couldn't see how handsome Oskar was; all she could see was the swastika on his coat.

The ballroom in the hotel was decorated to honor the Nazi guests. German flags hung from the ceiling, and a large photograph of the führer hung proudly behind the head table at the front of the room. The hotel manager, a Polish man who secretly despised the Germans, knew that these were esteemed guests, wealthy, high-ranking Nazi officers with their wives or girlfriends by their sides. And even though the manager hated them, he knew that the future of his job depended upon how well this party was executed. The women with their perfectly styled hair, wore expensive gowns; the men were in uniform. At the door, Oskar gave Kara his arm and they walked in together. Their entrance was accompanied by the sound of clinking glasses, and the music from a live band playing a piece by Wagner.

"Would you care to dance?" Oskar asked.

"Oh, I don't really dance much," Kara said.

"That's all right, neither do I. Please, just one dance before dinner?"

Anka and Ludwig were already whirling across the floor. Oskar took Kara's hand and led her to the dance floor. Then he put his hand on her waist and they began to dance. As Kara looked around her at all the healthy-looking couples, their laughter ringing through the hall, the faces of Abram, Hoda, and Yiskar flashed through her mind. The people at this party were lacking nothing, while the Jewish people were struggling just to survive. It hurt her heart to be at this party, and she silently apologized to Abram. At that moment, she decided that no matter what Anka said, the next time she was invited to a Nazi gala, she would refuse to go.

They finished the dance, and the band leader announced that dinner was served.

Oskar pulled out the chair at the table, and Kara sat down. Then he sat beside her.

Waiters in black suits served rare steaks, with creamy potatoes and fresh asparagus, all on beautiful china plates. The meal was lovely, but Kara found it hard to swallow the food. If Abram was, in fact, dead, and she believed he was, she was dining with his murderers.

Kara couldn't help but notice how refined Oskar was. His table manners were impeccable. The men at the table discussed how beautiful and private the lair was and how impressed they thought the führer would be when he arrived the following month. Kara was quiet. The steak was tender yet stuck in her throat. No one mentioned the Jews and she was glad. Even so, Abram and his family were all she could think about. After dinner, the musicians began to play again, and the other couples at the table got up to dance.

"Will you dance with me?" Oskar asked.

"Thank you for asking, but I think I am going to sit this one out," Kara said.

"You don't like me. Why?" Oskar asked.

She was surprised by his bold question. But something within her compelled her to answer honestly. "The truth?"

"Yes, of course."

"It's not you. It's just that I am not in love with the Nazi Party. I don't like the uniform and all that it stands for," she said.

A look of surprise flashed across his face, but that look was gone as quickly as it appeared. "And why is that? Hitler has been so good for our fatherland."

"Do you really think so? He is conquering the neighboring countries left and right."

"You mean Poland?"

"Yes, Poland, and what about Austria?"

"Austria welcomed us when we entered their land. The Austrians were pleased to be a part of our wonderful fatherland."

"And . . . dare I say it? What about the Jews?" Kara said boldly.

"The Jews?" he said, sighing. "Ah yes. The Jews. A problem for certain. They had to be dealt with. They were holding Germany back. Look at how our economy has improved."

"But what has happened to them? What has been done with them?"

"I don't know, actually. Exiled, probably." He smiled. "It's better for Germany if some other country is forced to deal with them rather than us. They kept us down. Now, we flourish."

"Exiled or imprisoned?" Kara persisted.

"Probably both, I suppose. I would venture to say that the ones who were able to leave, have most likely left. The others had to be sent to a place where we can keep watch over them. I promise you that the prisons are not bad places. They are fed and provided for nicely. But at least we have them contained, and we don't have to worry about them causing Germany any trouble."

"What is that place I saw called the Warsaw ghetto?"

"Oh yes, that's an area of town where the Jews have been sent to live."

"It looks horrible, from the outside at least."

"It wasn't terrible when we put it together for them. It was very nice, in fact. But the Jews are filthy people. They took that area and made it into a pigsty. Besides that, they are underhanded. There is so much illegal activity in that place that it would make you cringe. They steal and buy things on the black market. Jews are Jews, my dear. They can't be changed. They are like vermin. They have no respect for others and no respect for our father-land." he said, shaking his head. Then he added, "Why are we talking about this tonight? Tonight, when you look as lovely as a star. I would rather dance . . . please . . . won't you dance with me?"

His answers had not satisfied her. She felt as if he was lying and hiding things. But she couldn't ask anything else without raising suspicion. She'd already said far more than she'd planned to. Forcing a smile, Kara said, "All right, let's dance."

Kara danced with Oskar for the remainder of the evening. As he led her across the floor, she watched her sister dance with several different Nazi officers. Anka was beautiful and popular. She laughed and flirted with the men. And although Anka appeared happy in her life, Kara knew that her sister was not in love with Ludwig. And she wondered if Anka had thought about having an affair. It was late when the gala finally ended. Oskar walked Kara to her room. As they walked through the hall, Oskar turned to Kara.

"I wanted to tell you something," he said.

"Yes?" she answered in a soft voice, not wanting to wake the people sleeping within their rooms.

"I can see that you have a kind heart, and that is why you are so concerned about the Jews. I promise you they are not being mistreated in any way. I would never be a part of an organization that mistreated any living creature. However, just to set the record straight, in my position, I never have any contact with them."

"Ever?"

"No, never," he said, smiling, "and I must admit, I am glad. Like I said, I saw that Warsaw ghetto once. I went on a tour because I had to. It was part of my job to see it. But it was not a pretty sight. And that was the only time I had any actual contact with Jews. I prefer to work in an office designing beautiful buildings and gardens," he said, "but of course not a single design is as beautiful as you are."

Kara didn't answer.

When they stopped in front of her hotel room door, Oskar turned and took her into his arms. She felt herself tense up.

"You don't want me to kiss you?" he asked.

"It's too soon for all of that"—she looked away—"I-I would

rather we knew each other better before we . . ." She was stammering.

"I respect your wishes," he said, bowing slightly and releasing her.

"Well then, good night," she said.

"Good night."

CHAPTER EIGHTY-TWO

KARA DIDN'T SLEEP WELL. She could hardly wait to pick Karl up. They'd never been apart for an entire night, and all she could do was think about him. I wonder if he was able to sleep at all. I hope he didn't cry for me. Anka gets on my nerves sometimes. I don't know why I let her convince me to go to this ridiculous party and leave my son with a stranger. I must have been insane to agree. Well, thank goodness it's almost over. Everyone will be awake in a few hours, and then I'm sure I'll have to endure a quick breakfast. But after that, we'll be on our way to pick up Karl.

Anka knocked on Kara's door at ten fifteen. "Are you awake?"

"Yes," Kara said as she opened the door. She was already dressed for a day at the zoo.

"You certainly are awake and ready to go," Anka laughed. She was still wearing her robe and slippers. "I'm going to get ready quickly. Ludwig and Oskar are already downstairs having coffee. Here is the plan. First, we will have some breakfast. Then we'll go to Sonia's apartment and get Karl. But before we go to the zoo, Ludwig has agreed to drop Oskar off at the train station because he has to be back at work. I hope that's all right."

"Certainly," Kara replied.

"The two of you seemed to be getting along very well," Anka said.

"He's a nice man. But right now, the only man I am interested in is my son. I want to give him all my time and attention, at least until he starts school. So, I really don't have room for a man in my life."

"Kara, Kara, Kara . . . what am I going to do with you? Ludwig introduces you this wildly good-looking officer, and what do you do? You reject him." Anka sounded angry as she opened the door. "I'm going back to my room to get dressed. I'll meet you downstairs in about ten minutes. Then we can find the fellas."

Kara nodded and closed the door behind her sister.

Since Kara knew Anka was angry with her, and she wasn't exactly pleased with Anka either, she didn't wait for her sister before entering the restaurant when she got downstairs. Instead, she walked in alone. The maître d' asked her if she'd like to be seated. "No, thank you," she said, shaking her head, because she saw Oskar and Ludwig. They were sitting at a table with some guests she recognized from the party the night before. When Oskar saw Kara, he motioned for her to come over. And as she began walking toward the table, he stood up and pulled out her chair. The other men at the table stood up too. They seemed to follow his lead. *He appears to be refined and sophisticated. His manners are truly impressive, Kara* thought as she sat down.

"You look radiant. How did you ever manage to look so stunning after getting to bed so late?"

Kara smiled but she said nothing. Instead, when the waiter came around; she ordered a cup of coffee, which she sipped slowly until Anka appeared a half hour later. *She is so inconsiderate. Everyone has to wait for her. I want to get to my son. And she has to take a half hour putting on her makeup,* Kara thought. But then she reminded herself, *Anka is my sister. She may have her faults, but she is so good to Karl and me, I should be so grateful to her. God forgive me. I'm just so worn out, and I feel like I am drowning in secrets. All I want is to hold my son in my arms. I'm tired of all these people, and I'm tired of pretending.*

No one said much during breakfast. They all seemed to be tired and perhaps hungover. Still, it took a full hour after Anka's arrival before everyone was ready to leave. Once they said their goodbyes to the others, Kara and Oskar climbed into the back seat, and Ludwig and Anka got into the front of Ludwig's automobile. Then Anka gave Ludwig instructions as he drove to Sonia's apartment.

When they arrived, Kara got out of the car. "I'll only be a moment," she said. "I'm just going to fetch Karl."

"I'll come with you." Anka followed Kara into the building.

As they walked up the stairs to the apartment, Kara turned to Anka. "You didn't have to come."

"I wanted to," Anka said. "I want to pay Sonia for babysitting."

"I can pay her. I have some money of my own from tutoring," Kara said.

"I insist. After all, I sort of forced you to come to the party. I know you didn't have a good time, but I hoped you would. The least I can do is pay the babysitter."

"Anka"—Kara stopped on the stairs and took her sister's hand —"I did have a good time. And I want you to know that I appreciate everything you do for me and for Karl. If I seemed a little short, it was only because I am tired and I missed Karl so much."

"Are you sure you enjoyed our little trip?"

"Yes, of course I did. We had so much fun shopping and dancing," Kara tried to reassure her sister. "I love you so much; don't ever doubt that . . . even when I get irritable."

"I love you too, Kara."

Kara knocked on the door. They waited, but there was no answer. "What time is it?" Anka asked. "Maybe they went to the park and plan to return by eleven. I wish I had a watch."

Kara looked at her watch. "It's a quarter past twelve. We're late, but she should be here," she said.

"We did say we would be here at eleven to pick him up, didn't we?" Anka asked. "Where the hell could she have gone?"

Kara felt the hairs on her arms and the back of her neck stand up. "I don't know." She felt the sweat bead under her arms, and once again she knocked on the door, harder this time. But there was still no answer. "Sonia," Kara called out loudly. "Sonia . . ."

"Sonia," Anka cried, "Sonia, it's us, Kara and Anka—we're here to pick up Karl."

But no one answered. The hallway of the apartment building was eerily silent. The only sound that could be heard was a bird chirping outside. Kara looked at Anka, who had turned pale. Then without another word, Kara ran down the stairs to the car.

"Oskar, Ludwig, the woman who is babysitting for my son isn't answering her door. I'm afraid something has happened to her. Please come and help me. I must get inside. What if Karl is in there all alone?"

Oskar ran as fast as he could with Kara at his heels. When he got to door of the apartment, he kicked it hard and it sprung open.

"Sonia," Kara cried as she ran into the apartment, running from room to empty room.

"Sonia," Anka screamed, pulling her hair.

"Karl . . . Karl . . . Where are you?" Kara yelled.

Ludwig and Oskar ran through the entire apartment, but it was empty.

Then Oskar ran out into the hall and began knocking on the doors of the neighboring apartments. No one answered. He ran frantically from door to door in a panic. Kara followed close behind him, tears running down her cheeks.

"It's almost noon. You're going to miss your train," Ludwig said to Oskar. "Do you have to call anyone at home and let them know what is happening?"

"I will call my superiors at work later this afternoon and I'll explain. Right now, I can't leave Kara. I am going to stay in Warsaw until we find Karl."

Five minutes passed before an old woman with a hump in her back and frizzy gray hair opened the door to her apartment. "Who are you? Why are you knocking on my door, and what do you want?"

Kara saw the terror in the woman's eyes, and she realized that it was because of the Nazi uniform Oskar wore.

"My son . . . please, can you help me," Kara said, walking closer to the woman, trying to appeal to her as one mother to another.

338

"Your neighbor Sonia Smolak was babysitting for my four-year-old son. She was expecting me to come to pick him up this morning at eleven, but there was no answer when I knocked on her door. And we got inside, but there is no one home."

The woman looked at Kara, then she looked at Oskar and Ludwig. "I don't know anything," she said.

Anka came forward, crying. "Please," she said, taking the old woman's hands in her own. "Please, help my sister. I promise you that nothing bad will happen to you if you tell us the truth."

The old woman ran her tongue over her lips, then she said, "Men came yesterday afternoon. I saw them through my window. They took the Smolak widow and a young child away in a car."

"Who were they?" Anka said.

"I don't know."

"What were they wearing? What did they look like? Were they Germans or Poles?" Ludwig asked.

"I don't know. All I know is that they grabbed the widow by her arm and threw her in the back of the auto. They threw the child in too, and then they drove away."

"Where did they take them?" Ludwig asked.

"I don't know. I've told you all I know."

"They took my son?" Kara said. She was trembling. Her knees were weak.

"Yes," the old woman said.

"Dear God, help me," Kara said. Then she fainted.

CHAPTER EIGHTY-THREE

WHEN KARA AWOKE, she was back at the hotel with a wet rag on her forehead. Anka, Ludwig, and Oskar were beside her.

"We came back here and rented this room. Ludwig must return back to work at the lair, but Oskar and I are going to stay with you and help you find Karl," Anka said. Her face was red and tearstained. Then she added, "Kara . . . can you ever forgive me? This is all my fault."

Kara didn't answer.

"I'm going to go to the police station to see if I can find out anything about this widow Sonia Smolak," Oskar said, "and don't worry, Kara, I'll stay here in Warsaw with you for as long as I have to in order to find Karl."

"It could be weeks, or even months," Ludwig said.

Kara let out a cry of pain.

"It's all right. I'll make arrangements," Oskar said. "We'll find him."

CHAPTER EIGHTY-FOUR

Auschwitz
Two weeks later

ABRAM EHRLICH LAY on the bed of lice-filled straw where he slept. His body was covered in sores that itched mercilessly and oozed pus. He lay beside Moishe Strausman, a man he'd met on the transport to Auschwitz. When the train car was packed until there was only enough room to stand, these two men happened to be standing next to each other. The transport was unlike anything Abram had ever undergone. It still came to him in nightmares, the smells, the people moaning, the fear. There were no windows, only tiny rays of light that forced their way through the wooden slats of the train car. And although Abram was terrified, he was even more worried about Kara, and Karl. Moishe Strausman asked him, "Did you leave a family behind?"

Abram answered, "Yes, I left my mother, my wife, and son."

"They took me away from my house, leaving my pregnant wife behind. I am sick with worry about her."

"I'm worried about my family too," Abram said, then he added, "I'm Abram Ehrlich."

"Moishe Strausman."

And so began a friendship between two desperate men. Both of them being alone, in Auschwitz—the darkest of places—the friendship they forged was all they had to keep them from going out of their minds.

When they were assigned their sleeping areas, they had chosen to sleep next to each other. They talked and shared their fears and hopes. The men were lined up like sardines inside a can. They were unable to move at all; this was how close the sleeping quarters were. In another time, another place, Abram would have felt uncomfortable sleeping so close to a man. So close he could smell his breath. But here, in Auschwitz, the rules were different. Here, friendship was all there was. And as the time had passed, he began to see Moishe as the brother he'd never had.

The men surrounding them had fallen asleep. Some wept in their sleep; others snored because they were exhausted, having worked hard all day and little to eat. Most nights Abram was so tired he was able to sleep. But then there were nights, like tonight, when he lay awake knowing how desperately he needed to rest but unable to turn off his thoughts about his family.

Moishe, because they'd slept so close together, could tell by Abram's breathing that he was awake.

"Can't sleep?" Moishe asked.

"No. I am worried about Kara and the baby. And about my mother. I can only pray that somehow Yitzar has found a way to protect them all. I was arrested for fighting in the street, but you say that you were arrested for no reason at all. I am afraid my family could be arrested. Especially since Kara is not a Jew and my son is half-Jewish," Abram said. Moishe already knew the names of everyone in Abram's family, as they had talked about them numerous times. And, in turn, Abram felt like he knew Rebecca, Moishe's young and vulnerable wife. "I am hoping that Kara has somehow returned to her former life, and that somehow, she's found a way to hide the fact that Karl is half-Jewish."

"That would be the wise thing to do," Moishe said. "I am sure that she has done just that." He tried to comfort Abram.

"Sometimes I am terrified that they might all be dead. Murdered because of my selfishness. I should never have brought Kara into my world."

"You must try not to think that way. If you do, you will lose all hope. And hope is the only thing that is going to help us survive this."

"If they're dead, I don't want to survive," Abram said.

"But what if they aren't? What if when all of this is over, you can be reunited with Kara and Karl? And your mother and Yitzar? You must not stop hoping."

"You're right. I have to remind myself that one day when this is all over, you and your wife and newborn child will come to have dinner at my home. Our parents will be there and . . ."

"And there will be plenty of food," Moishe said.

"What shall we have?"

"Latkes."

"Yes, latkes. And chicken," Abram said. He could almost taste the food.

"Yes, chicken. Juicy chicken, so moist that the juice runs down your chin."

"I want a drumstick."

"You have one, I'll have the other."

They both let out a short bitter laugh. Then Moishe added, "And I'll play the piano, and everyone will sing."

"I don't have a piano," Abram said.

"NU? So, we'll buy one."

"Good idea."

The men could both picture the dream they'd created. Then Moishe asked, "By the way, have you noticed that the commandant hasn't been here at the camp for weeks. I hope to God they've transferred that bastard somewhere else. Somewhere far away from us. Maybe to hell?"

"That's where he belongs. It's rare that you meet a man who is so creative with his punishments. What a sadistic bastard," Abram said.

"You're telling me. I've survived two transports and a bunch of miserable sadists at another camp. The transports were horrible, and the Nazis were all demons, but of all the horrible Nazis I've had the pleasure to run into, this one has been the worst," Moishe said.

"That's for sure. I have to agree with you," Abram said. Then he added, "On a brighter note, maybe he's dead. That would be wonderful, wouldn't it?"

"Oh, yes. I must say that I would be relieved to say goodbye forever to the commandent as he leaves this world and goes to burn in hell," Moishe said, then he added, "You know what is very strange? Sometimes I hardly recognize myself. Before I was arrested and taken by the Nazis, I was a different fellow. I never hated anyone. And I never thought I would wish for the death of another human being. But I am wishing it now. I have become a monster, too, just like them. I would like to see someone beat him to death the same way he beat that teenage boy to death the day before he left."

"You are not alone. I have changed in the same way. I have become cruel and angry. Perhaps I am even worse than you, because I would like to be the man who beat Oberstrumfuhrer Oskar Lerch to death," Abram said. And, he thought, *I've killed before, and I'll kill again.*

AUTHORS NOTE

I always enjoy hearing from my readers, and your thoughts about my work are very important to me. If you enjoyed my novel, please consider telling your friends and posting a short review on Amazon of Goodreads. Word of mouth is an author's best friend.

I love hearing from readers, so feel free to drop me an email telling me your thoughts about the book or series.

You can write to me at roberta@robertakagan.com or sign up for my newsletters at my website - www.robertakagan.com!

In addition you can follow me on Facebook, join my Book Club and if you follow me on BookBub, you will receive emails whenever I am offering a special price, a freebie, a giveaway, or a new release!

Thank you so much for reading this book - and I hope to be hearing from you soon!

Keep reading to get a sneak-peak of *The Stolen Child!*

THE STOLEN CHILD

Kara paced the floor frantically in the hotel room where she was staying in Warsaw. Her hands trembled, and her knees felt weak.

"Do you think he will find him?" Kara asked as she turned to her sister, Anka, who was sitting on the bed.

"I don't know. I only know that I blame myself," Anka said, wringing her slender white hands together.

"Dear God, Anka, not everything is about you. My son, my little Karl, is missing. He's only three and he's missing. Somewhere, he is all alone and he's looking for me. I can hear him calling out *Mutti, Mutti*, and it's driving me insane. I can't go to him because, I don't know where to find him."

"And it's my fault. I told you to leave him with a babysitter who we hardly knew. It was me. I told you it would all be all right. Oh, Kara. I convinced you to do it. I had no idea that something so horrible could happen. All I wanted was to see you finally get out of the house. I wanted to see you laugh and enjoy yourself. I wanted you to attend a party. Perhaps meet someone. You've been so alone. I never thought this could happen."

Kara couldn't bear to comfort and reassure her sister as she'd always done in the past. She was in too much mental anguish to worry about Anka's feelings. *It was Anka's fault.* Anka had convinced her to leave her son with a Polish grandmother they'd met, in order to attend a Nazi gala, the night before. *This damn party was so important to Anka,* Kara thought as she paced the room. She couldn't even look at her sister, let alone comfort her. *How different we are. She is my sister, and we were so close when we were children. But things have changed. I have changed,* Kara thought.

Anka was married to Ludwig, a man who was trying to make a good impression in the Nazi Party so he could rise in rank. And although she wasn't in love with him, she was the perfect wife for him because she wanted the same thing. Anka made no excuses for how much she enjoyed the comfort of being married to a Nazi official. She loved the parties. She loved the good food and fine clothes. And she loved the nice home she and her husband had been given by the Nazi Party when he went to work on the Wolf's Lair, a luxury entertainment center for the führer and some of his high officials.

It had taken persistence, but she had finally convinced Kara to leave her son, Karl, with this Polish woman. Kara knew Anka would never hurt her or Karl on purpose. She was just thoughtless. And because she'd been so insistent, Kara had finally agreed. Everything should have been fine. But it wasn't. The following day, when they'd gone to pick Karl up, the old woman's apartment was ransacked, and the old lady and Karl were both gone. Kara, Anka, her husband, Ludwig, and Oskar Lerch, a high-ranking SS officer who was smitten with Kara, spent the rest of the day searching frantically for the boy. They went door to door, asking neighbors if they saw anything. No one wanted to get involved. Who could blame them? After all, Kara was accompanied by Oskar Lerch, who was intimidating to anyone Polish, in his black SS uniform. Poland was a newly conquered country. And the Polish feared the Germans, whose bombs and cruelty they'd witnessed firsthand. Kara could see the fear in their eyes. She wanted to throw herself on the floor and beg them to help her. But she knew it wouldn't make any difference. They were too afraid to speak.

Finally, Kara found a neighbor who was compassionate. She lived in the same building as the babysitter, Sonia Smolak. And she admitted to having seen the child and the old lady, Smolak, being shoved into a car by the Gestapo.

Kara turned to Oskar. "Gestapo?" she said. "Why would the Gestapo take my son?" She was hysterical. And although Oskar was scheduled to leave Warsaw and head back to work, he canceled his plans and insisted on staying to help Kara find her son. "I don't know," he said, "but I promise you this: I will find out, and we will find your boy."

"I wish he would get back here already," Anka said. She was referring to Oskar who had gone to the Gestapo headquarters in Warsaw to find out anything he could about the missing boy.

Kara was flushed. She felt faint. *Everything is out of my control,* she thought. *Dear God, how I wish my Abram was here. But I can't talk to Anka about Abram because none of these people knew of his existence, and that was because he was Jewish. Abram is the love of my life, and he is also Karl's father.* Abram was arrested right after Kristallnacht. His mother, Hoda, in order to protect Karl, insisted that Kara take Karl and go to live with Anka, who had married a high-ranking officer in the Nazi Party. Hoda and Kara decided it would be safest for Karl if he hid in plain sight. No one was ever to know he was half Jewish. Kara had lied to Anka. She told her that Karl was the son of a pure German man whom she had an affair with. She claimed the man was married, and he'd gone back to his wife and left her to raise the boy on her own. Anka took her sister and her nephew into her home to live. And because of his strong Aryan features, no one suspected Karl of having Jewish blood; he was accepted into Ludwig and Anka's world. All had gone well until this gala. Kara had not wanted to go. She had a bad feeling about it before she even attended, but Anka had assured her that all would be well. It wasn't.

MORE BOOKS BY ROBERTA KAGAN

AVAILABLE ON AMAZON

The Auschwitz Twins Series

The Children's Dream

Jews, The Third Reich, and a Web of Secrets

My Son's Secret

The Stolen Child

A Web of Secrets

A Jewish Family Saga

Not In America

They Never Saw It Coming

When The Dust Settled

The Syndrome That Saved Us

A Holocaust Story Series

The Smallest Crack

The Darkest Canyon

Millions Of Pebbles

Sarah and Solomon

All My Love, Detrick Series

All My Love, Detrick

You Are My Sunshine

The Promised Land

To Be An Israeli

Forever My Homeland

Michal's Destiny Series
Michal's Destiny

A Family Shattered

Watch Over My Child

Another Breath, Another Sunrise

Eidel's Story Series
Who Is The Real Mother?

Secrets Revealed

New Life, New Land

Another Generation

The Wrath of Eden Series
The Wrath Of Eden

The Angels Song

Stand Alone Novels
One Last Hope

A Flicker Of Light

The Heart Of A Gypsy

ACKNOWLEDGMENTS

I would also like to thank my editor, proofreader, and developmental editor for all their help with this project. I couldn't have done it without them.

Paula Grundy of Paula Proofreader

Terrance Grundy of Editerry

Carli Kagan, Developmental Editor

Made in the USA
Las Vegas, NV
23 January 2022

42176131R00215